His Perfect Plan

Laurel Ridge Series, Book #3

Tara Baisden

Sterling Ridge Press LLC

Cover designed by Sterling Ridge Press LLC

Published by: Sterling Ridge Press, LLC www.sterlingridgepress.com

ISBN: 978-1-966096-04-6 Printed in the United States of America

First Edition: October 2024

For permissions, contact: tara@tarabaisden.com or visit www.tarabaisden.com

About The Author

Tara Baisden is a Contemporary Inspirational Romance author who proudly calls the beautiful state of West Virginia her home. Nestled on a sprawling mountainous property, she is surrounded by the peace and serenity of nature. Her days are happily spent in the quiet of country life, writing heartwarming stories of love, faith, and second chances. Tara also enjoys quilting, working in her garden, tending to her beloved pets, and soaking in the beauty of her surroundings.

With deep roots in West Virginia, family is everything to Tara. One of her favorite pastimes is gathering on the front porch with loved ones, sharing stories, laughter, and enjoying the simple, meaningful moments that life offers. When she's not crafting her novels, Tara can often be found exploring the rich history of her home state, visiting local historical sites, and, of course, stopping by every bookstore she passes! Her passion for reading and discovery always fuels her next adventure.

Tara is the author of the Laurel Ridges Series of novels, which includes: Season of Hope, Finding Grace, His Perfect Plan, and Love Redeemed, all of which have been beloved by fans of inspirational romance. Her novels reflect her love for faith, family, and the timeless beauty of West Virginia.

Known for her sweet and clean romances, she creates characters that feel like family and settings that make readers want to visit again and again.

You can find out more about Tara and her latest releases at www.tarabaisden.com or follow her on social media for updates and behind-the-scenes glimpses of her writing process. Stay connected—you won't want to miss the heartfelt stories of love and family she has in store!

Also by Tara Baisden

<u>Laurel Ridge Series</u>

#1. Season of Hope

#2. Finding Grace

#3. His Perfect Plan

#4. Love Redeemed

Dedication

To everyone who's ever had their heart broken into more pieces than you thought could be fit back together...

And to everyone who's ever stared at life's big decisions like they were bracing for a New York cab in rush hour...

This one's for you.

Here's to taking leaps of faith (even if we're pretty sure there's no safety net), to wearing your heart on your sleeve again, and to trusting that God's plans are better than our perfectly color-coded timelines. May you find your own cozy bonfire moments, unexpected laughter, and the courage to take that first step down unplanned paths.

About Laurel Ridge

Welcome to the fictional town of Laurel Ridge, West Virginia!

Nestled deep in the heart of the Appalachian Mountains, Laurel Ridge is a place where time slows down, allowing visitors and residents alike to enjoy life's simple pleasures. With its quaint, brick-paved streets, historic storefronts, and the ever-present backdrop of rolling hills and dense forests, Laurel Ridge is a hidden gem that attracts tourists looking for both serenity and adventure.

A Rich History

The town was founded in the early 1800s by pioneering settlers who were drawn to the fertile land and abundant natural resources of the region. Laurel Ridge began as a small logging community, relying on the towering forests that covered the surrounding mountains. The New River, one of the oldest rivers in the world, provided an essential transportation route for lumber, as well as a lifeline for the early settlers.

As the years passed, the town evolved from a logging outpost into a thriving hub for craftspeople and artisans. By the late 19th century, it had developed a reputation for its hand-crafted furniture, textiles, and pottery, all made by skilled locals. The town's proximity to the New River also made it a destination for adventurous souls seeking to kayak, fish, or hike along the riverbanks.

A Place of Renewal

Though the logging industry faded by the early 20th century, Laurel Ridge adapted to the changing times. Its natural beauty and deep connection to West Virginia's mountain heritage drew travelers from near and far, transforming it into a beloved tourist destination. Local shops, run by generations of the same families, line the town square, offering handmade goods, locally sourced foods, and, most of all, warm hospitality.

The town's signature event, the Harvest Festival, began in the 1930s, celebrating the craftsmanship, music, and traditions passed down through the generations. Each year, visitors flock to enjoy live Appalachian music, taste locally grown produce, and witness demonstrations of old-world techniques like blacksmithing and weaving.

A Town of Faith and Community

At the heart of the town stands Laurel Ridge Community Church, a small, white clapboard building with a steeple that reaches toward the sky. Built in 1876, the church has been a pillar of faith and strength for the community for over a century. Its bell, crafted by the town's original blacksmith, has been ringing on Sunday mornings ever since, calling townsfolk to worship and reminding everyone of the enduring values of faith, hope, and love.

The church's history is intertwined with the town's, serving as a refuge in difficult times and a gathering place in moments of joy. Over the years, the church has grown to include an outreach center that supports local families and tourists in need, providing everything from free meals to spiritual counseling. The church's welcoming atmosphere reflects the town's deep sense of unity and service.

A Growing Tourist Haven

Today, Laurel Ridge has grown to a population of around five thousand people, yet it has managed to retain its small-town charm. Its thriving tourist industry draws visitors year-round. Tourists can stroll through mom-and-pop shops, and dine at the beloved Martha's Diner, famous for its homemade pies and retro charm. The town square, with its white gazebo surrounded by flowering bushes, is often the site of outdoor concerts and farmers' markets, creating a sense of nostalgia and small-town pride.

For nature lovers, the New River offers breathtaking views and the thrill of adventure, whether it's fishing in its crystal blue waters or hiking along the rugged trails that weave through the wilderness. Tourists and locals alike cherish the scenic beauty, often finding peace in the simple pleasures of watching the river flow or taking in the panoramic vistas of the Appalachian Mountains.

Laurel Ridge, with its rich history, strong community spirit, and natural beauty, is more than just a tourist destination—it's a place where past and present blend seamlessly, offering everyone who visits a chance to experience the best of West Virginia's mountain heritage.

You'll find that Laurel Ridge is a town that captures the heart.

Welcome to Laurel Ridge. I hope you fall in love with this charming small town and its residents.

Chapter 1

The narrow road wound its way through the mountains like a ribbon of uncertainty, curving sharply around each bend. The road twisted and dipped, sending small jolts through the car as Lily Reynolds gripped the steering wheel, her eyes flicking to the curves ahead. Each turn seemed to come faster than the last, the unfamiliar terrain keeping her on edge. Her heart racing every time she took a turn—yet another reminder of how far removed she was from the straight, sharp lines of Manhattan's streets. The mountains stretched endlessly into the sky, their ridges catching the last glimmer of the late afternoon sun.

"Come on, Lily. You can handle this," she muttered to herself as she navigated another sharp curve, her knuckles white from gripping the steering wheel. The towering mountains flanking the road felt almost as if they were closing in on her, making her acutely aware of how different everything here was.

Just a few weeks and then you're out of here.

A small part of her couldn't understand why anyone—let alone her cousin Grace Anderson—would choose to live way out here in the middle of nowhere, away from the hum of the city. As Lilly rounded the final bend, the cabin emerged against a backdrop of sweeping mountain views and thick forest. The property opened before her, the serene beauty of the Appalachian Mountains and the New River drawing her in. Even Lilly had to admit—it was stunning—if you were into the whole 'peace and quiet' thing.

The cabin looked like something out of a rustic home magazine, its wooden frame perfectly at home against the backdrop of the forest. On the front porch, Grace sat comfortably in her chair, a book resting on her lap, while one foot rested casually atop the porch railing.

Lily eased her car to a stop behind Grace's, the gentle hum of the engine fading into the quiet of the countryside. She stepped out, the cool breeze brushing past her as she caught movement up on the porch. Grace stood at the edge of the porch, barefoot in yoga pants, a t-shirt hanging loose over her frame, a smile across her face.

Lily watched her cousin for a moment, struck by how effortlessly she embodied something vibrant and untamed—like a gust of wind that swept through, full of life. Grace moved with elegant ease. Contentment radiated from her, like she had finally fit into a life that embraced her rather than demanded pieces of her. For Grace, peace had come in the simplicity of this small town, woven into the quiet cadence of its days.

It hadn't always been this way for Grace. Once, she had navigated an entirely different world. Back in New York, she had worn sleek power suits, heels that clicked with authority against marble floors, and carried herself with an air of corporate sharpness. A high-powered PR executive, always planning the next move, always maneuvering through a web of ambition and reputation. And she had been good at it—until the ground beneath her shifted.

She came to Laurel Ridge seeking a quiet place where the noise and chaos couldn't follow. What she found here was unexpected—a chance to rebuild. Here, away from the skyscrapers and scandals, Grace had touched on something new. She rediscovered parts of herself that had been hidden beneath the layers of corporate armor.

Now Grace wasn't just surviving—she was thriving, but in a way Lily couldn't quite grasp. Here, Grace had found more than just peace. She had found Ben, and in two short weeks, she would marry the man who had become the core of this simpler, more authentic life. The designer heels were long gone, traded in for hiking boots, and walks along the river at sundown.

Lily often wondered—How did Grace do it? How did she let go of city life so easily? The very thought weighed on her, pressing like a heavy stone against her already bruised heart.

Would she ever find that same peace, or had the world taken too much from her already?

"Lily!" Grace's voice carried over the short distance like a burst of sunshine, full of easy happiness.

"Grace! I've missed you," she said as they embraced.

"I've missed you too," Grace replied, squeezing her tight.

"Ugh, Grace." Lily gasped, though a part of her thrived in the kind of affection homecomings always brought. "You're going to crush me."

"Oh, don't be silly. It's been too long. I missed you, my wedding planner extraordinaire cousin." Grace said, "And look at you, all glamorous from the city, rolling up here like it's a catwalk. Girl, I don't know how you still look so perfect after that drive."

Lily chuckled, glancing down at her tailored slacks and soft wool blazer, a small smile creeping across her lips. "Trust me, I'm just holding myself together. That road... really put me through my paces." She gave a dramatic shake of her head. "I'm pretty sure I saw my life flash before my eyes on some of those curves."

Grace threw her head back and laughed, bright and full. "Oh, yeah. It gets everyone the first few times. But you get used to it. The view makes up for it, right?"

Lily gave a noncommittal glance over her shoulder at the stunning horizon, the sun dipping lower as it spilled rich hues of rose and amber over the hills. "I'll admit, it's not... terrible," she conceded with a playful grin.

As they turned to walk toward the trunk of the car, a furry, brown blur shot out from behind the cabin, tearing across the yard straight in their direction. Lily barely had time to register what was happening before an overenthusiastic bundle of energy collided with her legs.

"Whoa!" she exclaimed, stumbling.

"Daisy!" Grace called, laughing as the dog circled Lily, sniffing eagerly. "Yeah, she's a little much at first... okay, a lot. But she grows on you. Give her a minute."

Lily stared down at the whirlwind of fur, equal parts amused and baffled. "I didn't realize dog-sitting while you're on your honeymoon meant handling this much energy. I was expecting something a little more... mellow." Her tone was playful, tinged with disbelief as she crouched down. Daisy's response was instant: she flopped onto her back, legs flailing in the air, as though she'd suddenly forgotten how to exist as a normal dog.

Grace smirked. "Oh, that's Daisy's way of saying, 'Hi, please rub my belly and never leave me alone, and I'll love you forever and ever.'"

"Uh-huh." Lily reached out and gave Daisy a quick belly rub, which was immediately met with the dog's shameless attempt to roll closer and press her face into Lily's hand. "Great... I've made lifelong commitments to my cousin's dog, apparently."

"Speaking of lifelong commitments," Grace started with a mischievous glint in her eye, one Lily recognized immediately, "I'm so glad you came to help with the wedding plans! I wouldn't trust anyone else."

"Oh, I'm sure you could've managed." Lily said as she stood, brushing off her hands as Grace grabbed one of the larger suitcases from the trunk. "You've been out here, what? A few months and look at you... you're doing the whole country-living thing, and it looks good on you."

Grace shrugged. "Turns out all I needed was the right place and the right person."

A soft smile tugged at Lily's lips, but she fought it off, keeping her tone light. "Must be nice."

Grace didn't miss the guarded look in her cousin's eye, but she knew better than to push, at least not yet. "Come on, let's head up to the porch. I've got sweet tea waiting, and we can unload the rest later."

They made their way up the stairs, Daisy bounding ahead. Grace settled into the chair she'd been lounging in earlier, and Lily sank into the cushion of another porch chair. She leaned back, letting her eyes wander over the scene laid out before her. It was impossible to ignore—the sun casting its final golden rays of light over the valley, the trees swaying gently in the evening breeze, and the scattered birds serenading the descent of dusk.

"So, how's Ben?" Lily asked. "Ready for the big day?"

Grace's face lit up even brighter, though Lily hadn't thought that possible. "He's amazing. He's been so calm, so helpful... You know how he has that way of keeping everyone grounded. And the way he looks at me—" Grace broke off with a dreamy sigh, her smile widening into a grin that reached all the way to her eyes.

"Amazing," Lily repeated, arching a brow as she slid into a seat across from Grace.

She was happy for Grace, but it didn't matter how hard she tried; that small, familiar tug in her chest was impossible to ignore. It always resurfaced whenever someone gushed about how wonderfully in love they were. Lily had played that part once, too. She'd believed in love, the kind full of promises and forever afters, right until the moment it all crumbled beneath the weight of Bill's betrayal.

It had been six months since she'd stood before a mirror in her wedding dress, believing Bill Harlan was her forever. Now, as a seasoned wedding planner, she could orchestrate anyone's big day effortlessly—but planning her own? That was something she no longer dared to imagine.

That dream was long gone, along with the man who'd shattered her heart.

Grace's laughter brought her back out of her memories. "Come on, spill. What's been going on in Manhattan? Tell me someone exciting chose you to do their wedding—maybe the mayor's daughter?"

"Nothing nearly as dramatic. Just the usual stream of rich city couples looking for the perfect rooftop view or the latest trendy venue. You know—everything looks good on Instagram."

Grace's nose crinkled. "All the glitz without the soul."

Lily rested her chin on her palm. "Pretty much."

"And you, Lily? How's... everything else?" Grace asked.

Lily heard the question beneath the words—How's your heart?

It was almost funny, the way everyone just assumed that you'd keep chasing love. But for her, those doors had closed. There wasn't a future full of trust and laughter waiting for Lily. Not everyone got the fairy tale. Some people had to settle for building other people's 'happily ever after's' instead.

"As fine as it ever is," Lily answered matter-of-factly.

Grace didn't push, though concern flickered in her gaze. "Well, you know I'm always here if you ever need to talk... or complain about how much Bill Harlan deserves a few well-aimed pies in the face."

Lily let out a genuine snort at that. "I might enjoy seeing that."

"Just say the word," Grace grinned, "and Ben will gladly set it up for you."

Changing the subject, she added, "So, about the wedding... I know it's not quite your usual glamorous affair."

Lily chuckled. "You can say that again. No rooftop venues or 500-person guest lists. I think I'm actually going to survive this one without breaking into a cold sweat."

Grace gave her a playful nudge. "We only decided to get married a couple of weeks ago, remember? Ben actually wanted to elope, but I convinced him we could do something small, very low-key, just close friends and family at the church. Nothing big, just simple flowers, candles, and warm autumn colors... you know, something cozy and intimate."

Lily shook her head. "Low key, got it."

Grace sighed, tucking a strand of hair behind her ear. "I want it to feel peaceful... not overwhelming. Just us, the people we love, and God. That sounds cheesy, doesn't it?"

"It's your wedding. You can get away with being as cheesy as much as you want," Lily teased. "Besides, peaceful actually sounds pretty good right now. Better than rushing around downtown Manhattan, calming stressed-out brides about everything from table centerpieces to caterers being late."

Grace giggled. "Yeah, no bridezilla moments here, I promise. I've got you for all the stressful details!"

"Oh, please, I'll keep everything under control. Except maybe Ben's aunt's insistence on that green bean casserole for the reception. That might be a lost cause."

Grace laughed, throwing her head back. "Hey, don't knock a good green bean casserole until you've tried it. It's a staple around here."

Lily raised her hands in a playful shrug. "Small wedding, casseroles, and the venue already settled. Time to shift focus to the decor. I need to check out the church and the hall for the reception."

"That won't be an issue at all. Andrew, our assistant pastor, can help you access both," Grace said with a warm smile. "Lily, I can't thank you enough for being here to handle all the details. I know it's probably not as thrilling for you, planning something so... simple."

"Your family. And besides," Lily's voice softened, "It's nice to be reminded that weddings aren't always about giant productions. Yours is precisely how it should be, personal and intimate."

Grace glanced over at her. "You sound like someone who's maybe not as against the idea of weddings... or romance anymore?"

Lily waved her off with mock offense. "Don't get any ideas. You just caught me in a sentimental mood."

Grace didn't press further. "Well, sentimental or not, I'm so lucky to have the best wedding planner in the world." She gave Lily's arm a squeeze.

Laughter and conversation continued effortlessly, but Grace wasn't fooled by the easy back-and-forth. She knew Lily too well. Behind her cousin's bright smile and polished exterior, there were walls—ones that Lily wasn't ready to admit were there, much less bring down. But Grace could see them, clear as day.

"Anyway," Grace said, her voice bright with excitement, "I'm sure you'll want to settle in before I overwhelm you with all things wedding. We should probably get your stuff inside before the sun goes down completely. Plus, I need to show you where you'll be staying."

Lily stretched lazily, then stood, following Grace off the porch and back to where the car was parked. Daisy wove excitedly around their feet as they lugged the remaining suitcases into the cabin.

Inside, the cabin was even cozier than Lily had imagined. Thick wooden beams crisscrossed the ceiling, and the soft light from the windows painted the room with warmth. In the living area, a stone hearth anchored one end of the room, its rustic charm making the space instantly feel warm and cozy. There was a scent in the air—wood smoke from a recent fire and something sweet, like the remnants of a candle.

Grace gave a small, almost bashful smile as she gestured around the space. "Well, this is it. I hope the rustic cabin vibe works for you."

Lily took it all in—the simplicity of the space, the quiet elegance of Grace's life here. It was so... unguarded. So unlike everything Lily had built her world around. "It's... perfect, Grace. Really," she replied, her tone sincere.

Grace beamed. "Glad you think so. You'll be staying up in the loft—let me show you."

They made their way up the narrow staircase to the loft, where an antique four-poster bed took center stage. It was like the star of the show in the room. The bed was covered in a pile of handmade quilts that were so pretty, they looked like colorful works of art. The loft had a calm, stylish vibe, with a soft pink, white, and yellow color scheme. The bed had several decorative pillows in pastel colors and delicate lace, plus a couple of big, fluffy pillows to sleep on. There were cute vintage end tables on either side of the bed. A vase of fresh flowers on the dresser. There was even a small TV mounted on the wall in one corner. A huge walk-in closet for all her clothes. Another corner had a vintage rocking chair with more decorative pillows, and a bookcase filled with numerous paperbacks. From the large window next to the bed, the rolling hills stretched far beyond, like a painting that had come to life.

Lily lingered by the window, her gaze tracing the expanse of the mountains beyond. "You didn't have to go to all this trouble for me, Grace. I'm here to help, not to be spoiled, you know." She paused, her voice softening. "It just hit me... I've never stayed anywhere like this before." A trace of wonder crept in as she glanced back at her cousin. "I'm usually looking out over a skyline full of concrete, not...this."

Grace smiled and gently placed a hand on Lily's shoulder. "Out here, every window shows you nothing but pure beauty. And the best part? It's peaceful—no rush, no noise. While you're staying with me, just let yourself unwind. Consider this your chance to be pampered. So go ahead, settle in, relax, and make yourself at home."

Make myself at home...

Before she could linger on that thought, the sound of paws tapping softly against the wooden stairs broke through the quiet moment. Daisy trotted up the steps as if she owned the place. Without a second glance, the dog gave Lily's luggage a thorough sniff, her wet nose poking and prodding. Satisfied with her inspection, Daisy flicked her tail, hopped onto the bed, and curled herself into an unapologetic ball right in the middle of the quilts.

Lily watched her, a small chuckle escaping. "Well, I guess someone's already made themselves at home."

Grace grinned. "Oh, Daisy knows no boundaries. You'll have to wrestle her for that spot if you want it."

Lily shook her head, amused despite herself as Daisy sprawled out even more, heaving a contented sigh. "Yeah, I can see she's got a real knack for making herself cozy."

"Alright," Grace said, her eyes glinting with excitement as she clapped her hands together. "Now, on to some fun stuff! You've barely set your bags down, but we've got so much to catch up on. First things first—I can't wait for you to meet Ben's best man, Andrew! He's—well, let's just say Pastor Eli will be retiring soon and Andrew's the one that will fill his shoes when he retires. And he's single..."

Lily barely held back a groan, Andrew. Single, of course. The local preacher. Because what else did this quaint little town need to throw at her besides apple pie and a pastor gunning for heart-to-heart theology sessions?

Grace arched an eyebrow, catching the shift in Lily's mood. "Oh, come on. Don't look so dramatic, Lily. He's about our age, ridiculously kind, and nothing like what you're imagining. I think you two might actually get along."

Lily gave her cousin a dubious side-eye. "Grace, really? This feels suspiciously like matchmaking."

Grace's face morphed into a picture of wide-eyed innocence. "Who? Me? Matchmaking? Never."

Lily couldn't help the laugh that bubbled up. She rolled her eyes but smiled anyway. "Uh-huh. Sure. Whatever helps you sleep at night, Grace. But for the record—no pastor crushes, no 'nice guy' schemes, no playing cupid. I'm officially off the love market. Closed for business. Permanently."

Grace, unfazed, leaned in and kissed Lily on the forehead like she hadn't heard a word of it. "We'll see about that," Grace said with a grin. "Feel free to unpack. The dresser is all yours, and I've left plenty of hangers in the closet for you. I'll head downstairs and whip up a

Caesar salad—nothing fancy, but I'm starving, and I bet you are, too. How does that sound for dinner?"

"A salad sounds perfect, Grace. Thanks."

Lily glanced around the cozy loft and let herself relax for the first time since her car had hit that extremely curvy, winding road. She rummaged through her suitcase, pulling out only the essentials for now. She was too exhausted to unpack everything tonight. Instead, she hung a few blouses and trousers in the closet, tossing a quick glance toward the bed where Daisy was still sprawled out luxuriously. The dog hadn't budged an inch, still in her happy canine dreamworld.

Lily sighed, looking out the loft window again. The view was almost criminally peaceful, as if some unseen artist had labored over every detail—the rolling mountains, the sky that had deepened into rich hues of lavender and rose as dusk softly descended.

She could hear Grace downstairs, humming softly as dishes clinked together in the kitchen. The idea of enjoying a meal made at home instead of her usual takeout felt almost too good to believe.

"Come on, Daisy. Let's head downstairs and give Grace a hand, shall we?" A soft snore was her reply. With an amused exhale, she headed down the stairs to join Grace.

Chapter 2

Andrew Whitman stood at the edge of the overlook, as a gust of wind tugged at his jacket and tousled his dark, wavy hair. The crisp air carried the lingering scents of fallen leaves, rich forest soil, and the cool freshness of the river, but above all, it was tinged with the essence of autumn—fresh and full of change.

The New River stretched before him, a ribbon of silvery-blue winding through the landscape. The forest and mountains surrounding the river stretched out like a living tapestry, woven with threads of gold, copper, and crimson, as the Appalachian Mountains dressed themselves in the fiery colors of fall. The trees, towering and proud—dense thickets of oaks and maples, aflame with the season's dying embers. The wind rushed through their branches, making the leaves dance on their final descent; they swirled and spun in kaleidoscopic spirals before settling gently onto the forest floor.

The world felt impossibly vast yet intimate—a secret shared between the mountains and the sky.

Andrew's attention drifted toward the sky, where clouds floated lazily against soft pinks and purples, their edges brushed with gold as the sun rose in the sky. The beauty touched something deep inside him—something still and searching. This place—the river, the overlook, the mountains, the endless expanse of forests—it was more than a view to him. It was a refuge. A sanctuary. It reminded him, even when life was uncertain, there were constants. The earth beneath him. The wind overhead. God's creation spread out before him like a gentle reminder of something timeless.

As the wind swept past him again, it was as if it was reaching through him, pulling at the uncertainty knotted in his chest. The questions, the doubts—they were always there, beneath the surface. With every step closer to taking over Pastor Eli's role at the church, the weight of it all pressed heavier into Andrew's heart. Could he really do this—lead a congregation, carry their burdens and joys alongside his own?

He wasn't sure.

Somehow, though, being here—standing on the edge of the cliff where he could see how the sun kept shining despite the seasons changing, how the leaves turned brilliant and then fell to the earth promising new growth—it steadied him. It gave him a sense of peace, even as his mind whirled with possibilities and fears.

The wind tugged at the edges of the papers on Andrew's clipboard, a quiet nudge that even in the midst of all this grandeur, his day was still tethered to the ordinary—inventory to check, equipment lists to review. He'd come in early intentionally, hoping to steal a few moments of calm before the usual bustle at Adventure Tours began, when the eager crowds would arrive, ready for their trek through the rugged mountain trails.

Andrew's gaze dipped back to the mountains, drawing strength from their presence. They stood tall, unwavering, and seemingly eternal—the kind of endurance he longed to mirror. The kind of trust he wished he could claim.

But for now, he could only stand here and hold on to the peace that this moment gifted him.

The trees shivered again as another wind gust rustled through their leaves, setting them loose like fragile butterflies. Andrew couldn't help but think those leaves were much like life—beautiful, fleeting, and carried along by forces larger than any of them could control.

A small smile tugged at the corner of his lips. God, in all His infinite complexity, had a knack for creating beauty from change—perhaps even from uncertainty.

And if the wind could carry the leaves where they needed to go, faith could do the same for him.

"Hey, Andrew!" A familiar voice called out from behind him.

Andrew turned to see Ben, tall and broad-shouldered, walking toward him, his tousled brown hair catching in the breeze. Ben's confident, easy stride practically made the earth tremble underfoot. In his plaid flannel and cargo pants, it was clear the man was as much a part of these mountains as the trees. He wore ruggedness with the kind of ease that only someone who'd grown up in these parts could manage.

"Morning, Ben!" Andrew greeted, his breath visible in the cool morning air.

Ben waved one hand in the universal signal to hold that thought while the other balanced two large cups of steaming coffee. "Couldn't let my favorite assistant pastor slash manager freeze his tail off out here without a proper caffeine boost, now, could I?" Ben grinned, handing Andrew a to-go cup.

Andrew chuckled, wrapping his hand around it for warmth. "This shows a real understanding of the needs of your employees."

Ben winked, leaning against the log railing that bordered the overlook. "You know it."

They stood there in shared silence for a few moments, enjoying the tranquility of the morning—the peaceful hum of nature, the river rushing before them, and the birds singing their own morning praises.

Between sips of coffee, Ben shot Andrew a curious glance. "You've been awful quiet these last few days."

Andrew shrugged, his eyes still on the rugged landscape. "I guess I've had a lot on my mind. It's... you know, this balance thing I'm trying to figure out."

Ben nodded. "Church stuff?"

"Among other things." Andrew lowered the cup, resting it on the wooden railing. "It's... it's this feeling that I'm on the verge of something more... something bigger. Pastor Eli's been hinting about stepping down sooner than he originally planned, and it feels like everyone is expecting me to just seamlessly slide into his role. But it's more complicated than that."

Ben peered at Andrew, his brows knitting together in concern. "So, it's more like you're not sure if you're ready?"

Andrew exhaled slowly, the sound almost swallowed by the wind that swept through the trees. "That's part of it," he admitted. "But then, there's the other thing..."

Ben gave him a knowing look, waiting. "The other thing?"

Andrew tapped his fingers on the worn wood of the railing, the hesitation heavy in his posture. "It's just... what if I can't do both?"

Ben's eyes narrowed in thought. "Do both what?"

Andrew let the question hang between them for a moment, letting the weight of it settle before he spoke again. "Serve the church the way it deserves… and still have a life outside of it. You know, maybe find someone to share it with—someone to love, build a family with."

Ben's expression softened, understanding dawning. "Ah."

Andrew ran a hand through his dark, unruly hair, a hint of frustration creeping into his voice. "Sarah made it pretty clear that she didn't want to live in the shadow of ministry, and it's hard not to think… what if most women feel that way? Maybe this is God's way of telling me that I'm not meant to have a relationship—or a family, kids, any of that."

Ben took a slow, thoughtful sip of his coffee, giving Andrew's words the consideration they deserved. "And you really think that? That your calling and having love in your life are mutually exclusive?"

Andrew shrugged, the sting of doubt clinging to him. "I don't know. But sometimes… yeah. It feels like it."

Ben nodded, a long silence stretching between them. Then, setting down his coffee, he met Andrew's gaze directly. "Here's the thing, Andrew—just because your life path is different doesn't mean it has to be lonely. God's plans are complex, yeah. But that doesn't mean He's closed the door on love. It might just take a different form than you expect."

Andrew listened, but the thought still weighed heavily on him, unshakable.

"I guess," Andrew said, "but it's difficult to picture it all fitting together—the kind of life I have, the responsibilities of the church… and then making room for someone else in the midst of all that."

Ben gave him a thoughtful look. "Maybe there's more room than you think."

Ben continued, "I've known you all my life, Andrew. You're an assistant pastor, sure. But you're also young. A man like you… I don't believe God called you to walk this road alone."

Andrew considered the words, but those doubts lingered, gnawing at the edges of his faith in the matter.

"It's challenging to picture it," Andrew murmured. "Taking on the lead pastor role. It's more than just Sunday sermons. It's full-time care for people, preparation, and guidance. Entire lives. Where does a relationship fit into that?"

Ben chuckled, nudging Andrew with his elbow. "The same way it does for the rest of us. By trusting that God knows how to fit things where they need to go."

"Easy for you to say," Andrew teased, a smile cracking his otherwise serious face. "You've already found Grace."

Ben's grin only widened. "What can I say? I'm a lucky man. But you're dodging the point. You're not that different from the rest of us. God didn't write 'Pastor' next to your name and suddenly cut off access to the rest of life. You're still allowed to want love, just like anyone else."

Andrew's heart twitched at the words.

"You just have to believe you deserve it," Ben added.

"I guess I'm still working on that belief part." Andrew traced the rim of his cup before adding, "And let's be real—there's no one on the horizon, anyway."

Ben raised his eyebrows and looked at Andrew as if he'd just missed the most obvious clue in the room. "Uh, you sure about that? Grace's cousin just got into town. She's single and our age. You never know ..."

Andrew frowned. "Cousin?"

"Lily Reynolds." Ben said with a playful gleam in his eye. "She got here yesterday. Manhattan-based wedding planner. She's staying with Grace to help organize the wedding and then dog sitting while we're on our honeymoon."

Andrew's frown deepened, but there was a flicker of curiosity beneath it. "Wedding planner from Manhattan, huh?"

"Mm-hmm." Ben's lips curved. "And I'll bet you all my rafting gear she needs some encouragement and a break from her city life, just as much as she needs that wedding planner binder of hers."

Now Andrew was intrigued. "How so?"

Ben sighed, rubbing his neck. "Let's just say... she's been hurt before. A lot like you were, by the sound of things. Grace told me she's sworn off love, marriage, all of it. You know how it is with city folk sometimes—guarded, skeptical, always moving because stopping would mean feeling." He shrugged.

Andrew mulled over the idea, tipping his mug as the warmth faded with the cooling coffee. "So, she's a wedding planner who doesn't believe in love."

"That about sums it up," Ben said, chuckling.

Andrew chuckled. "Don't even try to play matchmaker."

"Hey now, you know I won't. But the possibility is there for you to meet someone new. You know, get your feet wet again and ease back into the dating scene."

Andrew raised an eyebrow.

Ben tapped the railing, grinning wider. "Look, all I'm saying is, Lily is here for four weeks and she's not seeing anyone. The rest is up to you."

Andrew stared down at his now-empty cup and shook his head, half-laughing, half-pondering.

***

Andrew moved on autopilot as he wrapped up the day's responsibilities—sending last-minute emails to vendors, reviewing tomorrow's scheduled tours, and running through the countless other minor tasks that had piled up. Even though his hands were busy, his mind was elsewhere, tangled with unresolved thoughts.

He rubbed his temples, glancing out the office window at the fading light of the evening.

Pastor Eli's retirement. The thought gnawed at him, always present in the back of his mind, like a distant storm cloud inching closer. Too soon... it was all coming too soon.

The congregation at the church had already begun murmuring about it—some speaking openly, others in hushed conversations after services. Everyone expected Andrew to step up when Eli retired. The thought left a weight on his chest.

Turning away from the window, Andrew's gaze landed on the task board pinned to the office wall. Beneath a haphazard collage of permits, laminated safety instructions, and snapshots of past clients sat a multicolored grid outlining the week's shifts, adventure tours, equipment reservations, and guide assignments. As he traced his finger down the schedule for Saturday, a frown set in. One of the lead guides, Jim, had been assigned to two different hiking groups at the same time—a clear oversight.

"Great," Andrew muttered, pulling out his phone to send a message. Fixing scheduling errors was far from the most glamorous part of his job here at Adventure Tours. While he preferred being out in the field—leading tours or climbing rock faces—he spent just as much time in the office wrangling logistics. In those moments, when he wrestled with payroll, vendor contracts, and the incessant email notifications, the sound of river rapids or the crunch of hiking boots on trails felt a lifetime away.

A far cry from Sundays at the church, where there was a different kind of stillness.

As he scrolled through his staff list, trying to find someone who could fill in for Jim, his phone buzzed.

"Perfect timing," he muttered before answering. "Adventure Tours. This is Andrew."

"Hey, it's Shelly," came the voice of their newest guide. "I'm down by the back shed sorting out the kayaking gear, but three of the harnesses are frayed pretty badly. Should I shelf them or just toss them?"

"Thanks for catching that. Toss them. I'll order replacements right now."

"Got it. Thanks, boss!" Shelly chirped before hanging up.

Andrew slid the phone back into his pocket and sat at his desk. It never ended—managing payroll, gear upkeep, safety protocols, staff training, not to mention balancing the books at the end of each week. There was always something to do, and though Andrew didn't mind hard work, the relentless cycle could wear anyone down.

It all felt so different from how he'd imagined it when Ben first roped him into co-managing Adventure Tours. Back then, he'd envisioned more time outside, guiding groups through the Appalachian wilderness, immersing himself in the natural beauty of the place. Now, most days slid by under fluorescent office lights or behind computer screens as he tackled the less glamorous side of running a business.

Still, it wasn't the chaos of management that weighed on him most—it was what loomed when everything went quiet. When the tasks were done, the tours scheduled, and the emails sent, only his thoughts remained restless and gnawing.

Could he balance it all—Adventure Tours and stepping into Pastor Eli's shoes?

The transition was happening, whether or not he was ready. The murmurs of the congregation grew louder each week, their expectations woven into every handshake and warm smile after Sunday service. They trusted him. They believed he could fill Eli's role when the time came.

But Andrew wasn't so sure.

Eli had been guiding him for months now, helping him grow into his role as the assistant pastor. Andrew hadn't known what to expect when he'd first agreed to take over. But Eli had been patient, allowing him to find his own approach while providing steady mentorship. Yet as the weeks and months went on, Andrew had noticed the signs—Eli rubbing his temples after a long sermon, leaving his Bible behind more often than he used to, fatigue etching lines into the older man's face. Soon enough, it would be Andrew standing at that pulpit every Sunday, managing crises day in and day out, preparing sermons, visiting homes—just like Eli had done for decades.

But did he have what it took to shoulder not only the practical demands but the emotional—and spiritual—heaviness that leading a congregation required?

Andrew leaned his elbows on his desk and scrubbed a hand over his jaw, feeling the slight scrape of stubble. Not that his faith wavered—his faith, if anything, was a constant, his anchor. God's love sustained him, even in his lowest moments. But could it sustain him while carrying the weight of the entire church on his shoulders?

Was that God's plan?

And was it selfish—feeling like something was missing? Wondering if there was a place in his life for love? For a partner to share all of this with?

The memories of Sarah still stung occasionally. She'd broken things off because she hadn't wanted to live a life of ministry—didn't want the burden of being the pastor's wife.

Andrew sighed and sat up straighter, pulling himself from his thoughts. Maybe love wasn't meant for men in his shoes. Maybe God's plan for him was different.

Even so, deep down, a small part of him wasn't ready to believe that.

"Pack it up for now, man," Ben said as he stepped into the doorway of Andrew's office, wiping his hands on an old rag. "We've got dinner at Martha's Diner soon."

Andrew raised an eyebrow. "We do?"

"Yup, all four of us. Grace insisted. You're coming."

Andrew paused. "And by 'all four of us,' I'm guessing that means her cousin will be there too?"

"Sharp as a tack, my friend," Ben said with a wink. "Lily's the star attraction tonight. Wedding details, yada, yada. But hey, dinner's on me."

Andrew chuckled, shaking his head. "Ben, I don't need to be—what's the phrase? Fixed up?" He folded his arms. "Besides, she's from Manhattan, right? I'm not exactly in the market for a long-distance relationship."

Ben leaned in, that mischievous grin never faltering. "Who said anything about a long-distance relationship? I'm just talking about dinner. Besides, it's not like you're married to the ministry, Andrew—you're allowed to talk to a woman once in a while who isn't one of Pastor Eli's widows."

Andrew snorted, rolling his eyes. "Yep, I'm surrounded by dynamo church widows. I get plenty of unsolicited introductions at the ladies' Bible studies."

Ben laughed and leaned back against the door frame. "Don't worry, I won't present you as a prize bachelor of Laurel Ridge this evening."

"Good," Andrew replied, trying to stifle a smile. "Because I'm not."

Ben raised his hands in mock surrender, still grinning. "Hey, come on now, you've got a lot going for you. But Lily, from what Grace has told me, is not looking for a relationship, so you don't have to worry. Maybe some friendly advice from your spiritual and emotional wisdom will do her some good because Grace said she's hurting."

Andrew gave him a sideways glance. "Is that so? Well, while the idea of playing Dr. Phil over dinner sounds riveting, I'm going to have to decline—on the grounds that therapy isn't exactly my area of expertise."

"Oh no, it's not therapy," Ben countered, his grin widening. "It's just... conversation. I'm not asking you to write up a diagnosis."

Before Andrew could respond, Ben continued. "Anyway, pack it up. Grace is starting to freak out about seating charts or something wedding-y, and you do not want to face her wrath if we're late."

Andrew sighed, but played along. "You sure this isn't just some elaborate scheme to fix me up?"

"One hundred percent sure." Ben grinned. "But if your plans involve staying single forever... I'd call that your choice. All I'm doing is offering a little Grace-approved socialization."

Andrew shot Ben an unimpressed glare. "Subtle, Ben. Very subtle."

Ben raised one slow, exaggerated shoulder shrug and tapped his temple. "Hey, I only use my powers for good."

Andrew chuckled as he grabbed his jacket. "Uh-huh. And if your schemes don't pan out? What's your backup plan?"

"Backup plan? Easy!" Ben said. "More free food at Martha's Diner until you come around."

Andrew shook his head as they walked out the door. "You've got quite the strategy. But I'm telling you, no one's looking for miracles here."

"Sure, sure," Ben called over his shoulder, voice teasing. "Although I've heard we might know a Guy who's pretty good at those."

Chapter 3

Martha's Diner buzzed with energy as Andrew and Ben walked in behind a crowd of hungry locals. The familiar scent of fried chicken and buttery biscuits wrapped around them like a warm embrace, while the low murmur of conversation hummed, giving the place its easy, small-town charm.

It was the type of atmosphere where everyone knew your name, and Andrew loved that.

Grace spotted them immediately from a booth by the window, her face lighting up with that smile she seemed to wear like it was part of her wardrobe.

"Right on time!" she called out, waving them over.

Ben slid into the booth beside her with the ease of someone who owned the space, while Andrew hesitated for just a second—just long enough for his eyes to lock onto the only unfamiliar face at the table.

Lily Reynolds.

She was undeniably stunning—sharp blue eyes that practically gleamed with the kind of keen, calculated observation people in big cities made a living off of. Her blonde hair, thick and wavy, cascaded softly around her face, catching the light in a way that highlighted the subtle golden undertones. She had a natural beauty that made her seem relatable, real.

Her handshake felt solid, but there was a firmness there, as if she were drawing a line, an invisible barrier separating her from anyone who dared to dig too deep.

"Nice to meet you," Lily said, her voice polite but clipped, like a person ready to politely disengage at any moment.

"Nice to meet you too," Andrew replied, masking his curiosity with a friendly smile. He could tell. She was a puzzle. And puzzles had a way of pulling him in.

"I hear you're working hard on Grace and Ben's wedding?" he added, hoping to draw her out just a fraction.

Lily gave a small nod, her posture poised and composed, before dropping her gaze back to the menu. She scanned it with the focus of someone preparing for a business meeting, rather than relaxing into the warm, informal vibe of a simple dinner.

Before the conversation could go further, Ben leaned in with his usual playful grin. "So, what's the verdict for our wedding, Lily? Biggest wedding disaster in the making, or manageable?"

That tugged the corners of Lily's mouth up just a bit, although the smile didn't quite reach her eyes. "I'll let you know when the wedding's over," she said dryly.

Everyone chuckled at the response.

Martha Kincaid, owner, waitress, and sometimes cook at the diner, appeared, her presence like a burst of southern hospitality wrapped in a blue-checked apron. The woman could light up a room with just her drawl.

"Well, well, look what the wind blew in," Martha said with a teasing grin. Her voice carried that warm charm she was known for—the way mothers and grandmothers spoke when they knew everyone's business but loved you anyway.

She clucked her tongue affectionately. "I love seeing young folks out and about. Ben, don't you dare start causing trouble here tonight," she teased, playfully waving her notepad in his direction.

Ben chuckled, throwing his hands up in mock surrender. "Who, me? I'm the model customer, Aunt Martha."

Grace leaned into Ben, her bright-eyed smile directed up at Martha. "You know he's always on his best behavior for you, Martha."

"Oh, I believe it," Martha responded with a wink. "But just barely." Her gaze then shifted to the unfamiliar figure seated beside Pastor Andrew. Martha paused for just a second, her eyes narrowing knowingly as she put two and two together.

"And you must be Lily, right?" she asked with the kind of sassy warmth that instantly put strangers at ease. "I've been hearin' about you all week long. I was wonderin' when I'd get to meet you."

Lily blinked, surprised but pleased, and nodded. "Guilty. I just got into town yesterday."

Martha gave her a once-over, nodding in approval. "Well, you picked a good group of folks to have dinner with this evening. Just don't pick up any of Ben's bad habits while you're here," she said, sending Lily a conspiratorial wink.

Lily smirked. "Noted. I'll be on my best behavior, too."

"Honey, please," Martha quipped, pausing to roll her eyes. "Now, what can I get y'all to drink? Root beer floats? Sweet tea? Coffee?" She nodded in Grace's direction before lowering her voice. "I can bring some hot cocoa your way. It's getting chillier every day."

Grace grinned. "You know me well, Martha. Extra marshmallows, whipped cream—the works."

"Of course, sweet pea," Martha replied before turning to Ben. "And what about you, Ben? Coffee?"

Ben leaned back. "Coffee's good—plain."

Martha scribbled it down, catching Andrew's eye with a teasing tilt to her lips. "And Pastor Whitman, sticking with the usual?"

Andrew leaned in. "Actually, let's go wild. I'll take hot chocolate too—no whipped cream. Gotta save some of my dignity." He threw a mock-serious glance at Ben. "Otherwise, I'll be bouncing off the walls like Mr. Trouble over here."

Ben snorted and Grace shook her head as she said, "You're impossible."

"And what about you, Miss Manhattan?" Martha's eyes narrowed playfully as she turned her attention to Lily, who was clearly still adjusting to this lively small-town vibe.

Lily blinked, giving a wan smile. "Just plain coffee, yes. No frills."

Martha's knowing glance lingered a moment longer. Then, with a wink, she whisked away, leaving a trail of warm energy behind her.

A contented buzz settled over the table, conversations flowing easily. Lily, however, remained quiet, occasionally letting a genuine smile slip out, but pulling back just as fast. Andrew couldn't help but sense how tightly she held her composure.

"So," Andrew ventured again, wanting to keep the conversation alive but easy. "Ben tells me you've got quite the wedding business up there in Manhattan, Lily?"

Lily's eyes flickered with the slightest hint of guarded amusement. "I stay busy," she said, her voice calm but tight. "Big personalities and even bigger expectations. Everyone wants the perfect day."

"What a shocker," Ben teased, leaning in. "Brides freaking out over flowers and hashtags on Instagram. Never saw that coming."

Lily smirked at the good-natured jab, clearly used to this line of thinking. Still, some of that tension around her shoulders relaxed.

Grace was quick to pile on, her face lighting up in that devilish way only siblings or close cousins could manage. "Tell them about that rooftop wedding with the swans. You know—the disaster."

Lily winced, though she was smiling now. She brushed a stray strand of blonde hair back, locking eyes with Andrew for a brief moment. "Oh, that fiasco? The bride insisted she needed two live swans from Central Park brought to the reception. Thought it would set the right mood."

She shook her head, laughing a little. "Have you ever tried convincing two public park swans to behave? Not exactly a dream job."

Andrew laughed, genuinely caught off guard.

So, beneath all that careful composure, Lily had a wicked dry wit tucked away. Interesting.

"Guess that's going into your 'Don't Panic: Disaster-Proof Wedding Planning book?'" Andrew teased.

Lily quirked her eyebrow. "Oh, the chapter on animal handling is going to be legendary."

Ben was practically howling at that point, while Grace just shook her head.

Martha returned with their drinks. "Now, what will you fine folks be ordering for dinner?"

"I'll take the Cobb salad with extra tomatoes, please." Grace said.

Martha raised a single eyebrow. "No fried chicken? Are we feeling alright today, Grace?"

"Just trying to eat healthy before the wedding. You know... fit into the dress." Grace shrugged.

Martha clicked her tongue and wrote the order down but leaned in conspiratorially with a loud whisper, "Honey, that's why they've invented sashays and Spanx. You can have your chicken and eat it too. Extra crispy, just the way you like."

Grace grinned. "I'll keep that in mind."

"Speaking of extra crispy, Martha, go ahead and sign me up for the double-fried chicken sandwich—with gravy on the side. No shortcuts tonight. If I'm going down, at least let it be delicious," Ben said.

"Now that's what I'm talking about," Martha said, jotting it down and giving him a nod of approval. "And for you, Andrew? Let me guess... the same ol' grilled chicken with vegetables?" she asked with a mock sigh.

Andrew grinned and shook his head. "Not tonight. I'll take the bacon cheeseburger, well done, with a side of fries, please."

Martha raised an eyebrow, clearly impressed. "Oh, well, look who's loosening up. Could this be the beginning of a new Andrew Whitman era? One with cholesterol?"

Lily snorted into her coffee at that. "You go from cautious to bacon cheeseburger in one meal? I'm not sure I even make decisions that big that quickly."

Andrew threw her an amused look. "You'd be amazed at the kind of major life choices I can make. Living life on the edge, one burger at a time."

Lily chuckled, tapping her fingers on her menu. "Well, I better keep up with all these daring choices. I'll take the steak sandwich with a side salad. No cheese, please."

Martha let out a dramatic gasp, her hand flying to her chest. "No cheese? Bless your heart, I ought to charge you extra just for the pain that causes me."

Lily smiled, enjoying the back-and-forth. "I'll take my chances."

"Alright then. Steak sandwich—no cheese. You're killin' me," Martha sighed, adding the order and sliding her notepad back into her apron.

As she sauntered off, Ben shook his head. "She amazes me. All that energy and humor wrapped up in one person."

Grace nodded. "Without her, I'm pretty sure we'd all just starve."

"She is a lively person all right," Lily said, her lips twitching into a smile as she sipped her plain, no-frills coffee.

Andrew leaned back, noticing how Lily had begun to warm to the group. Despite her careful facade, he could sense there was more to her—a depth and complexity that lay just beneath the surface.

"So Lily... How did you get into wedding planning?" Andrew asked.

Lily looked up from her coffee, the question catching her slightly off guard.

"Funny enough," she began, "I never really planned to be a wedding planner—at least not in the beginning. It all started when I was free-lancing as a graphic designer. You know how it goes—small projects here and there, helping friends with invitations, thank-you cards, little things just to make ends meet."

Her gaze flicked briefly over to Grace.

"But then things shifted," Lily continued, her voice taking on a more reflective tone. "I was working on a project for a friend when, out of nowhere, she asked me to organize her entire wedding. I guess she could see that I had a talent for details—designing invitations, place cards, event programs—it all came naturally to me. I could see how everything fit together, not just from a graphic design perspective, but as a cohesive vision for the whole event. I took the challenge, and before I knew it, I wasn't just organizing her wedding—I was coordinating every aspect. After that, word spread, and soon I was offered a position at one of the top wedding planning firms in Manhattan. I accepted—mainly for the stability of a steady paycheck.

"So, you kind of stumbled into it, but stuck with it because you were good at it. But is it something you love?" Andrew asked.

Lily's smile faltered for just a second before she composed herself. She gave a half-shrug, fiddling with the handle of her coffee cup.

"Well," Lily started, her voice shifting to something a little more contemplative, "I wouldn't say I don't love parts of it. There's something inherently magical about helping people create a day that's supposed to be the happiest of their lives. There's a rush when everything finally clicks—the flowers are just right, the lighting is perfect, the music starts, and all eyes go to the bride walking down the aisle. It can be... beautiful."

She paused and glanced out the window. "But somewhere along the way, that magic started fading for me. It's not gone, exactly... but I think I've reached a point where wedding planning isn't enough anymore—not for me, at least." she trailed off, searching for the right words, "I'm ready for a change."

"You're wanting to go back to graphic design, aren't you?" Grace asked.

Lily's eyes darted toward Grace. She gave a slight nod. "Yeah, that's it exactly. Graphic design was my first love, and I miss it. I miss the pure creativity of it—the part where I can sit with an open canvas and make something from scratch. Don't get me wrong, planning weddings takes a lot of creativity too, but there's something about graphic design that feels more personal to me. It's more fulfilling in a different way. I've known for a while that I don't want to be in wedding planning forever."

Andrew asked, "So... are you thinking about transitioning out of wedding planning completely?"

Lily bit her lip again and gave a small, tentative nod. "That's the goal, eventually. I've already started applying for graphic design jobs, but it's a tough market to break into, especially when you're trying to shift gears after being known for something else. It's a competitive field, and the freelance gigs I've taken on between weddings haven't exactly launched my new career the way I hoped." She sighed, but then gave a slight smile, lifting her eyes toward Andrew.

Ben leaned back in his seat, folding his arms across his chest, still studying her with that curious spark in his eye. "Well, sounds like you're making some bold moves. That's no small thing, changing course like that. Are you just burned out on weddings?"

"It's not exactly burnout, at least not in the traditional sense. Weddings are fine, but I think it's more about where I see my life going. When I was younger, wedding planning seemed so exciting—creating perfect days, making love stories come to life. But now... I don't know. I guess I'm realizing that love stories don't always pan out the way we dream, even when the wedding itself is perfect. And it's hard to keep giving so much of myself to other people's big days when..." She trailed off, and for a brief moment, something darker flickered behind her eyes, just enough for Andrew to notice but not enough for her to let it out fully.

"When what?" Andrew prompted.

Lily swallowed and mustered a dry chuckle. "When you're not sure if you believe in happy endings yourself anymore."

A quiet stillness followed her words, the kind of silence that only comes when someone has said something that hits a little too close to home.

Grace reached over and took Lily's hand. "Well, I think you should do what makes you happy, even if it takes time. The world could use more people following their passions and fewer swans invading wedding receptions, right?"

The group laughed, Lily's laugh genuine this time, though it still carried the weight of someone who was trying to figure out just where her heart fit in the picture she was painting for herself.

"Thanks, Grace," Lily said, her tone filled with warmth. "I'm trying, at least."

Andrew's gaze lingered on her a moment longer. She's trying, he thought. He could relate all too well. Like her, he was facing big questions—ones about life, love, about what came next. The paths they were each walking weren't all that different.

Chapter 4

The fire crackled in the hearth, casting flickering shadows across the knotty pine walls of the cabin's living room. The scent of burning wood mingled with the sweet undertone of the candles Grace had lit earlier—a mix of cinnamon and vanilla. It was the kind of comforting aroma that wrapped around Lily, almost daring her to relax.

Daisy, her brown head resting on Lily's thigh, let out a soft snore, perfectly content sandwiched between the two women. Grace sat on the other side of the dog, her legs stretched out across the big, poofy ottoman, holding a steaming mug of herbal tea in her hands.

Lily tapped her pen against the small notebook she had balanced on her knees, absently making little doodles in the margins between notes about centerpieces and ceremony details.

"So... Do you think things are shaping up? Are you planning to add an ice sculpture or fireworks for the reception? Something over the top?" Grace asked.

Lily chuckled, flipping through the pages of her neat, organized notes. "Tempting, but no. I think we'll stick to something that won't set off alarm bells with the fire marshal. Thank you very much."

Grace laughed and snuggled deeper into the cushions. "Well, you know if anyone could make that work, it'd be you. You've got the magic touch."

Lily grinned.

"What's wrong with my simple wedding that's got you in full-on business planning mode this evening? I just want a simple wedding, no stress." Grace asked.

"Oh, you're hilarious," Lily replied, grinning at her cousin. "These small, rustic weddings might seem easy, but they've got hidden complexities. Do you have any idea how hard it is going to be to source artfully 'disorganized' flowers?"

Grace gasped, mock horror on her face. "Oh no, not disorganized flowers! Where will the madness end?!"

Lily laughed.

"Somehow it will be a perfect simple wedding, Grace, just as you're hoping for." Lily said, flipping her notebook closed and resting it on the coffee table beside her.

"It doesn't have to be perfect," Grace replied. She pulled her knees up to her chest, wrapping her arms around her legs. "It just has to feel like us, you know? Simple. Warm. I don't need fireworks or towers of cake. Just me, Ben... and the people we love."

Lily's heart squeezed a little at that. Grace was so sure, so settled. There was no jittery uncertainty in her tone, no frenzied list of what-ifs blossoming in her mind the way they always seemed to with Lily. No, Grace knew exactly what she wanted, and she was ready to enter whatever came next with calmness and trust. It was beautiful... and a little heartbreaking.

"You're really excited, aren't you?" Lily asked.

"Yeah. I am." Her gaze drifted toward the fire, as if lost in thought for a moment, then she continued, her voice carrying that edge of joyful disbelief that people sometimes get when they're on the edge of their happily ever after. "Beyond excited, I feel... ready. I mean, I spent so long-running away from anything that looked like this—thinking love and life had to be bigger, louder, more chaotic. And somehow, it turns out the simplest things were what I needed all along."

"I'm happy for you, Grace."

"You are, right?" Grace's voice was gentle, but with that knowing edge only a loved one could get away with. "Because sometimes it seems like maybe wedding planning one too many love stories has left you a little disillusioned."

Lily waved her off with a good-natured snort, shaking her head. "Oh, here it comes..."

Grace laughed, but then leaned in. "No, but seriously, Lily—how are you? I mean, really? I feel like we've talked about weddings nonstop since you got here, but we haven't really talked about you yet. I mean, we did earlier this evening at dinner, but now it's just us. Girl talk...."

For a moment, Lily considered spinning another deflection, some joke about how she was just too busy to think about herself these days. But the way Grace looked at her—steady, without judgment but full of concern—made lying impossible.

Lily's shoulders sagged. She leaned her head back against the couch, staring up at the ceiling beams. "I'm fine," she said. "At least, I think I'm fine."

Grace waited patiently, knowing better than to rush her cousin when she was like this.

"I guess," Lily went on, "I'm just... I don't know. Tired. I've been doing a lot of thinking lately."

"About?"

Lily sighed. "About work. About life. And... how it really is time for me to make a career change."

The fire popped, a log shifting as the flame caught higher. Grace's gaze remained fixed on Lily, her expression tender and patient.

Daisy let out an adorable little grunt between them, pressing her head deeper into Lily's lap, as if sensing the shift in the emotional ties between the two.

Lily rubbed her hand along the dog's soft fur, her thoughts drifting to the career she dreamed of having years ago. "Yeah. I've been thinking more and more about making the switch. I love aspects of wedding planning, don't get me wrong. The creative juggling act, the design elements, seeing everything come together—it can be rewarding. But graphic design is where my heart is, you know?"

Grace's smile faltered, just for a second, but she composed herself. "You really miss it, don't you? The design work."

Lily nodded.

"And why haven't you just made the leap full time yet? I imagine there are plenty of remote or freelance jobs in graphic design."

Lily sighed, rubbing her temples. "Because wedding planning provides a steady paycheck. I can count on it."

Grace's gaze softened. "Makes perfect sense."

"I just," Lily continued, "I don't know if I can keep doing it for much longer. The more time passes, the more I feel like I'm losing the fire for it."

"You know what I've been thinking this whole time?"

"What?"

"I'm proud of you. It's not easy when life throws curveballs the way yours has the past few months." Grace said.

Lily's smile faded. "I don't always feel proud of me," she admitted, keeping her voice as neutral as possible. "But it's hard after everything... after Bill, after... trusting."

Grace nodded. She didn't need Lily to elaborate on Bill; she already knew the details—the betrayal, the disillusionment. How Lily's once unshakeable belief in love, and maybe even in God's goodness, had been shattered. She'd never blame Lily for her skepticism. This was what heartbreak did—it whittled away at your once-solid convictions until all that was left was cynicism and guardedness.

Grace tilted her head, her wide, honest eyes reflecting the glow of the fire. "I can't imagine how hard it must've been, walking through all that pain and betrayal. But... I think you're underestimating yourself. I mean, you've come out the other side, Lily. You're moving forward, even if you don't totally feel it yet."

Lily curled her toes into the soft rug under her feet, her throat tightening just enough to remind her how much she hated sympathy, even when it came layered in care.

It wasn't that Grace was wrong—Lily was moving forward... in some sense.

"It's not that simple, Grace," she murmured. "Every time I think about trusting someone, even with a small piece of myself, that old fear creeps in. It's all so... fragile."

Grace stayed quiet for a moment, contemplating her next words as though choosing them with the utmost care. "Do you think that fear is about more than just Bill, Lily?"

Lily blinked as she looked away from Grace.

Grace continued. "I mean, I get it—what he did, it broke something. You lived through something that would make anyone question everything. But I wonder if your fear of taking a leap—for your career, for love—it's rooted in more than just his betrayal. Maybe it's about trusting in something bigger again."

Something in Lily's chest tightened. "Trusting in something bigger."

Her mind flitted around that phrase like it was trying to escape. Trusting in what? In love? In God?

Lily reached for her mug on the coffee table and took a sip of her now-lukewarm tea, trying to gather her thoughts.

Grace had always been the gentle nudge—the one to peel back pieces of Lily's armor without making her feel like she was standing bare. But even Grace didn't entirely understand. She couldn't. Grace's life was now a patchwork of love and simplicity, where everything seemed to fit in place with an effortless grace Lily couldn't begin to imagine.

"I don't know," Lily admitted. "Maybe it's less about trusting something bigger and more about... I don't know, trusting myself again. When everything went down with Bill, I lost trust in my own judgment. I missed it, Grace. All the red flags. All the signs. I was supposed to be able to see those things, right? To know better? But I didn't. And... now, it's like I'm scared to trust my gut, whether it's about relationships or career or... anything."

"Lily, you didn't see the red flags because Bill was good at hiding them. He betrayed your trust. That doesn't mean your instincts were off. It means he was deceptive."

Lily twirled the pen between her fingers, trying to absorb her cousin's sincerity. Grace spoke from a place of wisdom, having rebuilt her life after her own struggles.

Grace leaned in. "You have an incredible capacity for knowing what feels right. Whether it's knowing the exact shade of flowers to match your bride's dress, or whether someone is walking into your life for a reason. But you have to stop blaming yourself for what went wrong back then. It wasn't your fault. And just because you want to go after something else now—graphic design or whatever your heart's tugging at—that doesn't mean you're about to fall into some new trap."

Lily said nothing, but her heart had started to beat a little faster, tension knotting between her shoulder blades as Grace's words filtered through her defenses. She wanted to believe them, but...

The wind outside the cabin lightly rattled the windows, reminding her of the world beyond this safe, fire-lit cocoon. They were here—two women curled up with a dog on a couch. Where life and big questions didn't seem as burdensome. But in a week? In a month?

"Lily?" Grace's voice broke through Lily's thoughts again.

Lily let out a long breath, the air tasting colder now as her mind retreated from its defenses. "I can't turn off the skepticism like you can, Grace." Her throat tightened as she spoke. "I wish I could. But I think I've been burned too badly. It's not as easy as choosing to believe in love or optimism or new beginnings. I look at you and Ben, and it's beautiful, it's perfect... but it scares me at the same time. I'm terrified of trusting again. And not just romantically. Everything—work, friendships, even in God. I'm suspended between waiting for something good to happen and bracing for the moment it all falls apart."

Grace moved closer, placing her mug on the end table next to her dog-eared copy of the bridal magazine they'd flipped through earlier. She took one of Lily's hands.

"I'm not saying it's easy to trust again, Lily. It wasn't easy for me to start believing in the quiet miracles happening in my life. But trust doesn't mean you won't ever get hurt again. It just means you're willing to believe the future could still hold something good despite the hurt."

Lily didn't say anything in response, but she let her cousin's words seep into her heart for a moment.

"What about you?" Lily asked. "How do you trust that this thing with Ben is going to last? I mean, after everything you went through, all your doubts... how do you know?"

Grace's lips turned up in a soft smile. "You mean other than him convincing me to swear off work heels forever and invest in hiking boots?" Her eyes sparkled with light teasing.

Lily chuckled, her lips curving upward despite herself.

"In all seriousness," Grace said, meeting her gaze, "I know because it feels different. It is different from everything I've known before. Ben is... steady. Our life together is steady. It's not about grand gestures, it's about making sure love is built in our everyday moments. Trusting that it's not fragile. Not like the superficial things I used to chase."

Lily's lips pursed into a tight line of thought.

Steady.

She didn't know if she'd ever experienced that kind of steadiness—not in love, not even in her career. Her entire relationship with Bill had been fiery, full of joy and ambition, but in the end, it had unraveled. Trust? Well, that had gone up in flames long ago.

"Hey," Grace said, nudging Lily's arm. "I'm not trying to sell you on some fairy tale. But I'm not going to sit here and pretend you don't deserve something good, either. Whether it's love, or graphic design, or—geez—something else entirely. Trust may start small, but it's always worth rebuilding."

Lily bit her lip, a corner of her mouth eventually twitching into a chuckle. "You've been saving up all these wise speeches, huh?"

Grace grinned. "I knew they'd come in handy one day."

"I'm not against trying," she said, her voice measured. "But... I haven't exactly worked up the courage yet. When I'm ready... I'll let you know."

"Deal," Grace said.

The fire was dying down, casting long shadows across the floor, but the evening felt far from tiring. There was something rejuvenating about their girl-time in front of the fire—a place where time could stop, and they could just be, wood crackling softly, silence rimmed with understanding.

"Thanks, Grace," she murmured.

"Always," Grace whispered, "Always."

Chapter 5

The Laurel Ridge Community Church stood peacefully amidst the grandeur of the Appalachian Mountains. The sun bathed the church in a warm glow. Every hill, valley, and ridge surrounding the church was painted with nature's last burst of life before winter—a rich, fiery tapestry of gold, crimson, and rusty orange, with leaves trembling and falling in slow motion from the ancient oak and maple trees that lined the property.

At the church's crest, the old bell tower rose toward the sky, its whitewashed steeple piercing the heavens like an arrow, stark and proud against the backdrop of the endless blue. As a gentle mountain breeze whispered through the trees, a fragile string of clouds, touched with a pinkish blush, floated across the sky, as if reluctant to disrupt the stillness below.

The church's wooden structure, though modest, held a quiet elegance. Its exterior was meticulously kept, the structure polished like a smooth marble, contrasting against the deep rich colors of the forested hills beyond. The arched, leaded glass windows—tall and stately—ran along either side of the building, stained-glass in vibrant patches of ruby reds, sapphire blues, and stunning emeralds.

The doors of the church stood open, a warm invitation to any passerby. The hand-carved wood doors bore marks of age, their grainy texture offering a tactile memory of hands that had passed through over generations. The polished brass of the door handles glimmered in the sunlight.

Beyond the church, the grounds stretched out into a blanket of green meadows, framed by towering trees and dense thickets of wild-flowers—some still clinging stubbornly to the last colors of the season. A gravel path wound its way around the back of the church to a small, rustic pavilion with thick wooden beams supporting a high, weathered shingle roof. Rows of long, worn benches sat beneath the open structure.

There was an unmistakable sense of tranquility. It was the kind of quiet that eased into a person's bones, a stillness that whispered with the murmurs of faith and the breath of rustling leaves. Birds darted among the branches overhead, their calls soft, almost reverent, as if aware they were guests in a place of peace. The air was filled with the sweet aroma of autumn leaves and wildflowers, pure and bracing in its simplicity.

It was a vision that might have graced any postcard—a scene so pic-turesque, so imbued with charm and serenity. It felt like time slowed under its spell. For all its simplicity, the church stood as a steadfast figure in a landscape that was nothing short of divine artistry—an unwavering testament to quiet grace against the rugged beauty of the Appalachians.

Lily stepped out of her car, her heels making soft clacking sounds on the gravel path leading to the entrance. She took in a steadying breath, smoothing down a few stray strands of hair that had been tousled by the breeze. The beauty of the church was undeniable, but it somehow sharpened her sense of alienation. Much like everything in Laurel Ridge so far, this place felt too peaceful, too settled for someone like her.

"Hey, Lily," Andrew greeted her from the church's open doors, his deep voice warm and relaxed as he appeared in the doorway.

He was dressed in dark jeans and a plaid flannel shirt, sleeves rolled up to the elbows. His wavy hair tumbled over his forehead, giving him a boyish but grounded look. He had that calmness that took her off guard—as if the weight of the world couldn't shake him.

"You're early," he noted with a small smile. "Grace and Ben texted. They are stuck behind a train—one of those long ones." His smile tugged into something more playful. "So it's just us for now. I can show you around if you'd like?"

Lily composed herself, putting on her usual polished professional face. "That's fine," she said, returning his smile but keeping a touch of detachment in her tone. "I prefer being early—it gives me time to take everything in and make sure things will work for what I have in mind."

"You strike me as someone who's good at making sure everything is under control."

Lily blinked, feeling an odd tug in her chest. His tone wasn't patronizing, just... observant. Like he saw more than she was willing to show.

"Let's take a look," she said, brushing it off.

Andrew stepped aside to let her in. The rich scent of polished wood and faint candle wax filled her senses. Inside, the church was... comforting. Late-afternoon light filtered through the stained-glass windows, casting soft pinkish, light green, and cobalt hues along the pews and floor, like fragments of a long-forgotten dream.

"The architecture's beautiful," Lily said, glancing at the high wooden beams crisscrossing overhead. Her voice echoed in the quiet, and she felt an unexpected reverence creep in. She cleared her throat. "Has Grace mentioned whether she wanted the flowers arranged at the front of the church, or more toward the sides?"

Andrew nodded as he walked beside her, his hands tucked in his pockets. "She's mentioned both options. She's flexible, but knowing Grace, she'll want it to feel personal... intimate. I imagine whatever you suggest will be fine."

Lily drifted further down the aisle. "I'll make it perfect," she said.

Andrew seemed to consider her for a moment as they reached the altar. "Perfection's great," he said, as if tasting the idea. "But it's fragile, isn't it?"

Lily paused, glancing at him with narrowed eyes. Was he giving her life advice now?

"Pardon?" she asked, her voice more clipped than intended.

Andrew smiled, but it wasn't arrogant. "Just thinking out loud. People plan everything down to the last detail. Want everything perfect. But sometimes, the best moments are the ones we don't plan for—the ones that catch us off guard. That's the beauty of it, I think."

Beauty? Lily shook off the thought, pretending it didn't stir something deep and tense inside her. She drew her posture straighter, her planner voice taking over. "Well, in my experience, I find that having a plan for everything is the best way to keep things from falling apart. Trust me... I've seen enough disasters to know that."

Andrew raised an eyebrow but didn't push. "I believe you."

Just then, a familiar voice cut through the silence, full of energy and barely contained excitement. "Sorry, we're late!"

Lily turned toward the entrance just as Grace and Ben hurried into the church, out of breath but all smiles.

"We got stuck behind that crazy-long train," Ben explained, giving Andrew a pat on the back. "Thought it would never end!"

"No worries," Andrew said with a grin. "We were just getting started."

"I imagine Lily's on top of everything, as usual. What have you two been brainstorming?" Grace asked.

Lily shifted gears, donning her efficient, no-nonsense wedding planner persona. "Let's talk about layout. The church lends itself to a more vintage style, so I was thinking of keeping it simple but elegant—candles in vintage lanterns lining the aisle, pews with autumn floral arrangements in muted golds, burgundy, and browns. It will complement the windows without overwhelming them."

Grace's eyes sparkled. "That sounds perfect! But... do you think we should have additional lighting, or will the candles be enough?"

Andrew chuckled next to Ben, shaking his head. "See, weddings are a whole different world. So much debate over candles, Pastor Ben."

Ben elbowed him with a grin. "Hey, don't knock it until you've planned one yourself, Pastor Andrew."

Lily raised an eyebrow, turning to Ben. "Wait—you're a pastor too?"

Ben shrugged, amused. "Yeah. I help with the youth group here at the church, and I minister during special youth events throughout the year. Andrew and I both lead youth Bible study once a week as well. I keep busy."

Lily was genuinely surprised. She hadn't picked Ben as the youth-pastor type. The outdoorsy adventurer? Sure. But youth ministry? The combination was... unexpected.

"You two?" Lily asked, glancing from Andrew to Ben. Her curiosity was piqued, her professional demeanor cracking.

Andrew's eyes held a playful gleam. "Yeah," he admitted. "We're not just working partners at Adventure Tours—we're partners in wrangling teenagers for a youth group as well. I guess we can add wedding assistants to our line of duties too..."

Ben nodded, throwing a conspiratorial glance at Andrew. "Stick with me. You might get some new material for some bridal emergency kits when you see the kind of chaos we deal with over the next couple of weeks."

Lily gave a half-smile, shaking her head.

As if on cue, the distant sound of chattering teenagers echoed in from the entranceway. Andrew exchanged a glance with Ben and nodded. "Speaking of chaos... Duty calls."

Teenagers began arriving, spilling into the back of the church in a wave of excitement and energy. There was Noah, Martha's wide-eyed grandson, already making some joke while a group of girls rolled their eyes good-naturedly. The rest of the group assembled, backpacks slung over shoulders or dragging on the ground, the clash of laughter and banter adding life to the space.

Andrew and Ben exchanged glances—showtime.

Andrew stepped toward the doors, throwing Lily a parting smile. "I'm sure we'll catch up later. But for now, youth wrangling is calling..."

Ben flashed a grin. "Consider ourselves dismissed."

Lily watched with mild fascination as Andrew disappeared into the crowd of teens, falling into his role. She looked over at Ben—just as energetic and easy with the group—and for the first time, she saw him as a youth pastor. Grace caught her look and smiled.

"Ben's great with the youth. They both are," Grace said, watching her fiancé work a room full of teenagers like it was second nature.

The teens clearly loved him, hanging onto his every word—even when those words were mixed with jokes and jabs.

Lily found herself struck by the sight. It was... unexpected. Endearing, even.

Grace nudged her after a moment. "Come on, I want to show you the recreation hall for the reception."

Chapter 6

Lily followed Grace outside the church and around to the back, where a modest, yet inviting recreation hall emerged from a small line of trees, tucked neatly on the church's property. The building itself was simple—constructed of worn, weathered wood siding—but well cared for and exuding a homey charm. The rectangular structure had a gently sloped roof, its natural finish blending seamlessly with the surrounding Appalachian landscape. Large windows lined the front, allowing natural light to pour into the spacious interior, where the church held its indoor gatherings—from youth activities to wedding receptions, and sometimes even community dinners when the weather didn't cooperate.

Beyond the recreation hall, to the left, was the outdoor pavilion—a larger rustic shelter supported by solid timber beams. The pavilion featured an open-air design, its high roof providing ample cover while still allowing the surrounding beauty of the mountains and trees to be part of the experience. Long wooden benches inside the pavilion, set for a more casual gathering—perfect for the congregation's outdoor socials after Sunday services.

In good weather, this space was often used for Sunday afternoon dinners or sometimes even outdoor services, the pavilion serving as a natural gathering point where the vibrant energy of the community came alive. Lily could almost picture the laughter and conversations shared there under the warm summer sun, the congregation coming together for fellowship after the weekly sermon, passing dishes of homemade casseroles and fresh-baked pies.

The entire layout—from the hall to the pavilion outside—was functional, but also cozy in a way that felt like home. To Lily, it wasn't just about the aesthetics—it was about creating moments that would linger long after the decorations were taken down, and the guests had gone.

"So, this hall is where you want the reception, right?" Lily asked, pulling out her notebook, walking toward the hall and making a few mental calculations.

Grace nodded as they stepped inside. "Yeah, it's perfect. It's simple, but that's what I want. Warm... intimate."

Long banquet tables stretched the length of the hall, practical yet easily transformed with the right decor. Lily could envision candles flickering upon skirted tables, the natural wildflowers that Grace wants spilling out of earth-toned vases, and garlands of greenery winding their way across the tables. Rustic details could be added to the allure, but Lily could already tell it wouldn't take much to turn this humble space into something magical for Grace's wedding.

Lily walked over to one table, running her fingers along the edge as ideas started forming in her head. "What about string lighting under the beams? Maybe mix some wooden accents with candles and fresh florals. We could do table runners along the banquet tables, paired with small glass jars of candles to add warmth and simple vases filled with flowers."

Grace beamed. "Yes! That sounds perfect."

Lily nodded, making more notes and sketches as she leaned into her planner mode, sectioning off the space in her mind. "We can keep the color palette the same as the ceremony. Maybe some burlap with gold and burgundy accent pieces. It'll keep things cohesive, but a few candles will add something soft and romantic."

"That sounds amazing, Lily," Grace said, placing a hand on her arm. "I really couldn't do this without you."

"Or without your youth pastor-fiancé," Lily teased.

Grace laughed. "That, too."

Lily walked outside toward the pavilion, her focus fixed, while Grace hurried to catch up.

"What about the pavilion area? I was thinking we could stage it with a photo booth," Lily said, her excitement creeping into her voice as the idea began to take shape. She gestured with a sweeping motion, like a painter envisioning the first strokes on a canvas. "Maybe—hear me out here—we line it with mums and pumpkins, really lean into the fall theme? We could use burlap for texture, maybe drape it around the poles or on the benches, and for the backdrop..."

She trailed off, her eyes bright with inspiration. Grace, standing beside her, could feel Lily's infectious energy buzzing to life.

"Oh, I love this already," Grace cut in, her hand pressing to her chest like she could physically contain her enthusiasm. "And maybe even some extra string lights overhead?"

"Yes—yes! Exactly! More string lights would be perfect," Lily replied, snapping her fingers like the lights had just clicked on in her mind, too. The possibilities seemed endless now that her creative spark was igniting. "We can run them across the beams, creating a warm, cozy ambiance once the sun sets."

"Oh ... Grace," she added, "for the backdrop, why not let the mountains do the heavy lifting? They're already stunning, and trying to compete with them wouldn't make sense. So, I'm thinking... let's set up the photo booth in a way that the mountains are the natural backdrop. We'll frame it with some fall-themed accents like bales of hay and go for something soft and romantic. Maybe a simple wooden arch, draped with more burlap, flowers, and vines."

Grace squealed, clasping her hands together. "Yes! A blend of rustic and elegant—exactly what I love."

"Oh!" Lily's eyes lit up with another idea, and she pointed toward the sky. "And don't forget about sunset. Imagine the photos people will get as the sun goes down. Warm light hitting the mountains, all those autumn colors coming through in the pictures."

Grace, clearly thrilled, threw her arms around Lily in a quick hug. "I knew there was a reason I asked you to plan this. You always know how to take a small idea and turn it into a dream."

"Hey," Lily said with a grin, brushing off the praise while still feeling a rush of pride. "It helps when the setting is as dreamy as this."

"I can already see all of us gathered there! People chatting, taking photos... we'll set up quilts on the lawn for people to sit on if they want, right?" Grace said, bubbling over with excitement.

Lily sighed dramatically, shaking her head with mock exasperation. "And to think, just yesterday, you were telling me you wanted to keep it simple. Now we're talking about quilts and a custom photo booth. I've created a monster."

Grace stuck her tongue out playfully. "What can I say, with our two heads together, we dream big, and your ideas...you're making it irresistible! Don't hold back."

"I won't," Lily promised, her grin widening. "But in exchange, I expect at least one pumpkin spice latte for every mum I have to place out here."

Grace laughed, "I imagine you'll end up drowning in pumpkin spice by the end of this wedding."

"Well, I won't complain," Lily shot back with a wink. "It'll fuel my decorating creativity."

Grace placed a hand on Lily's shoulder and squeezed, a soft smile on her face. "You know, I think this wedding is going to be wonderful, Lily. It's not like I imagined growing up, but it's exactly how it's meant to be."

Lily returned the smile, though a slight tightness surrounded it. "Well, that's the whole point, right? Wedding dreams change with the person you're with. You and Ben make it easy."

Grace glanced over at her cousin. "And your dreams, Lil? Do you think—"

Lily cut her off. "Let's not get into that."

There was a brief silence, broken only by the distant sound of laughter from some children playing in the distance. Grace didn't need to ask more. She knew Lily was still guarding that sore spot in her heart.

"Alright," Grace said, nodding, dropping the topic with that same understanding she'd always had.

Chapter 7

L ily leaned back in the rocking chair on Grace's back porch, the steady creak of its wooden slats joining the symphony of sounds from nature. Just a stone's throw away, the New River, its current gentle. The mountains loomed peacefully in the background, bathed in the dusky glow of the setting sun.

Lily cradled a Mason jar of sweet tea, its condensation slicking her palms. She took a small sip, letting the sugar and lemon dance across her tongue, a far gentler flavor than the sharp, bitter punch of the triple-shot espressos she usually gulped down in Manhattan to fuel her fast-paced days. As the sweetness soothed her senses, she felt a quiet calm that was unfamiliar, yet comforting.

The porch beneath her feet stretched wide, its wooden planks worn smooth by years of use, each one polished by countless footsteps and the passage of time. Several large pumpkins sat clustered next to pots of deep purple and yellow mums. The flowers spilled over the edges of their planters, adding splashes of color to the porch. The cushioned swing to her side, where Grace gently swayed in time with the rocking chair, its soft creak mingling with the twitters of birds hidden high in the surrounding trees.

Lily breathed in deeply, the coolness filling her lungs, and for a moment, she let herself forget the weight she carried. The usual tension at the back of her mind loosened just the slightest bit.

As she sat there, lost in the stillness, a thin wisp of hair escaped her loose bun, brushing gently against her cheek in the breeze. She absently tucked it back behind her ear, her thoughts living in a place somewhere between nostalgia and melancholy. She closed her eyes for a moment, half-wishing, half-dreaming that she could lose herself in the peaceful cadence of this place. The simplicity, the space to breathe—it was a far cry from the relentless pace of the city.

She took another slow sip of the tea, the ice clinking softly in the jar.

The creak of the porch swing to her left caught her attention, as Grace shifted and continued to swing. Gently pushing with her feet as she lazily swirled the remaining ice cubes in her glass.

"You've outdone yourself with this place, Grace," Lily said. "Really, it's... so peaceful."

Grace glanced over, a small smile tugging at her lips, cradling her glass in her lap. "I figured you'd like it once you got here. Once all the wedding madness settles down, you'll be able to really enjoy all of this. Sit by the river late in the afternoons, or come out here on the porch at dusk when the stars start to peek out."

"I'll consider it," Lily replied, tipping back her glass of tea and letting the sweetness slide down her throat.

"Mm-hmm," Grace hummed knowingly, her eyes flicking to the mountains beyond. "Anyway, I was thinking... about the flowers for the ceremony backdrop?"

"Yes! That wildflower arch we discussed earlier—I think it could work perfectly with the wood accents in the church. Adds some autumn warmth without taking away from the beauty of the space. I can play around with some matching candles, maybe bring in a few antique elements. Minimal but impactful."

Grace's eyes lit up, and she swayed a little faster on the swing, nodding her head. "See, this is why I asked you to help me. You just get it!"

Lily chuckled, slipping into her professional mode. Discussing color palettes and floral arrangements and what she envisioned for Grace's wedding.

But just as she started to relax into the conversation, Grace hit her with that familiar look. The one that said, I know you better than you know yourself.

"I get it, Lily," Grace said, her voice as soft as the breeze teasing the autumn leaves scattered across the porch. "You're back into all business professional mode. But... you seem a little off this evening. Distracted."

Lily blinked, forcing her fingers to loosen their too-tight grip around her iced tea glass. "Distracted?" she repeated, setting her jaw. "Ha, no, I'm just fine. Planning a wedding, you know? It's my job."

Grace didn't buy it for a millisecond. She leaned back in the swing, just watching Lily with those steady, patient eyes—the ones that drove Lily insane because they always knew. Grace had mastered the art of saying nothing, yet somehow, saying everything at the same time.

"Uh-huh," Grace murmured, still watching her. "You're fine? Really?"

Lily crossed her legs and sat up straighter, pushing a smile back onto her face. "Yes! There's just a lot to juggle, that's all. I've got under two weeks to pull everything together, so... yeah, my brain's buzzing."

Grace didn't move, didn't even blink. But that silence was louder than any lecture.

Oh, no—here we go—Lily thought, already feeling the knot tightening in her chest.

"Come on, Lil. I'm your cousin. You can talk to me. What's really going on...?"

Lily felt the porch close in around her. The breeze brushing her skin only made her feel more restless, more exposed.

"I'm fine, Grace," Lily insisted firmly, even though she could hear the strain in her own voice.

Grace didn't flinch. "You're planning the wedding perfectly," she said with a smile. "But I think there's something else you're... avoiding."

Lily sighed, sinking back into the rocking chair, frustration bubbling to the surface. She stared down into her cooling glass, watching the condensation slowly trickle down the sides.

Lily's lips tightened into a thin line. For a few moments, she just stared at the river and the mountains beyond the yard, her knuckles whitening around the glass.

"This wedding," Lily said, her voice quieter, laced with an edge she couldn't hide, "...it's got me thinking too much. Way more than I expected."

Curiosity flashed in Grace's eyes, but she didn't say a word. It was the soft, open invitation Lily hated. She felt stripped bare by it.

"This idea of forever," Lily continued, her voice hardening as she bottled back the wave of emotion threatening to rise, "It's all around me. Grace, I watch you and Ben, and it's like love feels easy for you two. Just... simple. But forever? It won't happen for me. Not anymore." She paused, feeling her heart tighten.

Grace stayed where she was, her full attention on Lily—no judgment, just quiet listening. That was worse because it made it too easy for everything to spill out when all Lily wanted was to keep it locked down.

Lily let out a bitter scoff, her gaze narrowing at the horizon. "Do you think... maybe some people aren't meant for love? I don't know why, but here... seeing you in love, it makes me think..." her voice trembled. "...it makes me think I'm just not cut out for it."

Grace furrowed her brow and then softened. "Lily, you believed in love once."

Lily let out a sharp laugh, though her smile never reached her eyes. "Yeah. Once." She gripped her glass harder. "Remember that, Grace? I was engaged to the perfect guy. The man who swore we'd start a family and grow old together. Said all the right things?"

Grace's face softened with empathy, but the undercurrent of tension rose like a wave between them. Her silence invited Lily to keep going, to let out the pain she'd obviously bottled up for months.

"I thought Bill was everything... and I fell for it," Lily admitted, her voice tightening, brushing her hand across her face as if she were wiping away a smudge, though it was so clearly about holding herself together. "We had all these plans—you know? Big, beautiful dreams. About the future. Except, the whole time, I had no idea I was just his side project..."

A flicker of confusion crossed Grace's face.

"He was married, Grace—to someone else. The entire time. I've never told anyone that part..." Her voice cracked like brittle glass, slicing through the stillness. She leaned forward slightly, as if pushing the next part out physically hurt. "So yeah, he made me feel like I was the one. But in reality, I was just the other woman in some twisted double life he'd created."

Grace's gasp was audible, her hand instinctively gripping Lily's harder. The pain in Lily's voice added weight to the truth—weight she'd carried alone for far too long.

"Oh, my goodness. Lily. I... I didn't know."

Lily shook her head with a joyless laugh as if to say, how could you have known?

"Grace," she said, her voice soft but tinged with bitter cynicism. "He shattered every bit of trust I had in myself—in others. I mean, I was convinced he was everything. I trusted God too, you know? I prayed for us. And then..." She swallowed hard. "It's not just the heartbreak. It's the betrayal. The manipulation. That's what gutted me. And honestly? I don't think I will ever get over that part."

"I'm so sorry," Grace breathed, her voice breaking as she pulled Lily into a hug. For a moment, Lily stiffened, but then, as Grace's warmth seeped in, something inside cracked. The cold control she'd clung onto began to melt, if just a little.

Lily pulled away and straightened up, pulling herself back together before she could fall apart completely.

"Don't be," she murmured, sounding more exhausted than angry.

Grace sat back again, quieter, absorbing the weight of what Lily had carried around for months.

"I can't blame you for feeling hurt, betrayed... all of it, Lily," Grace whispered, her eyes soft and understanding. "After everything with Bill, I get why you're struggling. But... you can't stop believing altogether. Not in love, and definitely not in God. Those things don't leave us, even when it feels like they have."

Lily shook her head, brushing hair out of her face and feeling fresh tension pull at her jaw. "After what happened, Grace, I don't want love. It's too dangerous. And if God's paying attention, I've been wondering why He'd let me fall into something that devastating. How could He let me trust so much, only to break me like that?"

Grace swallowed back her own tears. "Lily... heartbreak isn't the finale of your story. God's plans didn't end with that ugly chapter in your life with Bill. I still believe He's got something better waiting—even if you can't see it right now. It's still there."

Lily stared at her cousin, a sad smile tugging at the corners of her lips. "That's a nice thought, Grace. Really. But happy endings?" She exhaled, shaking her head. "I gave up on that fairy tale."

"God's love isn't some fairy tale. It won't always look how we think it should. But He doesn't leave us to face the pain alone. Even when it feels impossible, He's still working. You just have to trust that He's still there... even when He feels far away."

Lily let the silence fill the gap between them. Her head said no. But her heart? It was tired. And maybe, deep down, some small part of her wanted to believe Grace was right. That this wasn't the end of her story.

But she wasn't sure if she could risk it again. The wedding, the town... and Andrew—they all reminded her of what she was guarding herself against.

So she did what she always did. She shrugged, casually draping cool indifference over her shoulders like a well-worn cloak. "Maybe," she said, voice soft but deflecting. "But I'm just not there..."

Grace squeezed her hand again, not pushing. "You don't need to be there right now, Lily. But maybe, someday... you'll let a little bit of love back in."

Her eyes flitted up toward the stars that were starting to peek out. *No... Never again.*

Chapter 8

L ily stood in the gravel parking lot of Laurel Ridge Community Church, clipboard in hand, eyes scanning the scene with the no-nonsense precision she was known for. The setting sun dipped behind the Appalachian hills, casting a warm, golden wash over the church's white steeple and the quaint green shutters on its windows. Sure, the view was picturesque enough to grace the cover of a postcard, but Lily wasn't about to let herself be charmed anymore by this sleepy little town.

She shifted the clipboard, making a mental note of everything that still needed to be done count the pews, measure the aisle for ribbon placements, finalize her floral arrangements to ensure no one's view of the altar would be obstructed by an overzealous spray of flowers. After that, she needed to check out the recreation hall more closely for the bridal shower and rehearsal dinner setup. Piece by piece, it was all coming together, and with each finished task, she was one step closer to finishing the job and putting this wedding, and all its warm and fuzzies, behind her.

Purpose and control—that's how she'd get through. Becoming emotionally entangled? Not part of the game plan.

Then there he was.

Andrew, looking every inch the casual country pastor with his rolled-up sleeves, dirt smudged on one forearm like some kind of badge of honor, and that easy, disarming smile plastered on his face.

"Hey there, Lily," he said as he walked toward her.

His presence was like a strong ray of sunlight that blinded you suddenly, warm but unwelcome.

"You ready to tackle all this?"

Ready? As if itinerary boxes were a fun group exercise. Lily forced a smile, keeping her tone professional, cool. "Yep, ready as I'll ever be."

The last thing she needed was to entertain any distraction, especially in the form of an annoyingly charming assistant pastor with a sharp gaze that saw more than she wanted to show.

Andrew stopped just close enough that she could catch the scent clinging to him: woodsy cologne, a hint of sun-warmed earth, maybe even laundry dried by the breeze. The kind of simple, genuine freshness that had no business unnerving her the way it did.

"So, what's the game plan?" he asked casually, hands slipping into the pockets of his jeans, as if they could just casually chat like old friends instead of people tethered by nothing more than a shared task.

She glanced at her clipboard, letting it become a shield between them. "The plan is detail work," she said, flipping through her notes for something concrete to hold on to. "We need to count the pews, decide where the flowers and candles will be placed here in the church, then head around to the recreation hall and complete the seating arrangements for the bridal shower and reception dinner." She might've been talking too fast, but keeping it all down to business was necessary. It kept things orderly. Neat. And most importantly, it kept her detached.

Andrew tilted his head but smiled, as if sensing her need for efficiency. "Sounds like you've got it all under control. Lead the way."

He gestured toward the church entrance, that easygoing demeanor still in place. Lily stepped ahead, feeling the cooler air of the church wash over her skin the moment they crossed the threshold.

"This is a lot of pews," she commented, inspecting the rows of dark wooden benches, her voice clipped to keep things on track.

Andrew chuckled behind her, the low sound settling somewhere in the pit of her stomach—closer than she'd prefer. "Yeah, small towns tend to err on the side of church overpopulation."

Lily knelt, tugging the tape measure from her purse. She plunged into work mode, kneeling at the first set of pews to measure the aisle width, tuning out the way Andrew's presence hummed beside her. He just stood there, watching, exuding quiet patience.

After a couple of minutes, he broke the comfortable silence. "So, you do this kind of thing a lot, huh? The whole wedding planner thing?"

"Pretty much nonstop, year-round. It is my job," she replied, without looking up.

Andrew leaned a little against the pew beside her, crossing his arms as he watched her work, a hint of gentle amusement lingering in his tone. "And I'm betting it's a little different here?"

Lily straightened, moving to the next row, gesturing for him to hold the other end of the measuring tape. He complied, stretching it across the aisle. She tried not to notice how strong and solid his hands looked. How they lingered there, as capable as his easygoing persona.

"Just slightly," she answered, coldness tinging her voice, not lifting her gaze from the task at hand.

"So, what's the craziest wedding you've worked on so far?" Andrew asked, his voice light but curious. "Over-the-top brides? Celebrity couples?"

His question wasn't obnoxious, just genuine. But how could she take it lightly when her current reality felt far removed from the glitz of New York weddings? "There are definitely stories. Some of them are fun, others—eh, not the stuff of happy endings."

Andrew laughed, the sound of it sliding into her grasp far too easy to catch. "I guess everyone wants their perfect day, so long as someone else is handling the chaos."

Lily straightened, returning his gaze with a raised brow. "That's why they hire me."

She cleared her throat. "Let's head to the recreation hall." Hard pivot. Stay focused.

With a simple nod and a much-too-calm smile, Andrew followed her lead. Together, they left the church. His footsteps matched hers.

Upon reaching the recreation hall, the afternoon light streamed through large windows, illuminating long rows of folding tables lined up like soldiers, their plainness reflected in the folding chairs stacked to one side.

"Definitely not the grandeur some brides usually picture," Andrew remarked, flicking on the lights with a chuckle.

Lily circled the room, her mind already laying out the new seating arrangements she had in mind, planning how simple centerpieces with seasonal flowers and candles could transform the space. She pretended not to notice how he tracked her every move, casually yet attentively.

"Maybe not," she admitted after setting down her clipboard. "But simple works sometimes, and for this wedding, it will be perfect." Her voice softened as she allowed herself a moment to breathe.

"No argument from me. Simplicity has a way of cutting through all the noise," Andrew remarked, his voice low, his gaze steady.

For the next twenty minutes, they worked in relative silence—Andrew rearranging tables while Lily measured, planned, and made notes. There was no reason Andrew should've made this much functional silence feel so charged with energy, but he did.

When she'd finished framing out the space she needed, Andrew leaned on the edge of a table, folding his arms across his chest in a relaxed stance. His gaze lingered on her in that curious way of his, like he was trying to see beyond the professional polish she wore like armor.

"So... Mind if I ask you something?" he asked, breaking the quiet with a calm smile.

Lily glanced up, poised and ready to deflect. "Depends."

Andrew's lips curved, amused. "Fair enough. You've planned a lot of weddings... Do you ever run across couples who don't really want to be together?" His brow furrowed, like the question had bitten at him from the inside and refused to let go.

Lily remained still, blinking in surprise. She hadn't expected such raw curiosity. So many people asked questions, but very few wanted real answers. Yet, Andrew... he gave her the distinct impression he wasn't just asking for the sake of conversation.

"I mean... statistically speaking?" She stopped herself, realizing he wasn't looking for numbers. He wanted honesty. She sighed, softening. "Some people are just chasing a dream, clinging to an idea of happiness. Others believe in it enough to try making it real. And yes, I've seen couples who don't really want to be together. They put on a happy front, more for their families' sake than their own. Then there are those who think they need a partner to be happy, so they talk themselves into marriage, hoping it'll somehow lead to that 'happily ever after.'"

"And you?" There it was again—that gentle sincerity. No judgment, no push. Just... wonder.

"Me?" she echoed, glancing down at her clipboard as if it could save her from this conversation. "I'm just the one who makes sure the day actually works as planned. What happens after isn't my problem."

Even as the words left her, she could hear the fragility in her own tone—more telling than she would have liked.

What happens after isn't my problem...

Andrew nodded, watching the subtle shift in her mood. The silence thickened, a hum of unspoken thoughts swirling in the space between them.

Andrew smiled awkwardly, changing the subject. "Well... I'm sure that Grace will be happy with the plans you have for the recreation hall. What else is on your agenda for today?"

Lily blinked, still recovering from the shock of the harsh words she spoke just a moment ago. She scrambled for control as she tucked her clipboard under her arm. "I've got what I need for today."

She allowed herself a fleeting glance toward Andrew. A useless, warm feeling swam through her chest again, unsettling but real.

"I'll help you with your things." He grabbed her book of fabric swatches before she could refuse. His voice was calm, warm, and dangerous for a woman like her—a woman with no intention of letting her guard down again.

They walked side by side toward her car. The October sky washed in calming pinks and ambers as the sun dipped behind the mountains. The sight caught her off guard with its beauty, reminding her how serene and beautiful life could be if she let it.

Andrew set the fabric binder down on the hood of her car, his faint smile accompanied by that unwavering gaze of his. "I'll see you around, Lily?"

"Yeah…" she muttered, gripping her keys.

"Thanks for your help today." Her words came out polite, but fraught with something she wasn't ready to analyze.

"Anytime, Lily," Andrew replied, voice low and genuine.

She watched him as he stepped back with a small wave. When she drove off, the temperature inside her car felt far too warm.

Everything is fine. This is just another job. And Andrew? Well, pastors always seemed nice—didn't mean it had to mean anything else.

But as the church disappeared in her rearview mirror, she felt that sinking curl in her chest—the one that made her think of how she'd built her walls for a reason. And yet somehow, he made it all feel flimsy in a way no one else had in months.

Back at the church, Andrew watched her car disappear down the narrow road.

He exhaled, closing his eyes.

Lord, what are Your plans for me because I think I'm headed into something that's going to either change me or break me?

Chapter 9

Lily paused just inside the doorway of Leslie's Blossoms, surprised by how welcoming it felt—like stepping into a place that seemed to exist outside of time. The shop was a cozy haven, enveloped in warmth and brimming with the rustic charm of a small town that knew how to take its time and enjoy the surrounding beauty.

The first thing that struck her was the sweet scent of nature itself wrapping around her, beckoning her inside. Like a floral symphony, the fragrance of fresh-cut blooms filled the room, a soft harmony of rose petals, wild daisies, and the sharper, invigorating notes of eucalyptus blending together. It was fresh and earthy, in that nostalgic, sun-soaked way that made you feel you'd taken a walk through a blooming meadow and stirred the wildflowers with every step.

Overhead, large wooden beams stood like watchful sentinels, crisscrossing the ceiling with their age-worn richness. While newer shops back in Manhattan might have been sleek and modern, built for efficiency and social media snapshots, here, the shop was filled with natural whimsy. Bundles of drying lavender swayed from the beams, their soft purple hue adding a touch of faded beauty, while trailing green ivy cascaded down toward ceramic and glass vases overflowing with assorted blooms. The ivy was untrimmed but arranged so that its wildness felt deliberate, like a perfect accident, adding softness to the raw wood and structure.

The light filtering through the shop's wide front window painted the space with warm nudges of gold, casting long amber streaks which highlighted the flowers themselves in the late afternoon sun. Everything was saturated in color—the oranges, reds, and deep purples that only autumn could provide. The sunlight gave the room a dreamy feel, as if every petal, every blossom, was kissed by its glow, bringing out the lush vibrancy of living things.

Nearby, hand-painted terra-cotta pots, their edges weathered, sat clustered along shelves, each one bursting with smaller arrangements of daisies and chrysanthemums, their colors complementing the muted blue of the worn shelf beneath them. They were charmingly mismatched, arranged with a balance that made them feel as though they'd always belonged exactly where they were.

The shop was a patchwork of cozy nooks. Everywhere she looked, there were little touches designed to make a person feel at home—small clusters of candles beside potted succulents, vintage watering cans doubling as makeshift planters, floral-patterned tea towels hanging on wood pegs. Each corner had its own personality, as though the shop was alive with more than just the flowers, breathing contentment from its walls.

Alongside the flowers that spilled over counters and tables in every hue imaginable were tiny handwritten signs that described each bloom with care. They weren't printed on fancy card stock or embossed in bold fonts, but written in Leslie's elegant, looping script, giving each flower a personality of its own.

In another area of the shop, a rustic table displayed a bouquet-in-progress. The deep mahogany, stained with years of trimmed stems and scattered leaves, stood like the heart of the shop. The wooden surface was scarred with years of work—each nick and scuff speaking of countless seasons and endless bouquets. A basket of tools—shears, floral wire, and twine—sat beside the bouquet, all arranged in a way that suggested care and craftsmanship rather than chaos. Yet, nothing felt forced. There was an easy, lived-in quality to it all, like this had always been the rhythm of life in Leslie's Blossoms.

It was a shop that felt handmade and exquisitely imperfect, as though it had grown from the roots of the flowers themselves, thriving in the warm and patient energy of a town that never cared for the frantic pace of the city. A place as welcoming as a friend's kitchen on a chilly morning—full of history, comfort, and the cozy charm that wrapped around you like a thick woolen blanket.

Lily shifted her over-the-shoulder bag, almost wanting to sink into that unexpected warmth, but she shook off the moment. She wasn't here to admire the small-town charm. She was here for business—another task to check off her list. Yet, some part of her was not as convinced—a small, quiet part that lingered just a little too long.

Her heels clicked against the polished wood floor as she moved further into the shop. She glanced at her clipboard, but for once, it didn't entirely hold her attention. Not with a place that felt so alive surrounding her.

What surprised her the most wasn't how overwhelmingly beautiful it was, but how disarmingly human it felt. Like stepping into someone's home—warm, well-loved, made to be lived in.

"Lily! Over here!" the familiar voice of her cousin startled her, knocking her out of her thoughts.

Grace waved from near the back, where she stood beside a tall wooden rack of flowers—sunflowers, dahlias, and wild blossoms that looked like sunset petals plucked fresh from the Appalachian hills...

"Of course, you'd be deep in flower choices the second I walk in," Lily called back, a teasing note lacing her words, though she kept her tone playful.

"Well, it is my wedding," Grace beamed as she turned away from the flower display. "I can hardly help myself."

"I've noticed," Lily said with a faint smirk.

Grace didn't miss a beat as she motioned to a woman standing behind the counter, her hands busy trimming the stems of pale yellow roses. She was petite, her thick, vibrant, auburn hair pulled up into a ponytail that had once been neat but now sported a few escapee strands, giving her a down-to-earth appearance. She had an air of quiet authority, yet the kind that made you feel instantly comfortable.

"Lily, meet Leslie Williams," Grace announced, like she was introducing Lily to some VIP guest.

Leslie offered a gentle smile, her round glasses catching the sunlight just enough to give her a motherly–yet–mischievous appearance. Wiping her hands down the front of her faded green apron, she offered a hand across the counter. "It's a pleasure to meet you, Lily. Grace has told me wonderful things about."

Lily extended her hand, feeling an unexpected warmth in the florist's touch. "Nice to meet you, too. Grace hasn't stopped talking about how amazing your flower arrangements are."

Leslie chuckled, shaking her head as if to brush off the compliment, though the ease of her laughter suggested she didn't doubt the compliment's validity. "I don't know if they're amazing, but they're made with love—and a few good prayers, of course." Leslie winked.

"Well, I can appreciate that," Lily said, bringing her clipboard out to the forefront of the conversation. "Let's dive into the arrangements, shall we?"

Leslie's sharp eyes danced over to Grace—a silent, knowing look that made Lily feel as though the two had something planned. A faint amusement sparked in Leslie's gaze again as she turned back, gesturing toward a table filled to the brim with color. "Grace was just telling me you were thinking of something elegant and simple for the ceremony. Autumn colored flowers, mums, touches of greenery for balance. But... she's got her heart set on incorporating several more wildflowers. Simple yet whimsical."

Lily darted a knowing look toward Grace, narrowing her eyes playfully. "You're the queen of simple yet whimsical, aren't you?"

Grace beamed, shrugging one shoulder. "It's my wedding. Gotta have a little whimsy."

Lily exhaled, biting back a smile. Her cousin was impossible. And impossible meant adapting.

"I'm open to it, of course. It's your wedding, Grace," Lily said. "But keep in mind that wildflowers can overpower an arrangement if not handled delicately. Too much wild and the whole thing will look... chaotic."

She expected Grace to give a lighthearted retort, but Leslie beat her to it, glancing up from where she'd been arranging roses in vases. "Well, some of the best things in life are a little wild, don't you think?"

Lily blinked in surprise, but covered it with a polite laugh. She had to admit—Leslie had a point. Though she was firmly in the controlled elegance camp for organizing weddings, there was a certain something about letting a bit of loose unpredictability shine through. The trick was to balance it.

"You might be right," Lily admitted.

"I think with your added touch for detail, the flowers will end up exactly as they should. Sometimes we try too hard to perfect things. But working with flowers has taught me... they have a will of their own. They need little—just some patience and gentle care." Leslie said.

Lily blinked. "Patience isn't always my strong suit."

Leslie hummed as she worked, casting a glance at Lily with a mischievous smile. "You know... last year, we had a wedding here where the power went out right as the couple was about to say their vows."

Lily paused, mid-note, eyebrows shooting up. "The power went out?"

"Oh, yes!" Leslie nodded. "And guess what? Instead of freaking out, everyone just pulled out their cell phone flashlights. The bride even joked it was more romantic than she'd ever hoped."

"And she didn't panic?" Lily asked, incredulous. She couldn't help the surge of professional anxiety that bubbled up at the thought. A power outage during a wedding? That would be a nightmare in Manhattan.

"Not even a little," Leslie chuckled. "Sometimes the unplanned stuff becomes the best part of a romantic wedding day. That's something big-city brides might never understand, huh?"

Lily managed a small smile, though her mind was still racing. "I think I'd rather not test that theory."

Leslie stepped from behind the counter, walking Lily toward a display of pre-arranged bouquets, her eyes bright with curiosity. "Grace tells me you've been at this wedding business for a while. You must have some grand stories."

Lily raised an eyebrow, glancing at the bouquet of autumn-colored sunflowers Leslie was holding up next to a bundle of baby's breath. "A couple."

"Only a couple?" Leslie's grin widened. "I'm sure you must've seen plenty of bridal meltdowns, decor disasters, and last-minute rescues."

Lily smiled. "This one time, a bride insisted on releasing doves during her vows. She said they symbolized freedom and love. But just as they let the birds out of the cage, one dove flew directly into the groom's face."

Grace winced. "Ouch."

"After that, the bride spent the rest of the wedding in tears because she thought it was a sign," Lily continued, her tone somewhere between serious and amused. "Needless to say, I'm not a fan of animal releases at weddings anymore."

Leslie chuckled, her warm laughter filling the shop. "People can get so caught up in making everything perfect for just one day, can't they?"

"Perfection is sort of the goal," Lily responded, her voice harder than she intended. Almost defensive.

"Maybe... but perfection's a heavy burden, don't you think?" Leslie replied, turning to arrange some blooms. "Sometimes the most beautiful moments are the ones that don't go as planned. Like when a sunflower decides it's going to lean a little more toward the sky than you expected, or when wildflowers spill out of the vases and refuse to stay straight. It's all still beautiful in the end—you just have to let it be."

The shop fell quiet for a moment as Lily absorbed the words. It sounded an awful lot like the way Andrew talked.

"And with everything planned for Grace, I'm sure the day will be beautiful no matter what," Leslie added. She gestured toward one of the smaller arrangements of blooms nearby. "Now let's talk about wildflowers, shall we?"

"We'll add more wildflowers," Lily said, after scanning the various floral stems. "But let's mix it delicately. We don't want things to look haphazard."

"Of course," Leslie agreed, pulling together some samples with an effortless grace, and then walked back to her work space. She arranged different combinations of flowers and motioned toward them. "Does this look like what you had in mind?" she asked.

Lily circled the counter, eyeing the colors and textures. "It's perfect."

Leslie smiled, nodding to herself. "I thought you'd come around."

Grace slid up beside her, balancing several miniature sunflowers as if they were born to be part of her own wedding. "I knew you'd like the wildflowers," she mused.

"I'm humoring you," Lily smirked over the top of her clipboard.

Grace bumped her shoulder with a laugh.

Leslie leaned back, wiping her hands on her apron. "By the way, Andrew swung by last week. He was helping me out by stacking some flower crates. He just can't say no when someone needs a hand."

Lily's breath caught—just enough for Grace to notice.

"Oh, yeah?" Lily responded, her voice trying to sound neutral. Andrew's name alone sent an uninvited flicker across her consciousness.

Leslie chuckled. "He's got quite the soft spot for wildflowers, too. Always tells me they're the best because they're resilient—and they don't need much fuss. We could learn a lot from them, don't you think?"

"Andrew and his small-town wisdom," Grace teased as she sorted through the sunflowers. "He and Ben are so much alike."

Lily forced a smile, willing herself to maintain control of her emotions. "Right. Wildflowers and wisdom."

Grace shot her a knowing look, but said nothing further.

While they settled into the final decisions for colors, quantities, and arrangements, Lily couldn't shake the itch of Leslie's earlier remarks about perfection—about letting things take shape naturally.

"Hey, I have an idea." Grace said.

Lily blinked, coming back to the present. "What's that?"

Grace's smile had that unmistakable playfulness. "I think you should come out with me and Ben tomorrow. Lunch and then a small hike. I think it'd be good for you to take in some of the beauty of this area. Besides, you need to unwind, take a break, and enjoy some fresh air."

Lily scoffed, though there was warmth behind it. "Hiking? Me? I don't even own a pair of hiking boots anymore."

Grace tucked a strand of hair behind her ear, inching her shoulders up. "Why not? We can set all the wedding stuff aside for one day. Besides, it's a Saturday, a day to take a break. I have a couple of extra pairs of hiking boots. I'm sure one of them will fit you just fine."

Lily shook her head with a laugh. "Fresh air... hiking... sounds like a nightmare for this city girl."

"Trust me, you'll survive." Grace teased, batting her lashes. "Plus, a bit of fresh air will be good for your soul."

"And who doesn't need some soul-tending," Leslie chimed in, placing a bit of baby's breath into a floral arrangement.

Lily tilted her head toward the ceiling, feigning exasperation. "Now I'm being tag-teamed."

"It's all for your own good," Grace deadpanned.

Grace smirked as Lily rolled her eyes.

"Okay, be honest," Grace said, leaning in conspiratorially. "When was the last time you—oh, I don't know—breathed?"

Lily arched a brow. "I breathe all the time, Grace."

"Let me rephrase... When was the last time you breathed and enjoyed life without a color-coordinated calendar or checklist?" Grace crossed her arms, her eyes sparkling with mischief.

Lily shook her head with a mock sigh. "Hilarious. For what it's worth, I can be relaxed. I just... choose not to be when I have a million things to do."

"Oh, sure..." Grace drawled, grinning. "Relaxed? You're about as relaxed as a type-A personality at a spa without Wi-Fi."

Lily shot her cousin a deadpan look, though the corner of her lip tugged up. "Maybe I enjoy staying busy."

"Or maybe you have just forgotten how to unwind," Grace teased, nudging her.

"Life doesn't have an 'unwind' button, Grace."

"There's your first problem," Grace shot back, twirling a sunflower. "You're still looking for one."

Lily weighed her options for a second—the pull of routine, of safety, versus hiking in the mountains with her cousin.

"Alright," Lily conceded.

The excited clap that followed from Grace made Lily roll her eyes, though she couldn't suppress her smile.

"You won't regret it," Grace promised.

Lily wasn't so sure about that, but she figured one hiking adventure couldn't hurt.

Chapter 10

Lily, Grace, Ben, and Andrew stepped inside Martha's Diner, bringing with them a swirl of crisp October air. The rich scents of burgers sizzling on the grill, a hint of cinnamon sugar from freshly baked pastries, and the ever-present aroma of coffee brewing.

"Y'all's timing is perfect! The lunch rush just cleared out." Martha's familiar voice rang out from behind the counter, her tone as folksy as the surrounding decor. Her eyes twinkled, and she waved them toward a booth near the front window. Her apron, checkered like the floors, tied snugly around her, and the pencil tucked behind her ear completed the picture. "Sit yourselves down. I'll be right over."

Lily slid into the booth next to Grace. Across from her, Andrew settled in, a calm smile gracing his lips. His presence felt... full, solid—like a quilt on a chilly day. And not in a way that left her claustrophobic. But it still made her sit straighter, more aware. She wasn't used to noticing a man's presence like that.

Ben, ever the jokester, shrugged off his jacket, winking at his fiancée. "Now this," he declared dramatically, rubbing his stomach as though expecting the best food of his life, "is what I call the perfect afternoon. Sunshine, a hike soon, and Aunt Martha's cooking is about to hit the table."

"You say that now. We'll see if you're still feeling sprightly after we hit the trail on full stomachs." Grace said.

"Ha!" Ben leaned back against the booth, hands behind his head like he was king of the world. "A full stomach never stopped me before, Grace." He shot her a teasing grin, and Lily couldn't help but smile at these two—they were so in sync, so effortless in the way they just fit.

And it made Lily's stomach twist just a little.

Across the table, Andrew turned his attention to her, casual as ever. "So, Lily, have you ever been hiking before?"

Lily met his gaze, steeling herself against that undercurrent she would rather not acknowledge—the one that seemed to hum between them whenever he looked at her like that.

"I hiked quite a bit when I was younger," she replied, keeping her tone light. "Nothing major, though, definitely not as much as you all do here. Nowadays, a stroll in Central Park is about as rustic as it gets." She smiled.

Andrew grinned, his eyes still locked on hers. "The city's scenery has to be nice in its own way. I'll warn you, though—Grace likes her trails with a bit of grit."

Grace piped up, crossing her arms with a mock challenge. "I know Lily can handle it. We're made of sturdy stuff."

Lily offered a light laugh. "My work includes being tough with extra grit every day. I'm not too worried about a little dirt and uphill walking."

Grace's grin widened. "Exactly. You'll love it."

Before the conversation could stretch any further, Martha appeared at their table. With her signature sassy, grandmotherly charm, she slid four menus across the table with practiced ease and set a glass of water in front of each of them. "Well, don't y'all look as cozy as frogs on lily pads," she quipped, her Southern drawl thick like honey. "What can I get y'all to drink?"

"Aunt Martha, I've been counting down the minutes since our last meal here. We all decided earlier, before we got here, that we need burgers, fries, and coleslaw today." Ben said.

Martha smirked. "Got it, and I assume a round of sweet tea?"

Everyone nodded in agreement.

Martha chuckled. "And you, Miss Lily, welcome back to my diner. I hope you're starting to find yourself at home in Laurel Ridge."

Lily hesitated for only a beat before offering Martha a warm smile. "It's been... fun."

"Oh, I'll just bet it's been fun..." Martha's eyes twinkled as she cast a glance—not-so-subtle—between Lily and Andrew. "And I bet Pastor Andrew has been good company?"

Lily's face flushed with a sudden warmth creeping up her neck. She glanced toward Andrew, who—annoyingly—looked like he was enjoying this little exchange. "He's... been helpful," she mumbled, trying to dodge the giant, awkward balloon Martha had just thrown into the room.

"Helpful." Martha nodded, like this was weighty sage wisdom. "Well, good teamwork never hurt anyone."

"Teamwork... Right," Lily muttered, glancing at the ceiling, willing her blush to disappear. She could feel Andrew watching her again. That unnerved her more than she wanted to admit—how easily his attention threw her off course.

Grace, ever the savior, swooped in to distract. "Martha, we can't thank you enough for cooking for the wedding reception and asking everyone coming to bring a dish to share. Getting everything in line has been a whirlwind, but you've been amazing."

Martha patted her notepad with a gleam in her eye. "No thanks necessary, sweetie. Y'all are family. We take care of our own here." With a wink, she turned back toward the kitchen.

Ben and Grace fell into their wedding chatter again, Grace making notes on who still hadn't RSVP'd, while Ben playfully teased her about over-preparing.

Meanwhile, Lily tried to refocus. But Andrew's gaze lingered.

He broke the silence between them, his voice low and easy. "How's your weekend going so far?"

Lily felt herself tense, but she tried to play it off with a casual smile. "Busy, as usual," she said, maintaining her professional veneer. "Grace has had an entire list of things to get done, so it's been non-stop this morning. Plus, I've had to handle a few concerns from clients in Manhattan concerning their upcoming weddings." She grimaced. "Can't ever fully escape those, it seems. Keeps me on my toes."

Andrew nodded, his gaze warm and understanding—but not too prying. "Sounds like you've got a lot going on. Still..." He glanced out the window. "I'm guessing the scenery here at least beats the view from your office?"

Lily glanced outside. "It's... beautiful here," she admitted. "Much quieter than I'm used to."

"Quiet's not always bad," he said, his tone gentle.

Lily sighed. "No, it's not bad. But it's... different."

"Different." Andrew repeated, his eyes holding hers with an intensity that made her heart skitter against her chest. "Different can be good, sometimes."

The air between them felt charged. She glanced away, unsettled by how easily Andrew could slip past her guard.

Before she could dwell on it further, Ben leaned forward with his easygoing grin, cutting through the tension with a chuckle. "You know, Lily, I'm convinced even you will be converted to small-town living before long. These mountains have a way of working their magic on people."

Lily shot him a disbelieving look, a playful smile just twitching at her lips. "Magic? I'm not so sure I'm the kind who falls for small-town 'magic,' Ben."

Ben raised his hands in mock surrender. "I dunno... A few more days in Laurel Ridge, and I think you'll start to feel it."

Grace giggled, swatting at Ben before reaching for her ice water. "Ben thinks everyone should fall in love with Laurel Ridge. He's practically the town ambassador."

Ben puffed out his chest dramatically. "What can I say? Grace fell for it. Left New York behind, never looked back—and trust me, I'm counting my blessings."

"I'll admit," she said, her gaze drifting back to the view outside, "the mountains are... peaceful. I do miss them now and then. And the people here? They've been lovely."

"Exactly," Ben said, all charm and winning smiles. "You'll be dreaming about it all once you're back in Manhattan. Just you wait—this place sticks with you."

Lily's smile grew, this time real and undeniable. "Maybe," she said. "But I'd better survive your wedding first before you try planning my move."

Grace cocked her head and laughed. "Fair enough. But who knows? Once the wedding's over... things might just change for you, Lily."

Andrew, who had said little in the last few minutes, chuckled. "Sounds like they're all lining up for your slow-burn conversion, Lily.

Next thing you know, they'll have you organizing bake sales for church fundraisers and plotting out hiking trips."

Lily couldn't help the laugh that escaped her. "Bake sales? Now, that's a line I'm not sure I'm ready to cross."

Chapter 11

"So... who's ready to hike off those burgers?"

Lily threw up her hands with a groan. "Are we seriously doing this?" she mock-complained. "I'll need three weeks to recover from all this food I've eaten!"

Grace giggled, her eyes twinkling. "Don't worry, Lily. You'll manage."

The group made their way to the door.

"Thanks again, Aunt Martha," Ben called, adjusting his jacket with a wink. "We'll see you at the wedding, if not sooner."

"Don't you disappoint me now, Ben Turner," Martha retorted, placing a hand on her hip as she waved them off. "Y'all better come back sooner than that and bring me the best stories from today's hike!"

Grace made a playful face as she held up her hand in a parting wave. "I guarantee we'll make 'em good!"

Martha chuckled, raising an eyebrow. "I expect nothing less from you, Grace."

Andrew smiled as he tipped his head toward Martha. "You keep that coffee pot on for us."

"Always do," Martha replied with a wink. "Y'all stay safe out there."

Lily gave one last glance over her shoulder, catching Martha's eye. Martha waved, her smile softening. "Take care now, Lily."

Lily returned the smile, giving a small wave in response. "Thanks, Martha."

They all piled into the Adventure Tours van Ben had driven today to avoid everyone driving separate cars to the hiking trail. Driving up the winding mountain roads toward one of Grace's favorite hidden trails, the view was impeccable. Small talk and laughter bouncing between them as Andrew teased Grace about her less-than-graceful and laid-back hiking style, and Ben promised to keep them all on track. The farther they drove up the mountain, the more Lily found herself drawn to the scenery, her gaze lingering on the expanse of wilderness stretched out before her. The dense groves of trees slowly gave way as they climbed higher, revealing breathtaking views of the valley below, each turn in the road offering something more stunning than the last. And then, the shimmering blue thread of the New River came into view, winding its way through the mountains like a glistening ribbon of life. It wasn't just any river; it was a force of nature, its waters swirling in wild, surging currents, weaving through jagged rocks and bursting into frothy white rapids. The sight of it was raw and un-tamed. She couldn't tear her eyes away, captivated by the way the river danced, a contrast to the stillness of the surrounding mountains that framed it like a work of art. The beauty of it stole her breath.

The van came to a stop in a small gravel parking lot nestled between towering trees. Stepping out, Lily breathed in the crisp, woodsy air. She wasn't much of an outdoorsy person, but there was no denying the peace and beauty that weaved through these woods. There was a quietness to it all—a completeness that felt miles away from the tightly wound energy of Manhattan.

"Well!" Ben said, already adjusting his backpack and stretching his arms like he was preparing for some grand expedition. "Everyone ready to conquer the Laurel Ridge Short Loop?"

Grace chuckled, walking over, tightening the strap on her backpack. "It's hardly an expedition, Ben. Two miles, round trip."

Ben looked at Andrew with an exaggerated pout. "Man, everyone's a critic."

Andrew just gave him a solid clap on the back. "That's what happens when you're as humbled as you are."

They set off on the trail, with Andrew ahead of Lily, and Ben leading the way alongside Grace. The crunch of dirt and leaves under their boots became a rhythmic sound, steady and grounding against the backdrop of the forest. Lily stuffed her hands into her jacket pockets, her mind wandering as the silence settled around them.

Conversations would spark up now and then, but for the most part, the hike remained quiet—a reflective motion through the deep woods, interrupted by birdsong and the occasional squirrel darting up a tree trunk.

"So," Andrew said to Lilly as he slowed to allow her to catch up so they could walk side by side. "What's been the best part of being in Laurel Ridge for you so far, besides planning your cousin's wedding?"

Lily considered the question for a moment, eyes following the sway of tree branches overhead. She could give him a quick answer, something surface-level, but she felt like that would be an insult to the question. Andrew wasn't asking just to hear his own voice rattle.

"I guess... the stillness," she admitted. "My life—my world—it's always rushing forward at a hundred miles an hour. But here... I'm noticing that the quiet is sort of nice..."

Andrew nodded. "It's different when the world slows down around you, and you notice there is beauty in silence. Sometimes people need that pause in life to really understand what we're so busy racing toward... or even away from."

"It's funny," Andrew continued, "How nature has this way of reflecting faith sometimes. I've always believed that being out here... it simplifies things. Strips away complications. You just watch the trees or hear the water, and you can't help but know there's something bigger, something peaceful working underneath it all."

Lily kept her eyes on the ground, not sure what to say.

"I don't know, maybe that sounds strange," Andrew added.

"No," she said, surprised but relieved by her own honesty. "No, it doesn't sound strange."

Andrew's gaze flicked to hers, steady and searching, before he returned his focus to the trail ahead.

They continued walking, the sound of rushing water gradually growing louder, and soon the trees began to thin. The air cooling further by the nearby water.

Ben let out a mock cheer ahead of them, turning toward the group as they approached the waterfall. "Ladies and gentlemen, I present to you... West Virginia's crown jewel."

The waterfall came into view, an arresting cascade of water tumbling over dark, slick rocks, into a basin surrounded by ferns and smooth, polished stones. The sound infused the air, not loud, but constant—its rhythmic splash grounding and tranquil.

"It's beautiful," Grace murmured, slipping her arm around Ben's waist and leaning her head on his shoulder.

Lily stood at the edge of the overlook, staring at the waterfall. She let her breath out slowly, the scene before her filling her chest with an odd mixture of calm and unease.

The group settled on the flat rocks that created the overlook, chatting and falling into simple conversation. Grace rifled through her backpack, pulling out some snacks, while Ben recounted an embarrassing falling incident from one of their past hikes. Laughter bounced between them, light but real, the kind that left echoes long after the moment passed.

Ben recounted a hilarious story about a rafting mishap he'd had years ago that left even Grace giggling uncontrollably. Andrew chimed in with his own stories of misadventures in hiking, his infectious energy filling the space with light-hearted banter. Grace joked about her poor attempts at outdoor survival, insisting she'd get lost in her own backyard without a GPS.

Lily smiled to herself, content to listen and observe. The laughter, the ease of their conversation—it was nice, comforting. She wrapped her arms around her knees, trying to melt into the serenity of this place, letting the breeze cool her skin as the gentle rhythm of conversation flowed around her.

Andrew turned to her, his voice low and easy. "So," he began, "how long are you staying in Laurel Ridge after the wedding?"

Lily glanced at him, her expression thoughtful but soft. She stretched her legs out in front of her, her posture relaxing as she leaned back on a rock. "I'll be here for two weeks after the wedding," she said. "I'm dog-sitting for Grace while she and Ben are on their honeymoon."

Andrew smiled, nodding. "That sounds like a nice break after the chaos of wedding planning."

Lily chuckled. "Exactly. I'm really looking forward to it. I plan to spend those two weeks doing as little as possible. Just relaxing in her cabin with no emails, no clients, no vendors calling me with some last-minute disaster. During those two weeks, I'm officially on vacation from work."

He tilted his head, curiosity sparking in his eyes. "No plans at all?"

"Well..." Lily grinned, her shoulders loosening a bit. "I do have plans, but not the stressful kind. I've got a stack of mystery novels I've been wanting to read, so my goal is to knock out as many as I can. Maybe curl up on the couch and read, or spend my afternoons relaxing on the porch. Maybe explore the area a little, that sort of thing."

"Mystery novels sound great," Andrew said, his tone encouraging.

"Yeah," she breathed, a genuine smile touching her lips. "And then, once I'm caught up on those, I'll probably binge some of the Netflix series I've fallen behind on. There are a few thrillers I've been meaning to watch. Pure, unadulterated leisure."

Andrew laughed. "Sounds like you're going all-in on relaxing."

"Believe me, I deserve it after the last few years. I've been working nonstop and haven't taken a vacation." Her smile took on more of a playful edge. "In fact, if you see me even thinking about productivity during those two weeks, feel free to remind me I'm supposed to be doing nothing."

Andrew raised his hands in playful surrender. "You got it. No work talk for two entire weeks."

Lily leaned back further, pleased at the thought of her impending vacation—and then a spark of excitement crossed her expression as she remembered something else. "Actually, I have one little adventure in mind..."

"Oh?" Andrew asked, intrigued.

"I've been considering taking a day trip to Thurmond."

Andrew blinked in surprise, leaning a little closer. "Thurmond?"

"Yeah," Lily continued, her voice tinged with curiosity. "I came across this article about it while I was researching nearby towns. Apparently, it used to be a booming, prosperous town—tons of trains passed through there in its heyday—but now it's almost completely deserted. Only about five people live there. It's basically a ghost town now, just vacant buildings and abandoned streets, but the history behind it all? It sounded fascinating."

Andrew's eyes lit up. "It's actually a really cool place, great vibes in that little town. The people who live there are fascinating. I didn't realize you were into that kind of stuff."

Lily shrugged, a small smile playing on her lips. "I guess I like a little mystery and history combined. Plus, there's something haunting about a place that was once so vibrant, and now it's... just a shell of what it used to be. I want to see it for myself."

Andrew nodded, his voice thoughtful. "It is an intriguing place—like there's a story waiting to be discovered in those old buildings."

Lily glanced at him with a smile. "Exactly. It might sound strange, but I've always had an interest in places like that. A little off the beaten path, y'know?"

Andrew smiled back, a look of understanding flickering in his eyes. "I get it. Everyone needs something that pulls them in like that. Something that's just for them."

Lily's gaze softened as their eyes met for a brief, quiet moment. It wasn't much—just a small exchange in a shared space—but it felt like something.

Chapter 12

Eventually, the soothing lull of the waterfall wasn't enough to keep Lily's mind from filling with thoughts of Grace's upcoming wedding, flowers, and everything else on her checklist. She balanced a half-drunk bottle of water between her hands, her eyes drifting to the mountains in the distance.

This was supposed to be the part where she relaxed completely, right? But relaxation was proving to be more of a challenge than she'd thought it would be. It had been a long time since she had allowed herself to slow down. Back in Manhattan, if you weren't running from task to task, you would be standing still and not progressing. And here? Here everything seemed to move at half speed. She wasn't sure yet whether that was a blessing or a curse.

Andrew's voice rumbled nearby, breaking into her thoughts. He had been talking with Ben a few feet away, but now he was reaching into his jacket pocket, producing a cell phone. A slight frown crossed his features as he glanced at the screen.

Ben caught the look and raised an eyebrow, teasing already. "Calls even in the wilderness, Pastor?"

Andrew chuckled as he pressed the phone to his ear, stepping farther toward the edge of the overlook. "Martha? Hey, what's up?" His tone was casual, but warm as usual.

Lily straightened, glancing over at Grace, who was busy packing up some of their snack trash. Something in Andrew's posture caught Lily's attention, though. He wasn't smiling as much as before, but neither did he seem frazzled. More... thoughtful.

His gentle "uh-huh's" and "sounds great" drifted across the air, and after a couple of minutes, Andrew hung up, pocketing the phone again.

"What'd Martha want?" Ben asked, curiosity clear.

Grace glanced up, interest piqued as well.

Andrew turned back to the group and clapped his hands together in that casual, easy-going way he had. "Well, you all know how much Martha loves a good last-minute get-together, right?"

Grace's grin widened, piecing it together before Andrew even had to finish.

"She's throwing one of her classic impromptu bonfires," Andrew said, a warm chuckle in his voice. "She called to invite us all. Apparently, she's got a stash of marshmallows, chocolate bars, and a few extra logs that are practically begging to be burned."

Ben's face lit up, his usual enthusiasm bubbling over. "A bonfire? With Martha's homemade cider? We're in." He glanced at Grace with a grin, not needing to check in for her agreement. They were both as predictable as the sunrise in their love for good food and cozy, small-town gatherings.

Grace nodded, tugging the backpack onto her shoulder. "It sounds perfect."

Lily managed a smile, but her stomach flipped just a little. More new people. More small-town charm and casual chit-chat.

She had hoped to spend the evening in a quieter setting, maybe chatting with Grace about wedding details, figuring out their next task without the constant hum of people around. She needed to catch up on a few things, and—

"Lily, you're coming too, right?" Grace's voice cut through her thoughts, pulling Lily's attention straight into the spotlight.

Lily glanced down, already reaching for an excuse. "Oh, I don't know," she began, her voice casual, rehearsed. "I mean... I still want to go over some wedding stuff with you tonight, and I was kind of thinking we could get a head start on—"

"Oh, no, no, no you don't!" Grace interrupted, showing no signs of budging. She zipped up her bag with an exaggerated flourish, then leveled her cousin with a good-natured but determined look. "This is non-negotiable. You're coming."

Lily blinked, surprised by Grace's tone. "But we have a lot to cover. There's seating arrangements, and place cards, and I still haven't spoken with the baker about—"

"Lily," Grace said, stepping toward her and plopping down beside her on the boulder, her smile gentle but teasing. "You're always talking about wedding stuff. Give yourself one night off, would you? We've got over a week left before I walk down the aisle. It'll all get done, I promise. And whatever doesn't get done... well... we'll still be married, regardless."

Lily opened her mouth to protest, but Grace wasn't done.

"Besides," Grace continued, her grin turning sly. "I'm giving you the perfect excuse to sample small-town nostalgia in the best way—bonfires, hot cider, s'mores under the stars. Don't tell me you'll turn that down."

Lily bit the inside of her cheek as she thought about the list of wedding details she wanted to review and the emails she needed to send. Her brain was always going—one task to the next, never stopping to rest.

But now? Now Grace was asking her to... what? Relax? Sit around a bonfire and roast marshmallows like a summer camp girl?

"I..." Lily hesitated again.

Andrew's voice, calm but amused, drifted over from a few feet away. "You should come, Lily. Martha has this way of turning a simple bonfire into a fun time. Plus, she's baking her apple dumplings again."

Apple dumplings... the thought of those made Lily think of her childhood. Of state fairs and carnivals.

"You're going," Grace said firmly, standing and pulling on Lily's arm in encouragement. "End of discussion."

Lily let out a sigh of mild defeat, but the hint of a smile tugged at the corner of her lips. Resistance was futile when Grace put her mind to something. Anyone who knew Grace knew that.

Ben and Andrew exchanged amused glances.

"All right, all right," Lily relented, rolling her eyes but unable to suppress the slight laugh that slipped out. "I'm going. You win."

Grace let out a victorious whoop, throwing her arms in the air like she'd just won a championship game. "Yes! See? That wasn't so hard!"

Lily shot her a mock exasperated look. "You're impossible, you know that?"

Grace just grinned and winked back at her. "That's why you love me."

Andrew was already looping his pack back over his shoulders, his serene smile in place, as he caught her eye again. "Trust me," he said, "Martha's bonfires are pretty great. You won't regret it."

"Okay," she agreed. "Let's go make some s'mores."

The group fell into a casual rhythm as they made their way down the mountain. Lily walked beside Grace, while Ben and Andrew led the way a short distance ahead, chatting about some recent football game Ben had been hooked on.

Lily smiled to herself as she watched them. Ben and Andrew were a lot alike. Both easy-going, rooted in their faith, and content to simply be. They had that same small-town comfort vibe that made you feel you could let your guard down. Like you didn't have to be anyone other than yourself around them.

Unlike Manhattan, Lily thought. Every time she looked around, people had shields made of ambition, success, and heavy schedules.

"What's that look for?" Grace's teasing voice broke into her thoughts, making her glance over. Her cousin was shooting her a knowing smile, her eyes glittering a little too much with mischief.

"Nothing," Lily said, shaking her head, trying to dodge the subtle interrogation she felt coming on.

"Mmm-hmm," Grace drawled, entertained by her cousin's reluctance to share. "Oh, definitely... nothing. No big thoughts at all, right?"

Lily shot her a side glance. "Grace..."

"Oh, come on," Grace needled, stepping over a thick root in the trail and then half-turning toward Lily again as they walked. "You're doing that thing again, you know. The thing where you go quiet and start thinking deep thoughts. Some might call it brooding."

Lily laughed at the dramatic way Grace emphasized the word; it was impossible not to shake her head and chuckle. "Brooding? Really?"

Grace shrugged, giving her an innocent smile. "Brooding sounds better than overthinking, doesn't it?"

Lily sighed. That was fair.

Grace adjusted the strap of her backpack and grinned. "So... What do you think of Andrew?"

The question hit Lily out of nowhere, and she stumbled over the sudden transition.

"I—" she began, but Grace gave her absolutely zero time to buffer the shock.

"I saw the way you were looking at him while we sat on the overlook," Grace continued, hopping over a large rock, her voice light and teasing. "Don't try to deny it."

Lily's cheeks flushed. "What? I wasn't—"

"Uh-huh, sure," Grace interrupted with a playful roll of her eyes. "You totally don't find him at least a little charming, right?"

Lily blinked, still trying to catch up on the conversation. "Hold on," she said, her voice rising. "Wait a second. What exactly am I supposed to be denying?"

"Come on." Grace waggled her brows at her, a grin splitting her face. "I mean, he's single. He clearly enjoys spending time with you. And okay, okay—sure—he's a pastor, but I'm not saying you've gotta, like, run off and marry him."

"Grace!" Lily laughed now, her cheeks burning with embarrassment. "Stop. You're blowing this out of proportion."

Grace gave her an unbelieving look, enjoying Lily's discomfort a little too much. "Oh really? So his deep soulful eyes staring at you during lunch earlier today didn't make you feel at least weak-kneed?"

Lily groaned, throwing her hands up. "Grace... This is... This is a whole thing now."

Grace giggled like a mischievous schoolgirl. "What do you mean, a thing?"

"I mean…" Lily stammered, tripping over her words as she tried to catch her breath. "I don't know what I mean. Andrew is… he's a nice guy. He's been helpful, and friendly, and…"

"And what?" Grace prompted, leaning into the crazy anticipation like she'd just picked up a new favorite soap opera.

Lily exhaled. "And okay, okay. He's thoughtful!"

Grace let out a long, satisfied "ahhh" like she was getting to the good part of the story. "Thoughtful, huh?"

Lily threw a deadpan look at her cousin. "Don't. Make. This. Weird."

Grace grinned and nodded along. "Go on."

Looking up toward the sky as she tried to keep the rising nerves from showing, Lily sighed. "Okay, fine. Maybe I've noticed he's… different. But not in the oh my gosh, he's so cute kind of way."

Grace's eyebrow raised. "Not cute? Really?"

Lily second-guessed her words. "I mean… he's objectively… okay, yes—he's not bad looking. Handsome… but handsome can be dangerous. But that's not the point!"

Grace giggled again, swatting at Lily's arm playfully. She was having far too much fun with this. "Continue."

"He's just… different. If I had to put it into words, I guess… he's calm. He just… is. You know? He doesn't have that pressure cooker vibe that everyone in Manhattan has. Like he's just… steady. He is who he is."

Grace tipped her head from side to side as she considered that. "Hmm. So… I think what you're trying to say is… He's a nice change of pace for you."

Lily clicked her tongue, giving her cousin a look. "Maybe. I don't know. Ugh, I don't know what I'm trying to say."

Grace gave her a quick side hug, nudging her arm as they continued down the trail. "Look, Lil. I'm just messing with you, okay? Andrew's a good guy. And yeah, he's calm and steady. But more than that?" Her voice grew a little softer now as she glanced sidelong at Lily. "I think he's exactly what you need right now."

"I'm not looking... or needing... anything," Lily said, her voice dropping just a touch, more vulnerable than she meant to be.

Grace slowed their pace just a little as they neared a rocky portion of the trail. "I get it," she said. "Just... enjoy the bonfire tonight. Don't think ahead. Don't make it a project to figure out. Just... let the night happen."

Lily's heart tugged with something familiar—instinct. The instinct to control everything. But Grace had a point. Maybe for tonight, she could just be Lily—a woman at a bonfire, soaking in the warm company, the laughter of friends enjoying one another's company, and the easygoing delight of s'mores.

"I'll try," Lily conceded, offering a hesitant smile.

Chapter 13

The evening sky was a deep shade of indigo, dotted with stars that twinkled like they'd been loosely scattered by a gentle hand. Martha's backyard was glowing from the bonfire, set in the middle of a grassy clearing surrounded by a cozy arc of Adirondack chairs. The crisp autumn air danced with the smell of roasting marshmallows and apple cider.

Lily sat back, the chair creaking slightly beneath her as she cradled a mug of Martha's hot cider between her hands. She watched the flames from the bonfire as they licked at the air, sending sparks floating upwards. She almost wanted to laugh at how out of place she felt. Everyone else around the fire seemed so comfortable—so at ease. Her eyes drifted to Grace and Ben, who sat nearby on a shared blanket, close and warm, laughing as they chatted with Noah, Martha's grandson.

"Ah. S'mores. The true test of patience," a familiar voice interrupted her thoughts. Lily turned her head to see Andrew approaching, a marshmallow-tipped stick in his hands, a grin pulling at his lips. "Too short of a time over the fire and you've got an undercooked mess. Too long and it's charcoal."

She smiled. "Let me guess. You've mastered the perfect timing."

"Well, I don't like to brag," Andrew said with a playful twinkle in his eyes, "but I've been known to deliver a mean golden-brown marshmallow."

A laugh escaped her lips, surprising her more than anyone.

Andrew's grin widened. "Now, there's a sound we don't hear enough."

Lily's cheeks warmed. "Don't get used to it."

"Challenge noted," he said as he leaned back in his chair. "You survived the wilderness hike today. Did you enjoy yourself?"

Lily smirked. "Oh, I considered faking a twisted ankle. I think Grace would've seen right through it, though."

Andrew leaned back. "You think? I wouldn't underestimate her. Grace has a pretty decent sympathy streak."

"True, but then she'd rope me into something else, like... canoeing."

"Now that," Andrew said, his eyes sweeping over her, "would be a sight to see."

Lily squared her shoulders, mock offended. "You doubt my canoeing abilities?"

Andrew shot her a teasing grin. "I'm just saying, I've heard rumors about a certain person being overly fond of walking on solid ground."

Lily narrowed her eyes for a moment as she laughed.

"Well," she said, "I wouldn't mind a good canoe trip. Maybe one day."

"I'll remember that," Andrew said.

The group's laughter pulled their attention momentarily. Over across the bonfire, Noah, Martha's grandson, had half charred, half melted his marshmallow into a gooey mess. He waved it around as if showing off a new invention.

"Noah, that's not a marshmallow! That's a disaster waiting to happen." Rachel Turner said as she sat down beside Lily, laughing.

"I was going for 'extra crispy,'" Noah retorted with a devilish grin.

Lily's eyes fell on Rachel, noticing her vibrant energy.

Rachel was not only Ben's sister, but also Grace's maid of honor. Family ties were strong here, strengthening the already close-knit connections that seemed to weave everyone together effortlessly.

As Lily chuckled at Noah's marshmallow disaster, her gaze shifted back to Rachel. The flickering light of the bonfire cast warm shadows across her new acquaintance's face, highlighting the bright, animated energy that seemed to come so naturally to her. From what Lily had heard, Rachel was a bit of a town fixture—an artist with a quick wit and an infectious laugh, the kind of person who could make both kids and adults feel at home.

Rachel was now chattering away with Noah about the necessary "artistic value" of extra-crispy marshmallows, making dramatic gestures with her hands as if she were critiquing a painting.

"You see, Noah," she said, waving her marshmallow stick like a conductor directing an orchestra, "sometimes disasters turn into masterpieces. Just look at this thing!" She held up the charred marshmallow with mock seriousness. "This is more than just a s'more component... it's avant garde."

Noah giggled, utterly taken with her theatrics.

Rachel caught Lily watching them with an amused glint in her eyes. "Lily, what do you think?" she asked, gesturing towards the marshmallow-gone-wrong. "Should I hang this in my gallery? Call it 'Marshmellowing in Chaos'?"

Lily laughed. "I think you might need to refine it a little before it gets gallery space. A little more... fire control, perhaps?"

Rachel shot her a good-natured grin and waved her stick again in a helpless gesture. "Ah, well, I thrive on chaos. And I'm pretty sure Noah finds it an essential element for his artistic journey too, right?"

Noah nodded enthusiastically, pleased to be part of Rachel's antics.

Lily leaned in a little more, shifting in her chair. "So, how long have you been running your gallery here in Laurel Ridge?"

Rachel glanced over at her, her face lighting up with the kind of enthusiasm that came from someone who truly loved what they did. "Oh, wow. It's been about three years now, I think? Time flies when you're throwing paint at canvases and hoping for the best."

Lily smiled at the visual. "Three years? That's impressive. I'd love to see it sometime."

Rachel's eyes sparkled as she leaned forward in her chair. "I'd like that! I've got a new exhibit going up this week—of course, you're welcome to come by whenever you like. We're always playing with all kinds of mediums. And if you're interested, I'll even put you to work."

Lily raised her eyebrow. "Oh? What kind of work are we talking about here?"

Rachel clicked her tongue, pretending to size Lily up. "Mmmm, I'm thinking... abstract marshmallow masterpieces! You've already got the lingo down."

Andrew, who had been watching the exchange with a small smile, chimed in. "Don't let her talk you into that, Lily. The last time Rachel had me 'help' with a piece, I ended up covered in blue paint."

Rachel threw up her hands in exaggerated innocence. "Hey, I can't help it if my art is an immersive experience. Some people just don't appreciate the process."

Andrew shook his head, an amused grin tugging at the corners of his mouth. "Oh, I appreciated the process. I just didn't appreciate scrubbing blue paint off for a week."

Lily laughed. "So, you're telling me I should bring a smock if I visit?"

Rachel wagged her finger in faux warning. "Definitely. Or wear something you don't mind sacrificing."

"So, Lily," Rachel continued, resting her marshmallow stick back on the arm of her chair, "Tell me more about your life as a wedding planner. What's it like?"

Lily blew on her cider, the steam swirling into the cool air. "Well, it's not as glamorous as it sounds. Mostly, I manage a hundred tiny crises before the bride even notices something's gone wrong."

Rachel tilted her head. "And you enjoy that? The whole high-stress, super organized thing?"

Lily shrugged. "I used to love it. The fast pace, the sleepless nights... but now? I don't know. Lately, I really don't think it's what I want to do for the rest of my life."

Rachel's expression softened. "Hmm, I get that. Kind of like you're standing right where you thought you wanted to be, but you're looking at it all and wondering, 'Is this really it?'"

Lily blinked in surprise. "Exactly."

"I felt the same way before I opened the gallery here in town," Rachel continued, her tone more serious now, layered with her own history. "I thought I needed excitement—big cities, fast deadlines, high-flying art shows. But after a year or so chasing the big-city lights and trying to build a name for myself, I realized I didn't. I enjoy my life here and this is home. I enjoy the pace here. It gives me room to think and just be who I was meant to be."

Lily nodded, taking in her words.

Andrew, who had been listening, leaned forward a little. "She's right," he said. "Sometimes slowing down may feel unnatural, especially when you're used to being constantly on the go. But it gives you room to breathe. To figure things out."

Lily met his gaze. "I think... I'm still learning how to do that. The slowing down part. I struggle with that."

Rachel grinned, jumping back into her usual lively tone. "Well, you've come to the perfect place for it."

Grace caught the tail end of their conversation and raised an eyebrow with a grin. "You'll be here, roasting marshmallows and making apple pies with us full-time before you know it, Lily. I would love having you live nearby again."

Lily shot her cousin a playful glare. "Don't get ahead of yourself, Grace."

"Oh, I'm psychic," Grace teased before popping the rest of her marshmallow into her mouth.

Andrew smirked, his eyes meeting Lily's mischievously. "And from what I've heard... canoeing is also in your near future."

Lily groaned good-naturedly, rolling her eyes at Andrew. "You're all hopeless."

Martha pulled up a chair and sat herself down with an exaggerated huff. "Alright now," she began with a grin, eyeing the group, "I can't be left out of all this fun, can I? Besides, someone's gotta keep an eye on y'all and make sure you behave."

Martha crossed her arms and leaned back in her chair, looking directly at Lily with a glint of mischief in her eyes. "So, missy," she drawled, her words dripping with that unmistakable Southern charm, "how was that hiking adventure today? Did you survive?"

Lily laughed, shifting in her seat. "I survived, believe it or not. Although there were definitely moments, I thought I might not make it back in one piece. Especially when Grace tried to convince me uphill climbs were 'good for the soul.'"

Grace let out a mock-gasp. "They are good for the soul! You just need to embrace the experience."

Martha raised an eyebrow, still grinning. "Fresh air and a little dirt usually work wonders. Did it do the trick, Lily? Feeling all rejuvenated and at one with nature?"

Lily tilted her head, pretending to consider it. "Well, let's just say it wasn't quite a spiritual awakening, but I'll admit there's something peaceful about the mountains. I miss living in the mountains." She hesitated for a moment. "They have a way of making you stop and take notice of what's around you, which I guess isn't always a bad thing."

"Yeah," Andrew said, his voice thoughtful, "they do have a way of offering perspective, don't they? Kind of humbling, in a way."

Martha clicked her tongue. "Of course, they're humbling. A good trek up a mountain reminds you that you ain't invincible. But you know," she added with a wink, "from what I hear, you did just fine for a city girl."

Lily let out a genuine laugh. "I guess I did."

"Well, don't you worry," Martha said, leaning closer, "before you know it, you'll be leading the next hike like you were born here. We'll have you out there with a walking stick and everything."

"Oh, great." Lily laughed, shaking her head. "Next thing I know, you'll have me competing in one of Ben's wilderness survival challenges."

"You'd win," Grace interjected slyly, "if the challenge was organizing the group into efficiently timed stations."

There was a ripple of laughter, and even Lily had to grin at Grace's jab at her Type-A tendency.

"You're not wrong," Lily quipped, trying unsuccessfully to hold back another laugh. "Though I'm not sure the wilderness is ready for my brand of type-A efficiency."

Martha cackled in response, wiping her eyes. "Oh, honey, the wilderness would probably schedule a meeting just to keep up with you."

Andrew, chuckling beside her, leaned forward. "You'd definitely make the most organized campfire ever. Color-coded logs and all."

Lily shook her head. "I guess that's one way to bring some Manhattan to the mountains."

Martha reached over and patted Lily's knee. "You're doing real good, Lily. Sometimes, all we need is a little room to breathe, and Laurel Ridge has plenty of that. Reckon that's a big shift from all them skyscrapers you're used to."

Lily nodded, her expression turning thoughtful as her gaze wandered toward the bonfire. "Yeah... it's certainly different here. But maybe that's exactly what I didn't know I needed."

Martha gave a knowing smile, her eyes crinkling at the corners. "That's how it starts. Before long, these mountains weave their way into you. It's not just about slowing down either—it's about letting yourself be okay with that slower pace. Sometimes, in the stillness, we can finally hear what we've been running from."

Lily shifted, feeling that truth hit a little too close to home.

"And don't you worry," Martha added, now turning to Andrew, "we'll have our dear Andrew here to keep you in line. He's real good about reminding folks to take a breath when they need it."

Andrew chuckled, his gaze flicking to Lily. "I'm sure Lily can handle that just fine on her own."

Lily raised a brow. "Who knew I'd have so many people insisting I breathe?"

Martha grinned playfully. "That's 'cause you found yourself in a town where folks actually take the time to look out for each other."

Lily nodded, a quiet understanding settling in.

"Well, let me tell you this," Martha said, pointing a marshmallow stick toward the group. "Now that you've survived one mountain adventure, there's no escaping. I expect we'll be seeing you at all sorts of fun events here soon."

"Well," Lily began, a hint of a smile playing on her lips, "I'll have two weeks to myself after Grace's wedding to recharge and dog-sit while she and Ben are off on their honeymoon..." She paused, "Maybe by then, I'll have a little more time for some fun."

Chapter 14

Lily had just wrapped up a brief conversation with Pastor Eli after the Sunday service and made her way toward the wooden pavilion behind the church. Coffee and pie were being served as an after church form of fellowship. People chatted easily, some sitting on the long wooden benches under the pavilion, some sat at picnic tables nearby, others standing in small groups, their voices overlapping in joyful harmony.

As Lily walked closer, she spotted Grace and Ben sitting together at one of the picnic tables, animated in conversation. Martha was seated with them, laughing over a shared story. Their laughter was like music, blending beautifully with the background hum of the small-town gathering.

"Lily!"

She paused mid-step, turning to see Andrew approaching. He moved effortlessly through the gathering Sunday crowd, his easy stride matching the calm smile on his face.

"Hey," he said, flashing her a smile that was as simple as it was disarming. "What did you think of the service?"

"It was... different," she admitted, her voice softer than usual. "I'm used to a much larger church back in Manhattan and, well, I haven't been going regularly these last few months."

Andrew nodded, his expression thoughtful. "I'm glad you came."

"Thanks... I'm glad I came, too."

His lips twitched into a grin as he motioned toward the tables that held several pies and carafes of coffee. "Think we should grab some before the pie rivalry starts up?"

Lily chuckled as they wove through the small crowd toward the buffet. "Rivalry?"

"Pies are serious business around here," Andrew said, nodding, his eyes twinkling with humor. "Bonnie's got her lemon meringue game up at the top, but Marjorie's apple pie? Dangerous stuff."

"You're telling me there's a whole underground pie competition happening in this town?" Lily asked, raising a brow as she grabbed a plate.

Andrew laughed. "Oh, it's very real. You'll see."

Plates in hand, they made their way over to where Grace, Ben, and Martha were seated. The scent of wood smoke from nearby homes and crisp autumn air lingered as they slid onto the benches, immediately drawn into the lively, easy-going conversation that flowed like a well-practiced dance. Ben was in the middle of telling a funny story about a mix-up at Adventure Tours while Grace chimed in with her usual playful jabs, adding to the laughter bubbling around the table.

Martha, with a knowing smile, raised her cup, welcoming them to the fold. "About time y'all got here! You almost missed Ben's latest tale of disaster." Her wink was teasing, the warmth unmistakable.

Lily relaxed into the rhythm of a simple Sunday afternoon. As they continued to chat, Lily noticed how nice it felt to be surrounded by people who belonged effortlessly in each other's lives, with room to spare for her as well. It was a strange but welcome feeling—one that surprised her more with each passing moment.

"We're pretty blessed with some talented cooks in our church," Ben remarked with a grin.

"I couldn't agree more," Grace said, her eyes lighting up. "It's one of my favorite parts of Sunday afternoons—not just for the desserts, though those are definitely a bonus—but because it's so nice to spend time with good company and enjoy the afternoon together."

Andrew smiled and stretched. "How about a walk to burn off some of these calories, Lily?"

Lily glanced at Andrew, her fork hovering over a bite of Bonnie's prized lemon meringue, which, admittedly, had lived up to all the hype. She was surprised by the directness of his question. She could've dodged it—could've said something lighthearted, deflecting like she always did. But that same quiet ease that seemed to cling to Andrew pulled the honesty out of her. A walk? It wasn't a big deal. Just two people enjoying the autumn day. Nothing unusual.

Before Lily could respond, Grace chimed in, a glint in her eye. "You should go, Lily."

"Sure," she said, her voice steady despite her fluttering nerves.

As they strolled toward the back of the church grounds, Andrew turned to her with an easy smile. "So, any big plans for the rest of your afternoon?"

"Not much. Grace and I were going to finalize some wedding details, and then she suggested we unwind with a good chick flick. What about you—got any plans?"

"Not much, really. Ben and I were thinking about going fishing."

"So," Andrew continued, his tone light. "Grace mentioned you used to live in West Virginia when you were younger."

Lily sighed, her voice softening with a touch of nostalgia. "Yeah, we lived near Grace in Charleston for years. I have such fond memories from back then. It was great being close to family... but then Dad lost his job, and we moved to Philadelphia. After that, we only went back once a year to visit, and it just wasn't the same. Grace and I were so close growing up. Moving away in my early teens—it was hard, you know?"

"I can imagine. I was lucky enough to grow up here. The only time I ever left was for college, but as soon as I graduated, I came rushing back. I missed this place too much. Honestly, I've never wanted to live anywhere else," Andrew said.

"So, what did you study in college?" Lily asked conversationally, curiosity lighting her eyes.

"I majored in Business Management, with a minor in Religious Studies," Andrew replied with a smile.

"You're the assistant pastor here and also manage Adventure Tours? Sounds like you've got your hands full," Lily said.

"I most certainly do," Andrew replied with a warm, playful glint in his eye.

"What led you to becoming an assistant pastor?" Lily asked, her curiosity piqued as she shot Andrew a sideways glance.

Andrew's pace slowed slightly as they walked, and a thoughtful smile crossed his face. "Well," he began, his voice carrying the same easy, reflective tone she was getting used to, "I'd say it was a series of small moments rather than one big, defining moment."

"Oh really?" Lily tilted her head, intrigued. "So, no lightning bolt moment of clarity?"

Andrew chuckled. "No, no lightning bolts. At least, not in the dramatic sense." He shoved his hands into his pockets as they continued down the path, the sound of the creek quietly accompanying them. "Growing up, my family was always involved in the church—my dad was a teacher at the local high school, and my mom was a nurse. They taught Sunday school and helped out with youth groups, so faith was always a big part of our lives. But it wasn't something I felt called to in a formal way at first."

Lily nodded as she listened, drawn in by the calm cadence of his voice. It struck her how his words seemed so genuine—there was no rush, no dramatic flourish—just honesty.

"In college, I studied Business Management," Andrew continued, "thinking I'd get into something in the business world. Maybe run my own company one day." His expression softened. "But looking back, I think I always knew that my heart was somewhere else. I just hadn't figured it out yet."

"So, what changed?" Lily asked, fully intrigued now. "What pulled you toward ministry?"

Andrew's smile faded as he took a deep breath. "After I graduated, I had this whole plan mapped out, you know—get a great job or start a business, settle into a career. I even got engaged to someone I thought I'd spend my life with. But... that didn't work out."

Lily's eyes flickered with surprise. "Really? What happened?"

Andrew gazed up into the mountains ahead of them. "We were set to get married—everything seemed perfect on the surface, but deep down... I think we both knew it wasn't right. She wanted something different—a life far away from here, away from the kind of calling I felt. In other words, she did not want to be a pastor's wife. And when she left, it... well, it nearly broke me."

Lily's heart softened as she silently absorbed his words, feeling that familiar ache of heartbreak. She hadn't expected to hear anything like this from Andrew.

"After Sarah left," Andrew continued, his voice soft but steady, "I found myself pulling away a bit. Pastor Eli had already begun mentoring me to eventually take over for him, but I needed some time. I threw myself into various outreach programs, hoping to get some clarity, you know—find myself in all of it."

"But the more I searched and wandered, the more I realized that it wasn't really up to me at all. God was quietly leading me. Then, one night after helping out at a youth group in a small church nearby, it just... clicked. I finally understood that His plan was unfolding perfectly, even when mine had fallen apart."

He glanced at her, his brown eyes warm but serious.

"It wasn't anything particularly special—no big revelation. Just a quiet knowing. I realized I wasn't meant to chase a career that looked good on paper. I wasn't meant to start some massive business and make waves in the business world. I was meant to serve, to be there for people. The more I let go of my plans, the more I saw clearly where God was leading me. I began a serious discussion with Pastor Eli and, well, one thing led to another."

A small smile pulled at the corner of Lily's mouth. "So, no lightning bolt. But something definitely sparked."

Andrew laughed softly, nodding. "Yeah, you could say that. It took years of small nudges, brief conversations, and quiet whispers of truth I couldn't ignore."

Lily looked down, shuffling a few leaves with her foot as they stopped walking. "It's... refreshing to hear someone talk like this," she admitted. "So many people act like they have everything figured out. But I think most of us are just trying to put the pieces together."

Andrew shrugged, leaning against a nearby tree. "I think that's the case for everyone. We want certainty, but most of the time, we're just walking in faith, trusting that each step is leading us somewhere. God doesn't always give us the full map, but He gives us enough light for the next step."

Lily nodded slowly. His words hit close to home. The idea that someone could be at peace with not having all the answers? It stirred something inside her—something she'd been avoiding.

"When I took the job here as the assistant pastor," Andrew continued, "it wasn't because I felt like I'd finally arrived. It was because I realized I wanted my life to be about people. About walking alongside them, even when life is messy and uncertain. God calls us to these little communities, these tiny interactions that don't seem important at first, but... they're everything."

Lily met Andrew's eyes with a glimmer of admiration she wasn't sure how to express. "I think... that's something a lot of people don't really get," she said. "That life isn't about waiting for that one big revelation. It's about... just being there."

Andrew smiled again. "Yeah. Exactly."

For a moment, they simply stood there, letting the sound of the nearby creek fill the space between them.

"So," Lily said, breaking the silence with a smile, "you're officially a pastor-slash-business manager?"

Andrew laughed, shaking his head. "Guess I'm a man of many hats."

They both smiled, the air between them lightening again.

Nodding as they resumed their walk, Lily said, "It's so peaceful here."

Andrew nodded, taking in the surroundings. "Yeah, this spot has always held something special for me. Growing up, I'd spend hours out here… it's one of my favorite places. I guess the hiking trails come in a really close second, but this—this has a way of bringing me back to some of the best memories from my childhood."

As they walked, the sound of the creek grew louder. The trees soon opened up, revealing the rushing small stream through a break in the clearing. Lily stopped at the edge, watching as the water sparkled under the sunlight.

Andrew knelt down, tugging at his shoelaces.

Lily's brow furrowed. "What are you doing?"

He grinned at her as if it were the most natural thing in the world. "Wading in the creek," he said, peeling off his socks and rolling up the cuffs of his pants. "I'm sure you did this all the time growing up in Charleston."

"Sure, but that was ages ago, back when I was just a kid," Lily replied.

His bare feet stepped into the cool, rushing water. When she didn't follow, he turned back with a mischievous look. "Coming?"

Lily folded her arms, shaking her head in disbelief. "You're out of your mind."

Andrew splashed playfully in her direction, laughing. "Probably, but come on! Let yourself be a kid again—it feels good to loosen up every once in a while."

"I don't really do impromptu," she fired back with a raised brow.

"That's what makes it fun," Andrew grinned, splashing again. "Come on. You don't always have to overthink or manage everything, right? Sometimes it's okay to let go."

His words hit exactly where she didn't want them to.

Lily tried to maintain her resolve, but Andrew's infectious energy sparked her inner child, and she couldn't ignore. She thought about her life—how meticulously she planned, how tightly she held to control. Maybe for once... letting go wasn't so bad.

Taking a deep breath, she slipped off her shoes, steeling herself before stepping into the creek. The freezing water hit her like a shock of electricity, making her yelp, "Oh my goodness, this is freezing!"

Andrew held out his hand to steady her. "You'll get used to it. Let the water numb your feet and just consider it to be invigorating."

Lily rolled her eyes at him, trying to suppress her own laughter through chattering teeth. "Invigorating, sure. That's one word for it."

Still gripping his hand, she fought for her balance as they waded further into the creek. Andrew took a playful jump onto a large rock, holding out his other hand to her.

"I'm not hopping on rocks," she muttered, looking at the distance between herself and the slippery surface.

Andrew's expression softened, his mischievous grin turning into something more earnest. "You've got this. Just one leap."

Against her better judgment, Lily accepted his hand again. Gritting her teeth, she jumped, landing with a splash beside him. Andrew's laughter burst out in a victorious cheer.

"You did it!" he exclaimed. "I knew you had it in you!"

Lily grinned back at him, letting the joy of the moment bubble up inside her. Against all the odds—and the freezing temperature of the water—she laughed, really laughed for what felt like the first time in ages.

But then, before she could revel in the moment too long, she caught the mischief flaring in Andrew's gaze just before he scooped up a handful of creek water.

"No!" Lily squealed in mock protest, but it was too late. The water splashed across her arm.

With mock indignation, she retaliated with her own frantic splashes, dissolving into giggles. The two of them waded back and forth, hopping stone to stone with an ease she'd forgotten she was capable of, letting the moment unfold naturally.

The cold started to nip more insistently, and Lily began to shiver. Noticing, Andrew guided her back to the creek's edge, helping her step up onto the slippery bank.

"You're freezing," he said, his playful tone melting into one of concern.

"I'll survive," Lily tried to joke, but the teeth-chattering kind of gave her away.

Andrew shrugged off his jacket and, without hesitation, wrapped it around her shoulders. His warmth, lingering in the fabric.

"Better?" he asked, his voice lowering to a sincere murmur.

Lily bit her bottom lip, her eyes flicking to the ground as she nodded. "Yeah, thanks."

They stood there by the water, the church and those gathered around the pavilion, a distant blur of noise and laughter. The air between them felt alive, yet quiet, and charged with energy all at the same time.

Andrew's warm, calm smile softened as he met her gaze head-on. "See?" he said. "Feels kind of good to let go sometimes, right?"

Lily smiled, shaking her head in faux exasperation. "Alright, you win. Just this once."

Andrew chuckled, his voice melding with the gentle murmur of the creek. "Fair enough."

Chapter 15

The fishing rod bounced lightly in Ben's hand, the line cutting a thin trail through the air before landing with a gentle plop in the river.

The dock creaked quietly beneath Andrew and Ben as they sat on low, camping chairs that had seen countless days of sun, rain, and use. The river murmured along in front of them, carrying leaves, twigs, and small eddies downstream, flowing as effortlessly as the hours of the afternoon. In the distance, the towering trees of the Appalachian Mountains provided a stunning backdrop.

Andrew cast out his line again, eyes fixed on the gentle dance of the bobber bobbing in the slow current. He took a measured breath, inhaling the fresh, woodsy air.

"Can't remember the last time I actually caught anything out here," Ben said with a self-deprecating chuckle, eyes lazily following the movement of the fishing line.

Andrew smirked, shooting him a sideways glance. "Fishing's more about the sitting than the catching anything, right?"

"Exactly." Ben stretched his long, muscular arms above his head, groaning with exaggerated pleasure as the tension in his muscles released. "And sitting here with nothing on the calendar for the rest of the day? That's about as good as it gets."

Andrew leaned back. "True. Especially after how crazy things have been at Adventure Tours lately. Everything's blending together these days—tours, vendors, emails at every hour."

Ben crossed his arms, grinning like the cat who'd eaten a particularly smug canary. "You sound like an old man. What's that say about me?"

A laugh escaped Andrew. "You're too stubborn to admit you're getting old."

Ben shook his head, his grin widening. "Alright, I'll own that. How's your week been? You finally kick that cold?"

"Yeah, yeah," Andrew waved a hand, dismissing the concern. "Wasn't anything serious. Just typical fall allergy stuff."

The truth was, his allergies hadn't really been an issue. What had kept him restless and wired was the constant churn of responsibility that never seemed to stop—even for those in ministry? His role at Adventure Tours had become a behemoth of a task recently, especially since heading into the fall tourist season. Then there was the growing expectation from the church—Pastor Eli's hints about his stepping down coming more and more frequently.

"Bet things have been busier at the church too," Ben said.

Andrew ran a hand through his hair. "Definitely," Andrew replied. "Eli's been talking more openly about his transition this past week. Just little things here and there—commenting about being ready to take more time for himself, that kind of talk." He paused, his fingers adjusting the reel before casting again. "Feels like changes are coming pretty quick."

Ben nodded slowly. "Think you're ready?"

Andrew didn't respond immediately. It was a simple question, deceptively simple—and the kind of question Andrew had asked himself a hundred times lately.

Finally, he shrugged, his gaze fixed on the horizon beyond the river. "I think so. I mean, I've been preparing for this, right? Eli's been grooming me for months. But it's... I don't know." He rubbed the back of his neck, trying to defuse the tension creeping up his shoulders. "I still have this feeling like I'm one step behind what the job needs. Like there's this enormous weight that I'm not even sure I understand yet."

Ben's response came without hesitation, the product of years of steady confidence. "That's the thing about it, though. You'll never feel like you fully understand it. That's not how life works—not with the big stuff. Pastor Eli's been there for how long? Two, three decades?"

"Thirty-five years," Andrew confirmed, watching the bob of his fishing line.

"Yeah, well, I doubt he knew everything when he took that position, either. Doesn't mean you're one step behind; just means you're on track, learning like everyone else does as they go."

Andrew's laugh came out more resigned than amused. "Maybe. Still... I guess I keep thinking about how to balance it all, too." His fingers tightened their grip on the fishing rod. "Adventure Tours takes more out of me than I expect most weeks. Running that? And then diving into the full responsibility of leading the church?"

Ben raised an eyebrow, pulling in his fishing hook just enough to check the bait. "Have you considered scaling back? We could hire someone new to help manage things?"

A long silence followed.

"I have," Andrew said finally. "But in typical Andrew fashion, I can't seem to let any of it go. Feels like if I loosen my grip, something's bound to fall apart."

Ben cocked his head with a half-smile. "Ah, so this is a control issue."

Andrew shot him a dry look. "Easy there, Dr. Phil."

Ben chuckled. "Just saying, buddy. You might think you're the glue holding everything together, but news flash—God's got most of that covered."

Andrew snorted, a smirk tugging on his lips. "I'm aware."

"Yeah, but are you really aware?" Ben challenged, though his voice carried none of the hardness of judgment. "You've been juggling both Adventure Tours and the spiritual care of not only yourself but the congregation for months now, and... here's a very small-town friendly reminder—you'll be doing a whole lot more as the lead pastor."

Andrew exhaled slowly, the fishing rod still clutched in his hand but momentarily forgotten. "I think that's what scares me most," he admitted. "Not just stepping into that leadership... but wondering if it will gut me. There's this weight to ministry that I didn't fully anticipate when I first started."

Ben nodded slowly, casting his own line back into the water. "It's not all sermons and prayers over casseroles, huh?"

Andrew gave a small, humorless laugh. "Yeah... no. Don't get me wrong, I knew that going in. But when you see it up close? Week after week? The weight of people's pain, their struggles... it gets heavy. And it doesn't stay inside the church walls. You take it home. You take it everywhere."

Ben shifted slightly, the chair creaking beneath his weight. "You're good with people, Andrew. You've already proved that. You care for them... and that shows. Everyone at church knows it. But," he continued, pausing to reel in his line again, "you've also got to care for yourself too. You're no good to anyone if you burn yourself out trying to carry everything."

Andrew's gaze slipped down, watching the river lap gently against the dock. He knew Ben was right—he'd heard those exact words in various forms before. From Eli. From his parents, from other pastors he'd met. But it hadn't fully sunk in.

"All that said," Ben continued, his smile turning cheeky, "sounds like you might need to learn to relax a little. Maybe you don't need to outwork every single person in this town."

Andrew grinned despite himself. "Have you been talking to Grace? She said something similar over lunch the other day."

"Probably because she sees what everyone else sees, my friend," Ben teased. "The sooner you realize we weren't built to do it all, the sooner you'll stop tripping over yourself."

"You're probably right," Andrew admitted, his tone lighter now. "Guess I need to put more trust in both God and others."

"Wild concept, I know," Ben said, his grin broadening. "But here's another fun idea while we're hashing out life lessons—trust your gut too, especially when it comes to other people. Someone else might be just as good—if not better—at handling the things you think only you can handle."

Andrew chuckled. "So, basically... delegate. That's what you're saying."

"Delegate," Ben agreed. "Get others in the game... in other words, start interviewing for another assistant manager. And then there's something else."

Andrew's brow lifted, intrigued by the sudden shift in Ben's tone. "What's that?"

"Lily."

"Of course."

Ben's grin turned mischievous. "I can tell there's something going on there."

Andrew shifted uncomfortably in his seat, his gaze darting back to the water. "It's nothing... really."

"Uh-huh. Sure thing, Reverend 'I'm Just Being Friendly' Whitman," Ben drawled sarcastically. "We all see how you look at her, though."

Andrew sighed, instantly knowing there was no way Ben was going to drop this. "Look, I'm just... I don't know if that's something I can juggle right now."

Ben leaned in over his fishing rod, one eyebrow raised. "Because?"

"Because!" Andrew exhaled in frustration, searching for the words. "You know my history. After what happened with Sarah, I just... I question everything. A relationship and serve the church in the way I want to."

Ben gave him a long look, his usual easygoing nature softening as he recognized Andrew wasn't just being hesitant. "Andrew, I get it. Truly. What happened with Sarah left you pretty shaken. But man, that was years ago. Don't you think maybe this is God's way of showing you something else now? Some new direction?"

"Maybe," Andrew murmured, feeling the cautious hope forming in his chest. "But what if it's not that simple? What if things with Lily end up like they did with Sarah?"

Ben shook his head, a slow smile forming. "You're doing that thing again."

Andrew squinted. "What thing?"

"The thing where you expect the worst-case scenario because it's the only thing you think can happen. But trust me on this—life surprises you. Lily isn't Sarah. Just because she's reserved doesn't mean she's not ready for something genuine. And maybe she's waiting to see if you'll be the brave one first."

Andrew remained silent, processing Ben's words.

A soft gurgle erupted from Ben's stomach, breaking the silence. He slapped a hand over it, making a face. "Apparently, philosophical conversations make me hungry," he joked, rubbing his middle. "But I don't feel like cooking."

Andrew, grateful for the lighter moment, smirked. "What a coincidence. Neither do I."

Ben shot him a look, and in perfect unison, they both spoke the magic word: "Pizza."

Andrew pulled out his phone, flicking through his contacts. "I've got Sue's Pizzeria on speed dial. What do you think?"

Ben let out a low whistle. "Now we're talking."

Andrew tapped out the number, pressing the phone to his ear as it rang on the other end.

Meanwhile, Ben leaned back in his chair, sighing with contentment. "Think the girls are just hanging out watching a rom-com?"

Andrew grinned. "Probably. Lily mentioned something about a chick flick."

"I can see it now," Ben said with an exaggerated shudder. "All emotional dialogue and dramatic confessions of love."

"Pretty funny, considering how much you're all about emotional dialogue," Andrew teased.

Ben laughed, tossing a mock glare. "Hey, don't get ahead of yourself. I only sound this wise because I have to keep up with you."

After a brief conversation with the pizzeria, Andrew ended the call, a grin spreading wide. "Twenty minutes, and we've got ourselves two large pizzas. One with double everything, one Hawaiian."

Ben shuddered at the latter. "Of course you'd order pineapple on pizza. That's just wrong."

Andrew laughed, shaking his head. "More for me, then."

Ben laughed. "You know what? Call the pizzeria back and order a third pizza."

Andrew grinned. "And remind me why I should do that?"

Ben flashed him a knowing grin.

"Got it. I'm on it."

Chapter 16

"Can you pass the grapes?" Grace asked, nodding toward the porcelain plate resting on the side table next to Lily's chair. The plate was neatly arranged with an assortment of cheese, crackers, and clusters of juicy grapes—which Lily had been absently plucking from as they chatted.

Lily grinned as she leaned over to Grace, who was gently swaying on the porch swing. She held out the plate, and Grace popped a grape into her mouth with a satisfied hum before reaching for her mason jar of sweet tea. "Somehow, this tea just tastes even better out here," Grace murmured, stretching like a contented cat. She took a sip, smiling to herself as they both sunk deeper into their seats. Daisy was romping cheerfully in the grass beyond the porch, seemingly with endless energy.

Lily's gaze drifted to Daisy, who had run off to chase a butterfly for what must have been the fifth time that afternoon. "She reminds me of that dog you had when we were little. Max, right?"

Grace gasped softly. "Oh my goodness, yes! Max." Her face broke into a wide smile as she leaned forward, placing her jar down with a clink. "I haven't thought about him in ages! He was the best old boy, wasn't he? He loved chasing anything that moved. Do you remember the time he went after Mr. Clark's cat and chased it up in the tree-house? We had to beg that poor, terrified cat to come down for what felt like hours!"

Lily burst out laughing at the memory, her body shaking as she tried to control her giggles. "Oh, poor Max! He looked so guilty, pacing back and forth like he'd committed some doggy sin."

Grace leaned in conspiratorially. "And remember how we didn't dare go inside the house because we were certain Grandma was going to scold us for—what did she used to say? — 'letting that mutt run wild.'"

Lily winced dramatically. "Oh, I definitely didn't forget that. I was convinced we were both going to be doomed to chores for the rest of our lives!"

They both dissolved into laughter, the sound filling the air, mixing with the soft rustle of leaves and the far-off call of birds.

"Those were the days, huh?" Grace sighed contentedly, her gaze drifting off to the horizon. "Running through the woods, pretending we were explorers or fairy queens..."

Lily nodded, her heart tugging. "I miss that sometimes." She bit her lip. "How it all seemed so simple back then."

Grace shot her a knowing glance. "I think it's still simple, Lily. You're making it complicated."

Lily raised an eyebrow, trying to keep her expression light. "Oh, am I now?"

Grace nodded matter-of-factly. "You are. And you know what else?" She leaned forward in the swing.

Lily braced herself. "What?"

"You're not as guarded as you think you are," Grace said with a grin. "Ben and I snuck down by the creek behind the church after you and Andrew had been gone for a while. We saw you wading in it with Andrew. You two were acting like schoolkids splashing each other and laughing like it was the funniest thing in the world!"

"Oh no, here we go..." Lily dropped her face into her hands. The heat crept up her neck, settling into her cheeks.

Grace wasn't about to let her off the hook. "Come on, admit it. I haven't seen you loosen up like that since—well, since forever."

Lily groaned, peering at her cousin from between her fingers. "Okay, okay, maybe he's charming... in a silly sort of way."

Grace wasn't going to let her curb the topic that easily. "Silly? Or perhaps... charming in a handsome, thoughtful, pastor kind of way?"

Lily attempted a straight face, but a giggle slipped out. "Grace—"

"Oh, come on," Grace interrupted, laughing herself. "Don't try to deny it. You were grinning from ear to ear the entire time! And might I point out, he even wrapped you in his jacket like a proper gentleman."

Lily tossed a grape at Grace, hitting her directly on the shoulder. "Do not even start," she warned playfully. "You snoop!"

But Grace was relentless. "Too late because I'm already planning your outdoor wedding by the creek! A floral garland here, a string quartet there—oh, it's going to be divine!"

Lily laughed along despite herself. "You're impossible, you know that?"

"I know," Grace said sweetly, batting her eyelashes in mock innocence. "And I'm also right."

Lily leaned back with a huff, crossing her arms. "I have a wedding to plan. I'm not here to think about my own love life." Her voice was teasing, but beneath it all, she couldn't deny the hum of excitement that had begun to pulse through her lately—namely, every time she thought of Andrew.

Grace grinned and was about to respond when both women noticed something unusual. Daisy, who had been charging around the yard moments ago, was now standing stock still in the middle of the lawn, ears perked and head cocked.

"What's she doing?" Grace asked, her brow knitting as she leaned forward to get a better look.

Lily tilted her head, confused. "I have no idea. She's just... frozen."

Before either could investigate, Daisy went from completely still to full sprint, tearing off toward the front of the cabin with an urgency that took them by surprise.

"Daisy!" Lily called, but the dog was already gone.

Grace and Lily shared a baffled look before Grace's ears perked up, straining to hear. In the distance, the unmistakable rumble of an engine drifted over the ridge. Her eyes widened in realization as she bolted upright. "Wait. Is that... Ben's truck?"

Lily raised her eyebrow. "Ben? Here? Now?"

"Yeah, that's definitely his engine," Grace said, a hint of excitement creeping into her voice.

The two women scrambled to their feet and hurried around the side of the house, just in time to see Ben's truck pull into the gravel driveway. Daisy wagging her tail, excitedly prancing around the approaching vehicle.

The truck came to a stop, and the passenger door swung open. Andrew, wrestling with three pizza boxes, got out of the cab. He held them up in the air as if presenting a great prize, a broad grin stretching across his face.

"We bring food!" he called, his deep voice light and teasing. "Can we break up your girl time?"

Ben hopped out of the truck as well, looking equally pleased with himself. "These pizzas won't eat themselves. I know you two are probably gossiping about us, anyway."

Grace scoffed dramatically. "You bring pizza, and you think that gives you permission to interrupt our perfectly peaceful afternoon?"

Lily fought back a laugh, folding her arms across her chest. "Oh, we were just discussing... girl stuff."

Andrew took a step closer, still grinning. "Well, in that case, I'm sure pizza will help fuel the discussion."

Grace rolled her eyes in exaggeration. "Alright, alright—pizza wins. Come on, boys."

They all gathered around the wooden picnic table in the backyard. The smell of warm pizza crust and melted cheese wafted through the air as the group settled in for an impromptu feast.

"Let's see... we've got double everything, pepperoni, and Hawaiian," Andrew announced, laying the boxes open like treasures being unveiled then reaching in and grabbed a slice of Hawaiian pizza.

Grace put on a dramatic grimace. "I don't understand your obsession with that. It's...it's unnatural Andrew!"

Andrew winked at her as he took a gigantic bite. "Nah, it's the best."

"I wasn't sure what you'd like," Andrew said after swallowing, glancing at Lily with a playful smile, "so I went safe with pepperoni."

Lily returned his smile, gratefully accepting the slice he handed over. "Pepperoni's perfect, thanks," she replied before biting into the warm, cheesy goodness.

As the afternoon wore on, the conversation flowed around the picnic table, accompanied by generous helpings of pizza and even more laughter.

Ben, ever the storyteller, began one of his tales, his animated gestures making the others smile. "So there I was," he started, "at the Johnson wedding a few weeks ago. And let me tell you, it was high stakes." Ben paused dramatically, his eyes sweeping across their amused faces. "Now, everything's going great, right? The bride's smiling, the groom's not fainting, I'm supervising the background logistics like a total pro. And suddenly—disaster strikes!"

Lily raised an eyebrow, a grin already tugging at the corner of her lips. "Disaster, huh?"

"Oh, total disaster," Ben replied, nodding gravely. "The cake—this towering masterpiece, mind you—starts tipping! Some rookie groomsman grazed it with his elbow while sneaking a taste of the frosting. I didn't even blink. I was on it like... like a ninja!"

Grace stifled a laugh behind her hand, her eyes crinkling as she jumped in. "Oh, Ben. Sweetheart, you're forgetting the part where you tripped over the photographer's bag in your 'ninja' rush."

Ben's face twisted into mock horror. "That was a strategic stumble! I was diverting attention."

Andrew chuckled, shaking his head. "Right. I'm sure you were."

Lily, holding her stomach, couldn't help but laugh along, thoroughly entertained. "And did you save it? The cake? Was it some heroic leap across the room in slow motion?"

Ben raised his hand in a grand flourish. "Of course! I swooped in just as it wobbled and steadied that thing with my bare hands. The whole room went silent. I mean—could you blame them? And then, right there, I maneuvered everything back into place without dropping a single crumb."

Grace erupted into laughter. "Oh, you're so full of it! Who do you think iced over the dent you made on the side of it?"

Lily blinked, her cheeks flushing with laughter. "Wait—there was a dent?"

Grace nodded vigorously. "A massive one! Icing smeared all over the back. Ben's heroic moment came at great cost to the buttercream."

Ben waved a hand dismissively. "Details, details—the point is, I saved the wedding cake. The guests were none the wiser. I call that a win!"

"Besides," he continued. "It wouldn't have been a wedding without a little excitement."

Andrew rubbed his chin, joining in with a teasing drawl. "So let me get this straight—cake ninjas are a thing now? Good to know."

"You betcha," Ben replied with a wink before taking another bite of his double everything slice of pizza. "You never know when wedding disasters will strike."

Grace rolled her eyes affectionately and leaned into his side with a laugh. "Sure, cake ninja. Whatever you say."

"Hey, if the shoe fits..." Ben grinned, clearly enjoying the banter.

Lily smiled and took another bite of pizza, enjoying the lightheartedness of the moment.

"So, Lily, are you surviving the Laurel Ridge experience so far? I feel like we've thrown every hallmark of small-town life at you—bonfires, after church pie fellowships, and now, apparently, cake ninjas."

Lily chuckled and nodded. "I think I'm managing. It's definitely... interesting." She smiled a little wider, glancing around at the group. "In the best way."

"Come on, Lily. Admit it: 'managing' is underselling it. You're basically a country girl again now. I mean, wading in the creek earlier has got to count for something, right?" Grace said.

Lily threw a playful glare at her cousin. "Hey, I'm not swapping my high heels for cowboy boots just yet. Let's not get ahead of ourselves."

Andrew leaned back with a mock-serious nod. "Well, the transformation isn't complete until you've done at least one small-town dance or festival. Maybe you could come back for the Christmas festival in December. Really round out the whole experience."

Ben raised an eyebrow, barely hiding a grin. "That's true. No small-town membership is official without a dance or a festival."

"Oh, don't start," Lily groaned, though her smile gave her away.

Andrew picked at his last piece of pizza absentmindedly. "You'd do fine. You're already halfway there. Wading through a creek qualifies for something."

"See?" Grace added, reaching over to give her cousin a nudge. "You're basically one of us already."

Lily let out an exaggerated sigh and shrugged. "Fine. But I am drawing the line at riding tractors or ATVs."

Ben and Andrew exchanged mischievous looks.

Grace leaned in, grinning. "You've made a grave mistake, cousin."

Lily eyed them warily. "Why?"

Andrew chuckled softly. "Because Ben's got an old tractor in his barn. You know, for emergencies and things during the winter to help clear the roads... and for city girls who need a proper small-town initiation."

Ben's grin grew wider. "Don't worry, Lily. It's super safe. I've driven it a hundred times."

Before Lily could respond, Ben continued in a serious tone, "You don't want to miss the photo-op, trust me. It'll be something to remember when you're back in Manhattan."

Lily covered her eyes dramatically. "Why do I sense this is all a giant setup?"

Andrew, clearly enjoying the friendly teasing, didn't miss a beat. "Because it's probably exactly that."

Lily shook her head, her smile never wavering. "You guys are impossible."

Ben leaned back with an exaggerated stretch, hands behind his head. "We aim to please."

Grace tossed the last of the pizza crust to Daisy, who gleefully accepted her offer. "Look at us," she said with mock reverence. "Stuffed with pizza, sitting outside as the sun sets. I could make a postcard out of this."

Ben chuckled and squeezed her shoulder affectionately. "Or a documentary. 'The Quiet Drama of Small-Town Life: Pizza Edition.'"

Andrew, pretending to act contemplative, added, "Season one. 'The Rise of the Cake Ninja.'"

Ben laughed and glanced over at Grace. "So, what's next in the wedding plans?"

"There's always something. I think tomorrow we're finalizing the flowers with Leslie, and we need to recheck the catering menu with Martha, too," Grace said.

Ben quirked a brow. "More decisions to make?"

"Oh, plenty. But don't worry, we'll be sure and tell you all about it," Grace replied.

"I can't wait," Ben said dryly, though anyone could see the gleam in his eyes.

Lily smiled as she turned to Grace. "Oh, and just a reminder—tomorrow we need to tackle the wedding favors for each place setting at the reception. Still so much to do!"

"I can't believe I almost forgot about that!" Grace said, a bit surprised. "We're going over to Martha's house to make them."

Ben leaned over to Andrew with a grin, his voice teasing. "Meanwhile, we're over here busting our backs all day at work."

Grace rolled her eyes playfully. "You're welcome to join us if you'd rather stuff butter mints into cute little chiffon bags for the wedding favors."

Andrew and Ben exchanged a knowing glance, then responded in perfect unison, "Not a chance."

"Well," Ben drawled, "I don't know about you all, but I think I might have stuffed myself silly."

Grace giggled, nudging him lightly. "Ben Turner, are you actually telling me you ate too much? Never thought I'd see the day."

Ben groaned. "This might be a first."

Andrew shook his head with mock sympathy. "You'll live."

Lily laughed, savoring the easy camaraderie.

Andrew shot her a warm, subtle smile that sent an unexpected thrill through her. She looked away quickly, feeling a slight blush rise to her cheeks.

Chapter 17

"Alright, ladies, we've got a mountain of these things to stuff," Martha said, pointing towards little chiffon bags and bowls of pastel-colored butter mints. She wore a floral apron tied around her waist, her silver hair neatly pinned back as she busied herself arranging supplies. "Not to worry—there's only about a hundred or so bags." She winked, her tone all wit and mischief.

Grace groaned dramatically, but with a smile on her lips. "Are you sure we need quite this many?" she asked, scooping up a handful of chiffon bags and plopping them onto the table in front of her. The sheer number of them nearly spilled off the edge.

Rachel, ever the performer, grabbed a single chiffon bag, holding it like it was some royal artifact. "Oh, but think of the delicacy of it all," she said with a flourish, pretending to gently stuff a butter mint inside and tying it with extravagant precision. "These are no ordinary wedding favors, Grace. We're talking works of art here."

Lily smirked as she took a seat at the dining table, admiring the cozy space. The old farmhouse was undoubtedly the kind of picture-perfect home she'd imagine Martha to have—every corner filled with personality, from the family photos on the wall to the linen checkered curtains that adorned the windows.

"Well, at least someone is enjoying themselves," Lily said, tossing Rachel a gentle smile. Her hands moved methodically as she began stuffing butter mints into the chiffon bags.

"Hey…" Rachel continued, "I'm expecting high-end critics to review these in 'Wedding Quarterly'." She raised her eyebrows, muttering to herself in mock elegance. "Five stars, really. The perfect marriage of butter mint and chiffon."

Martha sat down and went to work. "Oh, honey," she teased, shaking her head. "You're using all that flair on candy and ribbons? If you put half that energy toward baking as you do toward flair, well now… I might have some actual competition with those biscuits of mine."

Rachel leaned over to Grace, whispering in a conspiratorial tone that wasn't quiet enough to keep Martha from hearing. "She's so humble—it's those biscuits that get people lined up at her door."

Martha, never one to be outdone, wagged a finger at Rachel, her tone gentle but amused. "Don't go thinking you can butter me up with flattery, Rachel Turner. It ain't gonna spare you from packin' these favors." She pushed a pile of bags toward Rachel with a tiny smile that held more kindness than any retort could ever mask.

Rachel grinned. "Wouldn't dream of it, Martha. I'm happily resigned to my fate."

"I can't believe my wedding is really happening in just a few days," Grace said, the reality of her approaching wedding setting in. She paused her busy hands to look over at Lily, her eyes shining with excitement.

Lily smiled, her heart twisting just a little, not out of sadness but something close enough—a reminder of everything good she'd planned for her own life once upon a time. "You two are perfect together, Grace. I don't see how it could be anything short of incredible."

Rachel chimed in, "She's right. You and Ben... well, y'all fit so seamlessly together. Almost makes a woman believe in the whole meant to be business."

"And... speaking of meant to be...." Rachel continued, feigning innocence—but the amusement on her face betrayed her mischievous intent.

Grace smirked. "Here it comes."

"I noticed a certain assistant pastor offering you his jacket the other day by the creek... I mean, come on," she continued, leaning on both elbows, completely invested in her own teasing. "If that wasn't a move, I don't know what is."

Lily nearly dropped the chiffon bag she was tying. "Rachel," she protested, shaking her head, trying to prevent the heat rising in her cheeks.

"Oh, c'mon, Lily," Grace chimed in with wide eyes, barely stifling her laughter. "You two did look awfully cozy."

Martha grinned. "I think they've got a point, sugar. Didn't look like just any kind of jacket-sharing to me."

Lily fought the urge to hide her face. "It wasn't... it wasn't anything serious," she mumbled, hearing how unconvincing she sounded. "It was cold, and he was being nice. Pastors are supposed to be nice, right?"

But Rachel wasn't letting it go. "You're telling me that sweet pastor didn't have anything more up his sleeve than warmth? Martha, remember what you've always said?"

"Well, of course I do," Martha said. "Actions speak louder than words."

Grace leaned in, her tone playful but encouraging. "I have to admit, I agree with Rachel on this once."

"Here we go," Lily muttered, sinking back into her chair as all eyes turned on her.

"It's true, Lily," Rachel said, as she stuffed a chiffon bag. "When a man offers you his coat, that's not just being nice… the man's smitten."

"Darlin' men don't just hand out jackets like that," Martha said.

"Look, maybe we're flirting a little, I don't know… but nothing serious is going to come of this. I mean, I'm going back to Manhattan in a few weeks. This whole thing? It's temporary, just mild flirting."

Grace and Rachel exchanged glances, their moods softening from playful to sympathetic.

"Well," Grace said, "If that's how you feel, Lily. But maybe don't shut the door on it just yet. Things can change when you least expect it."

Rachel leaned over, nudging her playfully. "Just don't forget… Manhattan's not going anywhere, but neither is Andrew…" she trailed off, leaning back in her chair with a knowing smile.

"Hello, hello! Permission to enter?" Leslie called from the front door.

Grace practically leapt to her feet. "Leslie!" she exclaimed, excitement overflowing. "What've you got for us?"

Leslie, arms full of flowers, entered the room in true dramatic fashion as she delivered her bounty. "Behold," she sang, setting an enormous bouquet made of lush greenery, ivory roses, wildflowers, and deep autumnal accents right on the kitchen table.

Grace's eyes widened. "Leslie… these are… stunning."

Leslie beamed, her hands already busy pulling more flowers from the basket she carried. "Wait until you see the bouquet for the maid of honor. I've outdone myself if I do say so."

Martha smiled warmly. "Leslie, that talent of yours just keeps growing."

Leslie nodded, accepting the praise with graceful modesty as she unveiled the second bouquet. "Come on, ladies... I didn't work all day just for a few oohs and ahhs. Keep them coming."

"Grace," Lily whispered softly, marveling over the exquisite bouquet. "Your wedding will be as beautiful as you are."

Grace teared up. "Thank you, Lily."

"Alright, alright," Martha cut in with a breezy laugh, "before everyone gets teary over flowers, let's dig into these appetizers I made." She brought over a fruit tray and a veggie tray with a quick flourish. "Can't be tacklin' all this serious business on an empty stomach!"

The food was quickly snatched up by eager hands as conversation meandered its way around the table once more. Discussions about wedding cake flavors and flower arrangements circled enthusiastically, typical hallmarks of wedding preparations.

Lily felt an undercurrent beneath all the laughter and joy in the room, a quiet stirring she couldn't quite name. It was the same feeling that surfaced whenever she caught Andrew's warm smile or heard his gentle words—subtle yet constant — pulling her toward something deeper. The sense of camaraderie in the room was overwhelming in the best way. These women were nothing short of wonderful—grounded, generous, and full of light. And they'd welcomed her into their circle without hesitation, making her feel like she truly belonged. It was a moment she wanted to hold on to forever.

Chapter 18

Andrew settled onto the worn seat of the picnic table behind Adventure Tours, stretching out his legs as he unwrapped his sandwich. It had been a long morning, packed with logistics for the busy week ahead.

Across from him, Ben sat with peaceful calm, as if the planning and chaos of running a business weren't weighing on him at all.

The late October sun cast long shadows on the grass, and a crisp breeze swept in from the river, sending leaves from nearby trees skittering across the table. It was one of those fall afternoons in the mountains where the sun was warm enough to feel good, but the air had a slight chill that reminded you how much you'd miss that warmth in about a month.

Ben unwrapped his sandwich with a dramatic sigh of appreciation, pausing, as if preparing for a Shakespearean monologue. "And thus a man doth find sustenance after the wilderness of paperwork and endless phone calls." He leaned back, biting into his sandwich like it was the answer to all life's problems.

Andrew, eating with less flair but no less enthusiasm, snorted. "You sound like you've rehearsed that bit."

Ben waved his sandwich in the air theatrically. "Hey, a man's gotta entertain himself after sitting through three hours of spreadsheets and waivers. If I have to process another trail permit for tourists who think they're going on a cozy woodland stroll and forget we're hiking near cliffs, I'm going to lose my mind."

Andrew chuckled, taking another bite of his turkey club. "Takes a special kind of person to run a business like yours. You ever take a group of tourists on a trail and wonder if they'll make it back?"

"All the time," Ben said with mock seriousness, pointing a finger. "That's why there's a waiver. Not that I want anyone to fall off a cliff, but you try telling Mr. Tech Man from some big city that jogging on an unpaved mountain path isn't a great idea after a rainstorm."

As they ate in comfortable silence, Andrew's thoughts began to drift—right back to where they always seemed to go these days. To her. A woman with city polish but a surprisingly tender heart. Somehow, she'd gotten under his skin, despite the short time they'd known each other, leaving him feeling more unsettled than he cared to admit.

Ben broke the quiet with a casual, "So... you ready to talk about her yet?"

Andrew paused, his sandwich halfway to his mouth, eyes narrowing at Ben. "Who are we talking about?"

Ben shot him a sly, cat-that-ate-the-canary grin before popping the last bite of his sandwich into his mouth with deliberate enjoyment. "Oh, I don't know... maybe the woman you spent yesterday morning wading through a creek with, like you were in some rom-com? And then shared a pizza with later in the day?"

Andrew chuckled, setting his sandwich down, already seeing where this was going but unsure how to steer it. "Please. It was just a little creek-wading."

"Right," Ben replied, putting on his best mock-serious face as he folded his arms and leaned in. "Because all 'just creek-wading' involves a head-over-heels pastor braving ice-cold water to show off his nature skills."

Andrew shook his head with a laugh. "Fine, fine. But really, let's drop it."

"No chance," Ben leaned in, his grin widening. "Mark my words—there's something there."

Andrew could feel the heat creeping up his neck. "I'm not—" he began, then cleared his throat, aiming for nonchalance. "It's not like that."

Ben's raised eyebrows made it clear he wasn't buying a word of it. "Mm-hmm. Tell that to the way you were looking at her in church yesterday."

Andrew blinked, caught off guard. "What are you talking about? I was just doing my job."

"Oh, doing your job, were you?" Ben said. "Looked to me like you were having an internal crisis every time her eyes so much as glanced your way."

Andrew rubbed a hand along his jaw, glancing away. "Look, yes. There's something there. I'm not denying it."

Ben threw up his hands in mock surprise. "Finally! The man admits it!"

Andrew shot him a look, brushing off the sarcasm. "Lily doesn't need any added pressure right now. We're just flirting, that's all. She's here to plan a wedding, not... whatever you think is going on."

Ben's voice softened. "And what are you afraid of?"

The question struck closer than Andrew wanted to admit. Ben knew when to joke and when to ask the tough questions, and Andrew wasn't ready for this one.

"I'm not afraid," he replied. "I'm just... being careful."

Ben studied him, his gaze steady. "I've known you long enough to know you're always careful. But this? This feels like more. It's like you're talking yourself out of something before it even has a chance."

Andrew's gaze wandered toward the parking lot, scattered with crisp autumn leaves, as if an answer might lie somewhere in the quiet. Admitting he liked Lily was one thing, but actually doing something about it? That was a different story—especially with the timing being what it was.

And that's what bothered him most: the timing.

"She's been hurt, Ben. And recently." Andrew's tone softened. "I don't know all the details, but I can see it in her face. The second things get close or uncomfortable, she shuts down. The idea of her trusting someone again? That could take a lifetime."

Ben was quiet for a moment, absorbing his words. Finally, he spoke, carefully. "So, you think getting close would feel like pressure on her?"

Andrew furrowed his brow. "Yes... possibly."

"And if you don't move at all...?"

Andrew didn't answer.

Ben watched as Andrew fidgeted with the plastic lid of his water bottle. "Look, Whitman, I get it. You don't want to overwhelm her. Makes sense. But maybe you're also trying to protect yourself here?"

Andrew blinked, caught off guard. "What do you mean?"

"I mean, it seems to me like Lily's not the only one afraid of things getting too close. You've always been the dependable guy, Andrew. But when's the last time you risked something?"

Andrew shifted uncomfortably, the truth hitting harder than he wanted. He knew Ben was right. His hesitation wasn't just about protecting Lily's heart—it was about protecting his own.

"There's a difference," Andrew said quietly, "between giving someone time and refusing to take any steps at all."

Ben nodded thoughtfully. "You're right. I've been there myself—wondering if Grace was ready to take a step forward when I knew where I stood. It's scary. But at some point, you have to trust that the timing, that pull you feel... it's God's way of reminding you. He's weaving your stories together, even when it's not obvious."

Andrew crossed his arms, letting the weight of Ben's words sink in.

"You're saying I should ask her out?"

Ben laughed. "Why not? What are you waiting for—Christmas? I can already picture it: some grand gesture with mistletoe, thinking you're being subtle."

Andrew rolled his eyes. "Now you're just making things up."

"Am I?" Ben teased. "Look, the whole town is waiting for you two to figure it out. Pretty soon, Shirley at the bakery's going to start placing bets."

Andrew smirked. "Sounds like something you'd start, actually."

Ben held up a finger in mock offense. "Hey, I respect people's privacy. I just happen to be invested in your happiness."

Andrew chuckled, shaking his head. Ben was right, though he hated to admit it. Having his hesitation laid out so plainly stung—but in a good way.

"I don't know," Andrew said after a moment, tracing a pattern on the picnic table. "I would rather not make Lily feel like she has to do something she's not ready for."

Ben tilted his head. "Has she ever told you she isn't?"

Andrew thought back to their recent interactions—the creek, the laughter, the way she'd looked at him. "No. She hasn't."

Ben raised an eyebrow. "Then maybe it's time to stop planning the entire relationship before it's even started."

Andrew's silence said it all.

Ben grinned, but his tone softened. "You've over thought it, as usual. Breaking news: Andrew Whitman likes Lily!"

Andrew groaned. "All right, enough already."

"But seriously," Ben continued, growing earnest again, "talk to her. Ask her out. Sometimes, you just have to step out on faith."

Step out on faith.

Andrew rubbed his temples, equal parts amused and frustrated. "Sometimes I wonder where you get your wisdom."

Ben grinned, pulling a cookie from his bag. "The secret is snacks during serious conversations. Keeps the brain sharp."

Chapter 19

Lily found a parking spot near the Taste of Heaven Bakery. The buttery yellow building with pink accents offered a whimsical charm. Twinkling lights framed the bay windows, woven with autumn garlands of rust-colored berries, autumn colored leaves, and sprigs of lavender. Cakes of all shapes and sizes sat on display, tempting anyone who slowed down to take a look. Above the entrance, the bakery's hand-carved wooden sign swayed in the breeze, beckoning customers in.

As Lily stepped out of her car, the scent of sugar and cinnamon mixed with vanilla hit her, and her stomach growled. She was just about to open the door when a familiar voice called out from behind her.

"Lily! Wait up!"

Turning, she saw Andrew jogging toward her, his trademark grin spreading across his face. The crisp fall air tousled his dark hair just slightly, giving him a carefree, relaxed look.

"Fancy running into you here," he said, slowing to a stop just a few steps away.

Lily raised an eyebrow, a playful smirk pulling at her lips. "Andrew, I didn't expect to see you today?"

He chuckled, holding up his hands in mock surrender. "Hey, I promise I'm not stalking you. Although,"—he gave a dramatic pause— "maybe we just share the same excellent taste in bakeries."

She tilted her head, repressing the smile threatening to grow wider. "Sure, that must be it. I need to check on Grace and Ben's wedding cake order."

"I need to order a cake for one of the congregation members. Mrs. Harlow's turning ninety next week, and we can't let a big birthday like that go without some celebration."

"Ninety?" Lily repeated, impressed. "I guess that warrants a cake."

"Absolutely." His eyes twinkled with mischief. "And between you and me, if we're lucky, Shirley might toss a free sugar cookie or two our way while we're in there."

Lily laughed. "I had no idea you were part of the Taste of Heaven Bakery's insider club."

Andrew winked. "Let's just say I have connections."

"Well, since it sounds like you're here for serious cake business too," she said, stepping aside and gesturing toward the bakery door like a hostess welcoming him into the finest establishment, "shall we?"

"Why, thank you, Miss. Reynolds. After you," Andrew said, giving an exaggerated bow, making Lily roll her eyes, unable to keep from laughing. He opened the door, and they stepped inside together.

The warm, inviting aroma of freshly baked cakes and sugary confections wrapped around them like a cozy embrace. Lily inhaled, savoring the sweet scent as Shirley Gallagher popped her head up from behind the counter. Her warm, round face broke into a smile when she saw them.

"Well, if it isn't Laurel Ridge's favorite duo!" Shirley greeted, wiping her hands on her apron, and coming around front. "What brings y'all here today? More wedding stuff, Lily?"

Lily nodded, smiling. "Favorite duo? I'm not so sure about that. I just need to finalize the details for Grace and Ben's cake. I thought I'd drop by to make sure everything was in order."

"And you," Shirley said, turning to Andrew, "I know you're not planning a wedding anytime soon, so what can I do for you?"

Andrew gave Shirley a grin. "It's not a wedding today. Lily already has me beat on that front. I'm in for something just as special—Mrs. Harlow's turning ninety, and I'm thinking we need one of your finest."

Shirley's eyes widened. "Ninety years old? Well, bless her heart! I've got just the thing for a milestone like that. You leave it to me, Pastor. We'll make sure she gets a cake fit for a queen."

Andrew shot Lily an exaggerated glance of approval, like he'd just made the best decision of his life. "I have baker friends in high places."

Lily rolled her eyes, smirking. "Impressive. You'll have to teach me your ways someday."

"Stick around Laurel Ridge long enough, and you might just pick up a few tricks," he teased, leaning casually against the bakery counter.

Shirley wiped her hands again and nodded. "Now then, anything else for you two lovebirds?"

Lily felt her face go hot, and she stuttered, "Oh no—no, we're not—"

Andrew shifted, rubbing the back of his neck with a sheepish grin. "Uh, not quite there yet, Shirley, but... I'll keep you in the loop if that changes."

His attempt at humor didn't quite mask the flush creeping up his neck.

Shirley, amused by the exchange, let out a lighthearted laugh as she scribbled down the details for Andrew's cake order. "Well, don't be too long about it, Andrew. Folks in this town love a good romance."

"About Grace and Ben's wedding cake," Lily began, lifting the clipboard she'd been clutching more out of habit than necessity. "Just need to go over the details."

Shirley waved her hand, scoffing at the seriousness of Lily's tone. "Oh, forget the clipboard, sweetheart. If you're standing in my bakery, we do things the fun way."

"The fun way?" Andrew chimed in, amusement swirling in his brown eyes as he met Shirley's gaze with a playful grin.

"Cake! And you two won't be leaving without tasting a few samples," Shirley said, turning on her heels and heading toward the kitchen. "I've got a fresh batch of cakes in the back."

Lily sighed, preparing herself to indulge in something she had little time for.

"You know we're not walking out of here without sampling a few flavors, right?" he teased, raising one eyebrow. "I mean, it would be rude not to."

"Rude?" Lily scoffed, already reaching for her planner as a shield. "Since when do cake samples count as a professional obligation on my part?"

"Let's just say I'm an expert in small-town hospitality," Andrew replied with a mischievous grin. "Trust me, this is part of the process. And just be prepared. Shirley's creations can get a little wild sometimes."

Part of the process? A little wild? Lily cast a skeptical look at him and glanced up to find Shirley already placing plates with small pieces of cake on the counter.

"All right, darlings," Shirley said. "I know Ben and Grace have already decided on their cake, but I insist you try a few different flavors."

Lily protested, "But I'm not—"

"No arguments!" Shirley interrupted with playful authority, pointing a cake server in Lily's direction. "You're in my bakery now, which means you're tasting heaven whether or not you want to."

Andrew laughed beside her. "You heard the woman."

Lily felt the protest dying on her lips. It was useless resisting. Between Shirley's charm and Andrew's infectious enthusiasm, she might as well surrender.

The first bite was harmless enough—a delicate slice of classic buttery vanilla with a hint of almond filling. But Shirley had other ideas in store. She grabbed two more slices. These adorned with violet-colored frosting and layers of what appeared to be… lavender petals?

"What… is this?" Lily asked, eyeing the cake with suspicion.

"That, darling, is my famous lavender lemon creation," Shirley announced. "It's perfect for any small-town wedding with a touch of elegance."

"Lavender?" Lily's eyebrow arched as she eyed the cake. "I'm not sure flowers belong in a cake."

Andrew, ever mischievous, grabbed the slice and held it out to her, eyes twinkling. "Come on, adventurous city girl. You never know until you try."

"I never knew you were such a daredevil," Lily countered before tasting the tiniest piece imaginable from his outstretched fork. The tangy scent of lemon mixed with the floral notes wafting up did nothing to assure her.

She chewed. The flavor was... odd. Not terrible, but certainly not what she expected. She wrinkled her nose, glancing at Andrew, who watched her with contained amusement.

"Well?" he asked, eyes glinting with humor.

"Let's just say..." She took a delicate breath before finishing, "... it's an acquired taste."

Andrew's grin broadened. "Acquired? Sounds like you didn't hate it."

"I didn't hate it," Lily conceded, smoothing her expression. "But I'm not so sure anyone would want a lavender lemon tea party wedding."

Shirley chuckled, watching the exchange with clear glee. "No need to break out the fancy tea sets just yet. That one was a definite no from Grace and Ben, but I have other customers who are into all that foo-foo stuff. I've got something a little more exciting for our next round."

Lily eyed the next plate. This one looked innocent—a soft golden brown with a light glaze.

"Pumpkin spice doughnut," Shirley announced proudly. "One of my seasonal favorites. You simply must try it."

Andrew didn't hesitate, taking the first bite before making a dramatic, exaggerated expression of pure joy that made Shirley laugh.

"Good enough to shout from the mountaintops." Andrew proclaimed. "This one's amazing."

Lily rolled her eyes, though she couldn't fight her own smile. "You're so over-the-top."

Andrew shrugged. "Life's more fun that way."

Lily took a bite, surprised at how much she enjoyed it. The spices were warm and comforting, reminding her of autumn nights spent wrapped in scarves with a hot drink in hand.

"You're right. This is fantastic."

Andrew laughed. "Told you it's more fun when you let loose."

Lily gave him a mock glare, trying to ignore the way his uninhibited laughter made the room feel lighter, less controlled.

Shirley returned with—in Lily's professional opinion—something not very eye-catching.

"This one," Shirley said, "is something new I've been experimenting with. A little unexpected twist—mango lemon ginger."

Lily stared at the plate, willing herself not to recoil at the description.

"What?" she asked, wide-eyed. "That's... an unexpected combination."

Andrew raised an inquisitive brow. "Shirley, have you gone mad?"

Shirley threw back her head and laughed. "Mad as a hatter! But this is where cake innovation happens, my dear. Trust me, this could be the flavor of the future."

Lily took one look at Andrew, whose expression was already full of mock bravery. Before she could dodge the situation, Andrew grabbed two slices—one for him and one for her.

Grinning impishly, he handed Lily a slice of cake, raising his own in a playful toast before taking a daring bite. Lily followed suit, albeit with more hesitation, her eyes never leaving Andrew.

The taste hit her like a brick wall. The combination of mango, ginger, and lemon created a flavor that was beyond unpleasant. Her taste buds rebelled, and she scrunched up her face.

Andrew, also struggling to swallow, stared at her in shock. "I'm not sure about this one," Lily gasped between coughing fits, clutching a napkin to her mouth.

Andrew waved his hand, choking back laughter. "Shirley, I think this one needs a little more testing."

Shirley's laughter echoed through the bakery, followed by tears of amusement running down her cheeks. "Oh, don't worry. Not all experiments are winners at first. I'm still working on this one!"

As Lily reached for her water bottle, she took a deep sip, struggling to control her laughter and not choke on the flavor. Meanwhile, Andrew gradually regained his composure, although his eyes still sparkled with amusement.

"Mango, ginger and lemon," he muttered, wiping his eyes with the back of his hand, "minus ten points for that one, Shirley."

Lily couldn't hold back any longer. The laughter continued spilling out—real, unrestrained, loud. She hadn't laughed like this in ages.

"Shirley," Lily said as she pulled herself back into professional mode. "We need to focus. The wedding is a few days away. Let's get to the details of Grace and Ben's cake."

Shirley, a merry twinkle in her eye and her brunette curls escaping from a haphazard bun, waved a dismissive hand. "Oh, darlin,' don't you worry your pretty little head. The cake's gonna be perfect. Three tiers of buttery vanilla cake with my raspberry filling that everyone seems to love these days. Topped with my best buttercream icing." She gave a wink, still looking more amused by the chitchat than concerned about any of the finer details.

"And it's still going to have the sugared berries and greenery that Grace requested, right?" Lily asked.

Shirley nodded, but then her brows furrowed. "Grace did say she liked the berries better than the roses, didn't she?"

Lily's mouth turned into a wry smile. "That's exactly what she said. Twice. Remember the consultation last week when Grace picked out the colors? Red berries to match the maid of honor dress."

"Berries, got it!" Shirley said, laughing.

"And," Lily continued, "you're sure the cake will be delivered to the reception hall behind the church by 10 AM, right?"

"No worries, the cake will get there in time," Shirley assured with a warm smile.

"Are you sure it's not too much trouble? Maybe jot yourself a note so you don't forget," Lily said, her voice laced with concern. "Or better yet... I can easily arrange for someone else to pick it up."

"You city girls fret too much," Shirley said with a dismissive wave of her hand.

"Worrying comes with the territory. I just want Grace and Ben's wedding to go off without a hitch," Lily said.

"Lily, stop worrying—it's all going to turn out just fine." Ben strolled into the bakery with a wide grin, his eyes twinkling.

"Grace might have the patience of a saint most of the time, but if this cake isn't exactly what she envisioned and delivered on time, trust me, I won't be the only one upset," Lily said.

Shirley let out a hearty laugh, the sound filling the cozy space. "Grace? Get upset about a wedding cake not being just right or delivered on time? Oh, honey, she's far too sweet for that."

Lily raised her eyebrow. "Maybe. But me? I'm not above bribing Andrew to whisper a few words of forgiveness into Sunday's sermon about someone who didn't pull through on their commitments."

Ben clapped his hands together, loving the playful tension. "Oooo, Shirley, I'd watch out if I were you. Lily's turned the big guns on you now."

Shirley squinted playfully at Ben. "Ben Turner, you hush now," she teased with a knowing grin. Then, her eyes dropped to the box in his hand. "Now, what've you got there?" she asked, nodding toward it with curiosity.

He opened the small box, removing the delicate contents. He held a beautifully hand-whittled wedding topper—a couple holding each other in a soft, intimate embrace, their features finely detailed in smooth wood.

Shirley's eyes lit up as she crossed her arms and leaned in for a better look. "Well now. Isn't that just a fine piece of work? It's gorgeous."

Lily smiled. "It's perfect, Ben. Grace is going to love it."

Ben's face softened, pride clear in his voice as he turned the topper in his hands, admiring the craftsmanship. "I hope so. Grace gave me the job of finding a topper for the cake, and I think this one is just right."

Shirley reached out to touch the wood, her fingers tracing the edges of the carved figures. "It's more than just right. This cake will be stunning. Whoever worked on this cake topper has some serious skill."

Ben nodded. "Local artist. He does all his carving by hand and only works with wood from the mountains around here. Thought it'd be a nice touch for the cake."

Lily tilted her head, looking at the intricate details of the couple's embrace—how their hands seemed just about to move, and the way their carved faces mirrored a quiet, shared moment of love. "It's more than a nice touch. Grace is going to be surprised and probably speechless when she sees this."

Shirley grinned, nodding appreciatively. "If the cake turns out half as good as this topper, Grace might just mistake me for an angel!"

Ben laughed, slipping the topper carefully back into its box.

Chapter 20

As Lily, Andrew, and Ben exited the bakery, the bells above the door chimed merrily, announcing their departure into the crisp fall air.

Lily clutched a small box of cake samples, a token of appreciation from Shirley for being a good sport.

Ben stretched his arms overhead, letting out an exaggerated yawn. "Well, folks, I better get a move on," he said, sounding half-regretful. "I've got a hiking tour calling my name in a few minutes. You know how it goes, keeping the masses from wandering off cliffs and all," he added, grinning.

Andrew gave him a mock salute, hand to his forehead. "Go save the day, Turner. Your adoring fans await."

Lily and Andrew stood on the sidewalk, their eyes following Ben as he strolled toward his truck with a casual wave. "Y'all have fun without me," Ben called over his shoulder, winking before climbing into the driver's seat.

Andrew cleared his throat, glancing down at the package of cake samples in Lily's hand. "So... Have you eaten lunch yet?"

Caught off-guard, Lily blinked. "Oh—uh, not yet actually."

He raised an eyebrow. "Well, that's a good thing. Because Martha's Diner is calling our names." He winked. "And rumor has it the burgers today are legendary. Bigger than anything you've probably ever seen."

Lily laughed, shaking her head. "Is that your best marketing pitch?"

Andrew flashed her a grin, those warm brown eyes of his crinkling at the corners—a grin that was disarming, yet also impossible to refuse. "So... lunch?"

Lily hesitated for just a moment. She enjoyed being around Andrew, but she wasn't entirely sure what she was getting into. Still, it wasn't as though she had any other lunch plans.

Her lips twitched into a reluctant smile. "Alright, fine. I'll have lunch with you. But this burger you speak of better live up to the hype."

"It will," Andrew said.

As they walked toward Martha's Diner, Laurel Ridge unfolded around them in all its small-town charms. The sidewalks were dotted with pumpkins, cornstalk displays, and hay bales lovingly decorated for autumn. The whole town had that distinct feeling that only fall in the mountains could bring—the air was crisp with slivers of a chill, but the sun still stretched just enough warmth to make you smile.

Inside the diner, booths were filled with locals chatting over burgers and coffee, a hum of conversation blending into the clatter of dishes from behind the swinging kitchen doors.

Martha herself was behind the counter, chit-chatting with Earl Smith, the owner of the hardware store in Laurel Ridge. But as soon as the door closed behind them, her keen eyes met theirs. A wide, knowing grin immediately bloomed across her face, and within two seconds, she was bustling over.

"Well, well, well," she crowed, playfully wagging her finger. "Look what the wind blew in."

Andrew shook his head. "Now, Martha, don't start."

But Martha, with all her Southern charm and spunk, would not be deterred. "Hush now, Andrew," she teased. "When two people walk into my diner together, it's as good as a headline in the town newspaper!"

Lily blushed a deep scarlet. "Oh, no. This is just... lunch. Really."

Martha raised her eyebrows, lips pinched together like she was holding back a thousand teasing words. "Just lunch, huh? Well, by all means. Sit down, relax. I'll be there is a second."

With a chuckle, Andrew motioned toward an empty booth near the wide front windows. "Let's grab a seat."

With a lingering flush still warming her face, Lily approached the booth and slid into a seat opposite Andrew.

"Let me guess... you both are here for the burger special, am I right? Oh, and fries, of course," Martha said as she set glasses of water on the table.

Andrew nodded. "You guessed right."

With a wink and a happy hum to herself, Martha disappeared into the kitchen.

"How do they manage to do it?" Lily inquired.

"Do what?" he asked.

"Every single person!" she exclaimed. "Whenever you step into a store or even this diner, it's as if everyone is part of a shared secret. They act like they've already written the next three chapters of your life."

A grin spread across Andrew's face. "That's the charm of small-town living for you," he explained. "Here, everyone knows everyone else's business before the first sip of coffee hits the table. You just have to adjust to the way of life here."

Lily huffed out a small laugh, shaking her head. "Well, I'm not used to it yet."

"That's alright," Andrew said, his eyes holding hers for just a beat longer than necessary. "You don't have to be."

Before she could respond, Martha returned with two giant plates, each bearing burgers that lived up to every bit of Andrew's earlier hype.

"You weren't kidding," Lily murmured, eyes widening as she stared at the burger towering on her plate. "This thing's... it's monstrous."

Andrew laughed. "Told you. Martha does burgers right. Let's say grace."

Andrew bowed his head, and Lily followed suit.

"Lord," Andrew began, his voice soft but steady, "thank you for this food, for the hands that prepared it, and for the chance to share a meal together. Bless our time and let it be filled with laughter and joy. Amen."

"Amen," Lily echoed, a warm hush settling between them as they lifted their heads.

They both bit into their burgers at the same time, and for a moment, conversation ceased in favor of appreciating the food.

Lily wiped her mouth with one of the diner's paper napkins, wide-eyed. "Okay, you weren't exaggerating about this burger. It's delicious."

Andrew nodded, still chewing, but gave her a thumbs up in agreement. After swallowing, he added, "I told you. Martha doesn't mess around."

"So," Andrew said between bites, "tell me more about your job. How do you handle wedding after wedding?"

Lily laughed a little, wiping her hands before taking a sip of her water. "Organizing a wedding is like corralling a group of children with attention spans shorter than a goldfish. But somehow, I make it work. I think I've developed herding skills along the way."

"Sounds like there's never a dull moment in your line of work."

"You could say that," Lily admitted, resting her hands on the table. "But honestly, I like being the one making sure things run smoothly. It's satisfying to orchestrate everything and watch it all come together. I guess it keeps me busy... keeps me in control."

Andrew arched an eyebrow. "Control. Something tells me there's more to that word for you than just getting the flowers right."

For a moment, she hesitated. But something about Andrew's presence—the way he listened without judgment, the way he never pushed her to share more than she wanted—gave her the courage to be a little more honest.

She shrugged, looking down at her plate. "After my breakup with Bill... things felt out of control for a while. Planning weddings is orderly. It's something predictable that I can manage. Even when things go sideways, like mismatched bridesmaid dresses or last-minute catering disasters... it's still fixable." Lily took a breath, leaning back in her seat. "It's easier to fix someone else's mess than to face your own."

Andrew's expression softened. "I can't imagine that was an easy time for you."

"No, it wasn't," she said. Then, after a beat, she added with a small smile, "But I'm still here, right?"

"Yeah," Andrew replied gently. "You are. Tell me more about your passion for graphic design. Do you think you'll find it easy to shift gears from wedding planning and dive back into that world?"

Lily's eyes widened slightly as Andrew brought up graphic design, surprised he remembered.

"I really miss graphic design. Wedding planning has been reward-ing, but it's not something I see myself doing forever. Lately, I feel a bit like a hypocrite—planning other people's weddings when I don't really believe in love anymore. Graphic design, on the other hand, has always been my passion. It's where my genuine talent lies, and I've been trying to find a job in that field again. Wedding planning just doesn't feel like the future for me."

Andrew leaned forward slightly, his tone gentle yet curious. "It sounds like you've got a pretty clear handle on your passions, but I have to wonder—what's behind your hesitation? Why is it you say you don't believe in love anymore?"

Lily set her burger down. She hadn't expected this—not here, in this cozy little diner, with their lunches only halfway eaten. Her fingers twisted the napkin in her lap as she avoided meeting his gaze.

"It's just..." she said, her voice softer now, almost fragile. "After everything I went through with my ex... Bill? It's like something broke in me. I lost faith in it—all of it. Love, trust, even God's plans for me. It felt like everything I believed in went up in smoke. And now? Now it feels safer to just... not believe."

Andrew studied her, his brow furrowing slightly, but his gaze was full of quiet understanding. It wasn't pity—he had enough respect for her to know that pity wasn't what she needed. It was something else. It was as if he was seeing her—not her defenses, not her walls, but the real Lily, sitting there, raw and vulnerable.

"You know," he began after a moment, his voice gentle but de-liberate, "I get that. I do. With Sarah, I thought I had everything figured out. I thought I knew how my life was going to go, how my future was going to look. And then it didn't happen, and it felt like I'd been left broken trying to understand why God abandoned me in that moment."

Lily blinked, surprised.

Andrew smiled a little, as if reading her thoughts. "You probably can't imagine me having tons of doubts or fears," he continued, fiddling with a fork beside his plate. "But we all do. Even pastors believe it or not. I went through months of wondering if I'd ever be able to trust God's plan again. But, over time, I realized something. God doesn't abandon us in those moments of pain. He's there, waiting for us to look up."

Lily's throat tightened.

Andrew glanced out the window before his gaze landed back on her. "I don't want to preach at you, Lily. That's not what this is. But I do know this... Love and faith, they aren't about having control. They're about trust—even when it feels impossible."

"And you think," Lily said, her voice just above a whisper, "that I should just... let go of my fears and start trusting again?"

Andrew leaned forward, his expression earnest. "Not just trust blindly. But open your heart, even if it feels like the hardest thing to do. It's a process. You don't have to figure it all out right now, but maybe start by trusting that God's plan for you is bigger—so much bigger—than the pain you've been through."

Tears crept into the corners of her eyes, ones she quickly blinked away. Lily didn't want to cry, not here, not in front of Andrew. Still, there was something about his words, his presence, that made her feel like maybe—just maybe—it was okay to feel what she hadn't let herself in a while.

"I don't know if I'm ready for all that," she said, her hands now resting still beside her plate.

"I understand," Andrew said. "Just take it one moment at a time. You don't have to have it all figured out by the end of lunch." His tone lightened, a small grin spreading across his lips. "But you do have to finish that burger. No one leaves Martha's Diner without demolishing their food."

Lily laughed, the sound tinged with something bittersweet, but genuine. She took a moment, lifting her burger for another thoughtful bite, letting the discussion hang between them, allowing its weight to dissipate naturally.

"So," she said, her tone lighter as she eased into a new topic, "tell me more about the youth group you and Ben lead at the church."

Her eyes met Andrew's, a subtle shift away from her vulnerability, but there was warmth there, an invitation to continue the conversation at a gentler pace. Andrew welcomed the shift in conversation, recognizing that sometimes people needed space to process. He smiled, soft but genuine, appreciating her willingness to connect.

"Ah, the youth group," he said, leaning back in his seat, his shoulders relaxing a bit. "Well, it's one of the most rewarding—and sometimes chaotic—things I do at the church. Ben and I started leading the group together a few years ago. The kids are great, a mix of all ages, full of energy... and questions. They keep us on our toes."

Lily raised an eyebrow, her lips tugging into a smile. "Questions?"

"Oh, you'd be surprised," he replied, humor lighting his eyes. "They come up with the most profound—and sometimes bizarre—ones. We were having a Q&A last week, and one twelve-year-old asked if dinosaurs and humans coexisted because of something he saw in a movie. And a ten-year-old was straight-up wondering if heaven had Wi-Fi because, you know, eternity without the internet is apparently unfathomable."

Lily laughed, shaking her head. "Sounds like they keep it interesting."

"Interesting is an understatement," Andrew laughed. "But they're also genuinely curious about life, faith, purpose. Their questions cut deeper than the stuff we adults sometimes avoid. Last week, one of the kids asked, 'How do you know God really loves you, even when you feel small?'" Andrew's voice softened, as if the memory still tugged at his heart.

Lily paused, her expression thoughtful. She glanced down at her plate, chewing on her next words before speaking. "How'd you answer that?"

Andrew looked at her, something sparking behind his eyes. "I told her that love isn't about how big or small you feel at the moment. It's about knowing that no matter how lost or insignificant you might think you are, love—true love, God's love—sees you where you are. Knows you by name. You don't have to earn it or prove yourself worthy of it. It's there, constant, even when you can't see it clearly."

Lily swallowed, Andrew's words sinking deep into her heart.

"You make it sound so simple," she said, the doubt in her voice tinged with just a hint of hope.

Andrew reached for his water, taking a sip as he watched her carefully. "It's not simple. Not always. But sometimes, we overcomplicate it. God's love—it's there even when things fall apart... especially then."

Lily glanced out the window. "You're good with them," she said after a pause, her voice thoughtful as she turned her attention back to him. "The kids, I mean. You seem to know just what to say."

Andrew smiled, but there was a hint of modesty in the curve of his lips. "I try. But honestly? They teach me just as much as I teach them."

Lily chuckled. "I could see that. Kids don't hold back. There's something refreshing about that."

"They keep me grounded," Andrew agreed. "There's a purity to how they see the world, and even their doubts. They remind me of all the things we adults sometimes forget when we get busy in life."

She took another bite of her burger, chewing thoughtfully. "So... what's up next for the youth group? Another big Q&A session?"

Andrew chuckled, noticing the way she shifted the conversation just before it tipped too far into heaviness. "Something like that. We're actually planning a weekend trip to help the local wildlife center with some trail restoration. Get them out into nature, work with their hands a bit."

"I bet they'll love it," Lily said, her voice genuine, intrigued by the idea. "And you'll love trying to keep them all in line, right?"

Andrew shook his head, laughing. "Oh, absolutely. Herding a group of teenagers in the wilderness? It's my idea of a relaxing weekend."

Lily smiled, her heart feeling uncharacteristically light in Andrew's company. For the first time in what seemed like a long stretch of loneliness, she was starting to believe that maybe—just maybe—she didn't have to carry everything alone.

Maybe, as Andrew had subtly implied earlier, not every moment had to make sense, as long as there was space to hope for something better.

As Martha passed by the table, dropping off extra napkins, she winked at the two of them. "Well, don't go making things too serious right now. Nothin' wrong with just sharing good company."

Andrew grinned, and Lily shot Martha a playful glare, though no annoyance accompanied it—just a sense of lightness.

"See," Andrew said after Martha walked away, leaning back in the booth, "small towns—everyone's a part of your story, even if you didn't invite them."

Lily laughed despite herself. "I'm learning that very quickly."

Chapter 21

T he air smelled of pumpkin spice and apple cider as twilight descended over the small town of Laurel Ridge. Outside the Laurel Ridge Community Church, strings of orange and purple lights twinkled overhead like tiny stars, casting a soft festive glow on the community's annual Halloween event. The church pavilion, usually simple and rustic, had been transformed into a festive wonderland. Jack-o'-lanterns lined the gravel path leading to the pavilion, their toothy smiles flickering from within.

Lily tugged her light jacket tighter around her shoulders, bracing against the crisp autumn air. The sounds of children laughing and running filled the space, their excitement obvious as they raced from one trick-or-treat station to the next. Candy wrappers crinkled, and the occasional peal of delighted shrieks from kids trying to outdo each other in their costumes echoed through the grounds.

It was perfect. Almost too perfect.

Lily stood near the edge of the pavilion, watched the controlled chaos unfold as kids in pirate hats, fairy wings, and miniature superhero suits weaved between the candy booths set up for the event. She had told herself she was just here to help, to support Grace with organizing the trick-or-treat stops and making sure all the kids had their fill of candy. Her thoughts, though, swirled with dreams and new possibilities, each one painting a picture of the future she hadn't dared consider before.

"Well, well. Thought I'd find you lurking on the sidelines again."

Grace's voice came from behind her. Lily turned, finding her cousin holding two steaming cups of cider, balanced precariously in one hand. Her other arm cradled a pumpkin-shaped bucket filled with candy.

"You make me sound like I'm hiding," Lily shot back with a smirk, taking one cup from her cousin. The warm Styrofoam cup was a welcome to her icy fingers.

Grace gave an amused huff. "You are hiding. Come on, Lily, it's Halloween. You're supposed to be having fun."

"Grace, I'm really not trying to hide—I'm just... having a moment, I'm trying to work my courage up," Lily said with a sigh.

"Care to elaborate? Because, honestly, I'm a bit lost." Grace said.

"You know, Grace," Lily said, her voice tinged with a rueful smile, "I think I'm standing here in the middle of a churchyard, having my own come-to-Jesus moment."

"Okay, so..." Grace said with a playful grin.

"I never thought I'd be saying this, but I've genuinely enjoyed my time here in Laurel Ridge so far. When I first came here, I figured I'd help plan your wedding, watch you walk down the aisle, dog-sit for a few days, and then be on my way, no strings attached..." Lily admitted.

"I'm going to need you to spill it because, honestly, I have no clue where you're going with this," Grace said, raising an eyebrow.

"I have no idea where this is all heading either," Lily admitted, her voice steady yet raw. "But I do know one thing—I'm exhausted. I'm done just taking baby steps in finding a new career. I want a career that has more meaning for me. I'm done letting fear run my life. I'm done letting Bill live rent-free in my mind, constantly pulling the strings."

"I'm glad you're finally coming around..."

"I'm on a roll, Grace, so just let me get this out," Lily started, her voice laced with frustration. "I'm thirty-two years old, acting like my life has completely fallen apart because of one man who shattered my trust. But here's the irony—he was the one cheating, living a double life, lying to both his wife and me. So why am I the one trudging through life, feeling stuck and broken? If anything, he should be the one living in misery."

"I agree, but what brought about this sudden change? How did you come to see things differently?" Grace asked.

Lily looked toward Andrew, laughing and tossing beanbags with the kids, his carefree spirit lighting up her surroundings.

"You know," Lily began, her gaze shifting back to her cousin, "after lunch with Andrew today, I decided to take a drive around town, just to clear my head. And as I was driving, it hit me—I don't think I'm here just to help with your wedding. I mean, let's be real, Grace. Your wedding would be perfect, with or without me. There's something more going on. This trip... this town... the people I have met... it's all opened my eyes in ways I didn't expect."

She paused for a breath, her fingers toying with the edge of her jacket as the weight of realization settled over her. "For so long, I've been stuck—trapped in this job that doesn't fulfill me anymore, feeling like everything ended when Bill broke my heart. But being here, in Laurel Ridge, I'm starting to see that life doesn't end because of one man's betrayal. There's so much more—more than I've been allowing myself to see. And Andrew..."

Lily glanced back at Andrew, who was guiding a young boy with the beanbag toss, his laughter warm and genuine. Her eyes softened, and her voice grew quieter. "I think God brought me here for more than just wedding planning. He put Andrew in my path for a reason—to help me see things differently. To remind me that there's love, hope, and purpose beyond the walls I've built. I've realized that maybe... just maybe... it's time to let go of the past and trust in what God has in store for me."

Grace smiled, listening intently, and the evening air felt full of possibility swirling around them.

"You're going to make me cry, Lily," Grace said, her voice soft with emotion.

"Believe me," Lily said softly, her voice wavering as she fought back the emotions welling up inside her. "When I was out driving this afternoon, I couldn't hold back the tears. It hit me all at once—like a brick to the chest—just how overwhelming everything really is."

"And so... what's your next move?" Grace asked.

"I don't have all the answers right now, but one thing I won't do is let fear sabotage my future—or my chance to become who I'm meant to be," Lily said confidently.

"You know, Lily, you never cease to amaze me," Grace said, her voice filled with admiration. "Now, tell me about your lunch with Andrew today. What happened that really made you start thinking?"

"Well," Lily began, biting her bottom lip as if trying to choose her words carefully, "it wasn't so much about what he said—though that was definitely part of it—but more about how he really listened. Like, deeply listened. No judgment, no interruptions. Just this... steady, quiet patience that felt so different from anything I've experienced before."

Grace sipped her cider, her eyes twinkling. "Andrew has that way about him. It's why the whole town loves him. But clearly, he's made more than an impression on you."

Lily tilted her head, gazing out toward where Andrew stood, now untangling a cluster of giggling kids as they attempted to tackle him in some mismatched pile of superhero costumes and pirate hats. His laughter rang out, free and light.

"I think it all started when we got into this half-serious, half-playful conversation about trust," Lily said, swirling her cider. "I told him about Bill—about how I feel like I can't trust my own ability to love without it breaking me again. And instead of giving me the usual comfort lines, you know, 'Oh, not all men are like that,' or 'You'll know when the right one comes along,' he just... got it."

Grace leaned in slightly, her attention fully on her cousin now. "How so?"

"He told me a little more about himself and some of the things he's gone through. And I realized... he's scared too. He even admitted that he's used his pastoral role as a way to distance himself from getting too close to anyone again, convincing himself that love would somehow distract him from his calling. It was... I don't know how to explain it, Grace. But hearing him say that? It made me feel less alone."

Grace tilted her head, studying Lily's face with a knowing smile. "So, you shared your fears about love with each other?"

"Yes," Lily said, her voice almost trembling. "But it wasn't just that. It was the way Andrew framed love—not as a perfect, safe thing, but as a choice, despite the messiness. He didn't try to offer a fix like everyone else always does. He just... acknowledged it, like he was telling me, 'Yeah, it's hard—but it's still worth the risk.' And I don't know, it hit me in a way that I didn't realize at the time... I was ready to hear that honesty and truth."

Grace let out a soft hum of understanding. "That's just like Andrew. When things get real, he knows exactly when to hold space for a person without taking over. You know that's rare, Lily."

Lily nodded, her chest tightening with the weight of that truth. "It is. And it goes beyond that. For so long, I've been running this script in my head—that I don't deserve love anymore or that I've somehow misplaced the right to have it because I didn't see Bill's lies. But Andrew's words—they challenged that. He challenged it."

Grace reached out, placing a hand on Lily's arm. "Because that belief of yours isn't true, Lily. You didn't lose anything except the version of love you thought was real—but all that did was make room for something that truly is."

Lily's eyes flicked up to meet Grace's, her resolve beginning to harden into something more tangible. "Yeah. I think I know that now. And honestly? I'm scared out of my mind. Because everything in me wants to pull back, to retreat to safety—like I've done since Bill, like I've done ever since coming here. But when I was sitting there with Andrew today, for the first time in months... it didn't feel scary. It felt different."

Grace's gaze softened, her lips curving into a gentle smile. "You're falling for him, aren't you?"

Lily lowered her eyes, her cheeks flushing with warmth. "Maybe," she said, her voice barely above a whisper. "No... actually... yes. Yes, I think I am. Which is terrifying in its own way, but it's also... it's nothing like what I felt for Bill. It's like I don't have to pretend with Andrew. I don't have to be this perfect version of myself that I've always tried to present to the world. I can be... me."

Grace grinned, her eyes sparkling with excitement for her cousin. "And maybe that's the whole point—that real love isn't about perfection at all. It's about being vulnerable, being messy, and still showing up for one another."

Lily sighed, a mix of relief and trepidation. "Exactly. And I think that's why I'm terrified. Andrew... he's rooted here, Grace. His entire life is bound up with the church, with this town. And I'm.... I don't even know how this could work. I'm afraid of dragging him into my craziness."

Grace considered that for a moment, her brow furrowing. "Here's a thought, Lily—what if you're not dragging him into anything? What if... just what if... you're both stepping into something new together, creating a life neither of you expected, but both want?"

Lily paused, mulling over Grace's words. "I don't know if I'm ready to leap. I mean, we've barely scratched the surface of what's between us."

"Yes," Grace agreed, her voice brimming with encouragement, "but there's a reason you're thinking about that leap in the first place. Look, Lily, you're not going to have all the answers on day one. You are smart enough to know that, but maybe that's the beauty of it. God brought Andrew into your life for a reason. And maybe He's inviting you to let go and trust that wherever you land will be beautiful—even if it looks different."

A moment passed, then Lily, smiling through the mix of excitement and fear that churned within her, let out a soft breath. "I don't know what to do, Grace."

Grace shifted toward her, her expression resolute but tender. "Take the next step—talk to Andrew. Tell him what you're feeling, what your fears are. I guarantee you he's having the same thoughts about the future. He's probably wondering how this all works with his ministry and your life in Manhattan. But keeping this all inside—doing everything on your own—won't help either of you."

Lily nodded. "Maybe you're right,"

"Not maybe—I am right, Lily!" Grace said firmly before her expression softened again. "Look, I know you hate it when I push, but seriously—this is your chance. Don't let yourself overthink it until you've buried every good thing before it even starts. Andrew might just be the man who's willing to walk through the uncertainty with you. But you've got to meet him halfway."

Lily fell into silence.

Grace gave Lily's shoulder a playful nudge. "So, when are you going to talk to him?"

Lily shot her cousin a teasing glance. "No pressure, right?"

"You know me. I firmly believe in cheering my cousin on—preferably with an obnoxious sign," Grace said with a wink. She tilted her head and glanced to where Andrew was handing out candy to costumed children near the beanbag toss game. "But seriously, the longer you wait, the harder it'll get."

Lily knew her cousin was right. This was her moment—a chance to break the fortress she'd built around her heart and trust.

"I think I'm going to just set my thoughts and worries aside for the evening and go have fun," Lily admitted, her voice shaky but determined.

Grace's smile widened. "There it is! That's the Lily I know." She nudged her again. "Go on, before someone else calls dibs on his beanbag toss skills."

Lily laughed.

"Alright, I'm doing it," Lily said, standing tall, a mix of fear and hope dancing beneath her calm façade.

"Go get him, tiger," Grace whispered, watching her cousin take those first steps toward Andrew.

Chapter 22

The lively sounds of Halloween—the carefree laughter of children, the soft rustle of leaves, and the occasional whoop of excitement—faded into the background as Lily made her way toward Andrew. Her heartbeat thudded in her ears, a rhythm of anticipation.

Lily quickened her pace and approached Andrew just as he was helping a little pirate with a beanbag. He looked up, spotting her, and a smile spread across his face.

"Oh, look who's ready to have some fun and toss a beanbag in a pumpkin," Andrew teased, his tone playful. "I was thinking you were avoiding me."

Lily rolled her eyes but couldn't suppress her grin. "Avoiding? Well, that is partly true. I'm always up for a good bean bag challenge, though."

Andrew raised an eyebrow. "Oh really? So... you think you can toss this bean bag into the pumpkin on the first try?"

Lily cast a glance at the plastic pumpkin. "I think I could manage."

Andrew stepped aside, mockingly sweeping his arm to signal the floor was hers. "Alright, Miss Lily. Impress us with your skills."

With a playful narrowing of her eyes, Lily shifted her stance, squinting at the plastic pumpkin as if it were an Olympic target. She tossed the beanbag, and it sailed through the air with a perfect arc, landing directly inside the pumpkin.

The kids whooped and cheered as if she had just landed the winning shot in the NBA finals. Lily shrugged, feigning nonchalance, and turning to Andrew with a coy smile. "What can I say? I aim for perfection."

Andrew chuckled, his smile widening. "A born natural. Who knows, maybe you've missed your true calling in life."

Lily bit her lip, holding back another laugh. "Don't let my clients hear that—I might just switch careers."

Andrew grabbed a bean bag himself, tossing it up and down idly before looking at her. "I can see it now—'Lily Reynolds, Championship Bean Bag Coach.' Has quite the ring to it."

She laughed—really laughed—and something loosened in her chest a little.

Andrew tossed the beanbag toward the pumpkin, and it missed—by a significant margin.

"Oh, okay," Lily teased, biting back her amusement. "Not everyone can be a champion on the first try."

"Beginner's mistake," Andrew said with heavy mock seriousness. He narrowed his eyes, studying the pumpkin like a football coach planning a strategy. "Next time."

"That's what they all say," Lily quipped, nudging him lightly with her shoulder.

Andrew grinned and tilted his head. "What do you say we grab some cider and... settle this with a rematch later?"

She nodded. "You think you can handle the pressure of a rematch?"

"I think I can handle whatever you throw at me."

They walked side by side toward the cider table, the hum of the festivities lingering behind them—the warm glow of the Jack-o'-lanterns guiding their way. Lily noticed that walking next to Andrew felt... natural. Unhurried. The kind of thing that didn't need a plan or agenda.

As they reached the cider table, Andrew deftly plucked two steaming cups from the table, handing one over with an exaggerated flourish.

"Your beverage, madam," he said in a sophisticated tone, only to break into a broad smile.

"Why, thank you, kind sir," Lily played along, feeling lighter with every passing moment.

They found a bench near the church's side lawn, a little quieter but still close enough to feel the festive energy pulse around them.

For a moment, they sat in comfortable silence, watching the kids run around, the soft rustling of leaves and the occasional burst of laughter filling the space.

Lily cleared her throat, breaking the silence. "Andrew, can we talk? I mean, really talk?"

Andrew set down his cup on the bench, shifting so that he could face her more fully. The way his brow furrowed ever so slightly showed he was already sensing the vulnerability beneath her calm demeanor. He nodded slowly. "Of course, Lily. What's on your mind?"

Taking a deep breath, Lily dropped her gaze to the amber liquid swirling in her cup. "I just... I want to apologize. I know I've been, well... cold. Quite a few times over the past several days, to be honest." She gave a rueful chuckle, shaking her head. "I'm sure you noticed."

Andrew didn't confirm or deny—he simply watched her with those warm, attentive eyes that made it impossible to hide.

Lily's voice softened. "I didn't mean to push you away, but I guess that's precisely what I've been trying to do, isn't it? I've been throwing up walls every chance I get. And it's not fair to you."

He remained quiet for a moment, clearly choosing his words with care. "I won't lie... I did notice. But I also knew there was more to it. People don't throw up their armor without a reason, right?"

Lily huffed softly, glancing away. "Yeah, well, my reasons are... complicated. And I probably haven't given you—or anyone else close to me—the benefit of understanding that."

She was quiet for a beat, unsure how much to share, but then the words started tumbling out. "After everything with Bill," she began, heart quickening at the mention of his name, "I just... stopped believing. In love. In trust. In happy endings. It felt safer to keep everything at a distance, you know? Protect myself. What if it all falls apart again?"

Andrew's gaze never wavered. "And so you did what anyone would—you chose to protect your heart."

"Yes." Lily's voice was barely a whisper now. "But I see now... that fear, it's kept me stuck. And in the process, I've been pushing away people who never deserved any of that... including you."

Andrew reached for her hand, his touch warm against the cool evening air. "Lily, I want you to know something. I've been exactly where you are."

She looked up at him, surprise flickering in her eyes.

"No, really," he continued, his voice steady. "When Sarah left, I did the same thing. I threw myself into my work at the church, into the community, anything to avoid the possibility of getting close to someone again. I was terrified of letting someone new into my heart, only to end up broken a second time. People would call me kind or patient, but really? I was just... playing it safe."

Lily gazed at him, taking it all in.

"So," Andrew said, squeezing her hand gently, "I get it. I get why it's hard for you to let someone in, and why it feels safer to retreat. But the truth is, those walls just end up keeping us from everything good, too."

Lily's eyes softened. "You make it sound so simple, like you've already mastered all this."

Andrew chuckled, shaking his head. "Oh, far from it. I'm still learning daily how to trust. Trust in God's timing, trust in this—the potential between us. But one thing I do know..." He paused, searching her face. "Whatever this is, you and me? I'm willing to offer patience, to build that trust together. But I need to know... are you willing too?"

Lily swallowed hard, her heart thudding in her chest.

"I am," Lily said, locking eyes with Andrew. Her voice held a quiet strength, a newfound resolve that shimmered beneath the surface of her vulnerability. "I'm terrified... but I'm done letting fear control me. I just—" She hesitated for a beat, gathering her thoughts, "we have to be open with each other... really open. If I falter—if I hesitate or get scared—I need you to call me out. Don't let me retreat into my own fears. We need to talk about them. Deal with them head-on."

Andrew smiled, the warmth of it reaching his eyes. "That's what I want too. Just us, no walls, no games. Honest, adult conversations."

Lily met his gaze, her heart clenching at the sincerity behind his words.

"I've... I've been holding back too much," Lily admitted, "Especially with you, and I'm deeply sorry for how I've treated you."

"Lily, apology accepted, but I do get it."

They sat there in comfortable silence for a while, absorbing the weight of their words, letting them settle between them. Lily couldn't remember the last time her heart felt so... light. Vulnerable, yes. But light.

Lily took another sip of her cider, letting it warm her from the inside out. "So, about that rematch?"

Andrew grinned, his eyes glinting in the soft light. "Oh, I'm ready whenever you are. But don't say I didn't warn you—revenge is sweet."

"I'm not worried," she teased, standing up from the bench and tossing him a playful glance over her shoulder. "I've got a championship title to defend."

Chapter 23

Lily stood on Grace's porch, tugging her scarf snug around her neck as a crisp breeze blew through the hills, and though the coolness was biting, it was also invigorating, waking her senses—reminding her she wasn't in the city anymore. Here in Laurel Ridge, autumn wasn't just a background season. It was something to be worn, like a cozy sweater, wrapping the town in soft oranges and reds, the air laced with the promise of bonfires, cider, and something to look forward to.

Lily shifted from foot to foot. Grace sat on the porch swing, swaying back and forth, reviewing a list. Her brows furrowed with concentration, but a smile kept tugging at the corners of her mouth whenever she stole glances in Lily's direction.

"Cold?" Grace asked, glancing up while tucking a stray lock of hair behind her ear.

"Just a little," Lily replied, though in truth, the nip in the air wasn't her only reason for feeling restless. Her tummy fluttered with anticipation, and not just because of the logistics of picking up the wedding mums today. No, the flutter had more to do with a certain someone who would soon arrive with a truck bed spacious enough for the large flower order.

Andrew had offered to drive her to the farm, his silver pickup the perfect vehicle to transport the potted mums she'd ordered. Despite her best efforts, Lily couldn't deny that spending more time with him made her anxious and excited.

Grace set the list down. "Everything's all coming together now." She shot Lily a wide, excited grin, her joy uncontainable as the wedding day crept closer.

"It is," Lily said, nodding in agreement, though her mind was still elsewhere. "I checked off most of the big items on the list yesterday. We'll be ready. Just a few last-minute details. Plus, we can start setting up the church and the hall starting today. There are no more activities planned at the church, so Pastor Eli gave his blessing and told me to have at it. That gives us three full days for decorating, and I'm not used to that luxury."

Grace's eyes sparkled. "I seriously wouldn't be sane right now without you. I can't believe it's all happening so soon, though. Just a few more days..." Her voice held that unmistakable quality of someone whose dream was about to become a reality.

Lily smiled and glanced out over the mountains. Despite the wedding looming around the corner, Lily felt calm. Everything seemed to be running smoothly. Which was odd since weddings hardly ever went off without a hitch, at least in her experience.

"Are you okay?" Grace asked, her voice filled with casual concern, though her warm smile showed she already knew the answer.

Lily grinned, shrugging one shoulder as she cast her cousin a side-long glance. "Yeah, just... thinking about today. Nervous about picking up all the mums."

Truthfully, it wasn't just a bunch of flowers making her nerves prickle. Her mind had been spinning since the Halloween festival at the church last night.

"Oh, the mums, huh?" Grace teased, tilting her head. "And picking them up with Andrew. Funny how that works out."

Lily felt heat rise to her cheeks, and she glanced away. "I asked him to help because he has the truck," she said, a little too defensively, crossing her arms to feign nonchalance.

Grace snickered. "Sure, sure. The truck. That's all it is."

Lily turned back, narrowing her eyes for effect. "You're delusional. I'm in full wedding mode right now."

Grace raised her hands in surrender. "Hey, I'm not saying anything except…" She drew out the pause, glancing toward the horizon where the gravel road led around the bend. "Well, here comes your 'just helping me because he has a truck' now."

Sure enough, the rumble of Andrew's pickup truck echoed through the early morning stillness, growing louder as it approached. The truck crested over the hill and navigated the driveway with ease, pulling to a stop behind Lily's car. A faint cloud of gravel dust billowed behind it, catching in the sunlight, as Andrew stepped out of the cab.

Grace gave Lily one last amused look before rising from the porch and brushing the wrinkles from her jeans. "Alright, that's my cue. I better get going, too. I've got decorations to track down in the city."

Lily managed a smile, but was too busy smoothing the front of her own jacket to offer a snappy comeback.

"Andrew," Grace called, waving as he approached the porch steps with a confident, easy stride. "Thanks for driving Lily today. She's got her hands full, same as I do."

Andrew grinned, tipping an imaginary hat to Grace. "Happy to help. Besides, getting out in this weather's better than being cooped up in the office."

As Grace stepped off the porch, she headed towards her car, shaking her head and repeating the word "Office."

"Oh, come on, Andrew," Grace said gently. "I know Ben told you to take it easy at work this week so you could help us with all this wedding stuff. You're covered at the office. There's no need to worry about it."

Grace's sedan disappeared down the driveway, and Andrew turned his attention back to Lily. "Everything good to go with the mums?"

Lily nodded, trying to keep her words light and professional. "Yes. They promised to have them ready, so we should be able to just pull up, load them in the truck and go... no frills."

"No frills?" Andrew quirked an eyebrow. That playful gleam in his eyes again. "I'd expect nothing less from a wedding planner like you."

Lily rolled her eyes and swung her purse over her shoulder. "Hilarious."

Andrew opened the passenger door of the truck for her, bowing in an over-the-top, chivalrous gesture. "After you, m'lady."

She fought the smile that threatened to pop up. "Your trouble, you know that?"

He just winked as she climbed in. As soon as Lily was buckled up, Andrew shut the door with a soft click and rounded the front of the truck, climbing in beside her.

The engine rumbled back to life as they set off down the gravel driveway, the early morning light flickering through the trees lining the road.

Sitting beside him, Lily allowed herself to lean into the peacefulness—something she was still getting used to in this town.

Andrew glanced over with a casual smile. "Hope you don't mind a pit stop before we pick up the mums. I need to drop off groceries at Wilma Netherlands's. Her place is just down the road from the farm, and it won't take long."

Lily hesitated for a moment. "I wasn't expecting a social call this morning," she admitted. "But I guess a quick stop is no big deal. Who's Wilma Netherland?"

Andrew chuckled, like he was in on some inside joke. "A quick stop by Wilma's? Well, let's just say quick and Wilma rarely goes together." His grin widened. "She's a member of the congregation and her eyesight is getting bad. Wilma doesn't drive anymore, and so either I or someone else from the community delivers her groceries to her every week. She's a wonderful woman, really—sharp as a tack, too. Always has a story or two up her sleeve. You can't help but love her once you meet her."

The truck bounced as Andrew took a turn onto a dirt road. Lily glanced out the window, noting how the trees grew denser, the quiet stretching uninterrupted except by the occasional rustling of leaves in the breeze.

Wilma's house peeked through the trees like a relic from another time—a place that had seen its share of seasons and stories. The porch, with its weathered wooden boards and peeling white paint, spoke of years of steadfast resilience. Despite the wear, it held a certain charm. In front of the porch, an untamed flower garden spilled over the edges of its beds. Though it had clearly been a long time since anyone had tended to it, late-blooming marigolds and daisies still clung to life, their bursts of color defying the cool October air. It was a place full of character—a mix of beauty and stubbornness, where life pressed on.

Andrew cut the engine and hopped out, motioning for Lily to follow. The moment her feet hit the dirt, the scent of wood smoke reached her, mingling with the earthy aroma of autumn leaves.

Andrew frowned as they approached the house, his eyes landing on the front steps. One board sagged crookedly, as though it had borne the weight of years and just gave way under the strain.

"Well, what do we have here?"

The voice that greeted them was high and raspy, but full of life. Standing in the doorway, leaning on a wooden cane, was Wilma Netherland herself. Her silver hair was swept back in a tight bun, and her hazy blue eyes twinkled.

"Come on up and set those heavy groceries down," Wilma called out. Her gaze shifted to Lily, and a mischievous grin spread across her face. "Well now, who's this lovely young lady you've brought with you, Andrew?"

Lily offered a tentative smile, unsure of what to expect. "I'm Lily Reynolds. I'm... I'm helping Grace Anderson with her wedding."

Wilma's eyes narrowed, but not in a threatening way—more like she was sizing Lily up. "Reynolds, huh? So you're the city girl everyone's been talking about. The one tryin' to help folks say I do."

"Yep, that's me," Lily nodded, offering a smile, and feeling self-conscious under Wilma's penetrating gaze. The elderly woman had the kind of presence that demanded respect.

Wilma's grin widened, a glint of amusement dancing in her hazy eyes. "Well, welcome to Laurel Ridge, city girl," she cackled, leaning a bit more on her cane. "Bet our little town's a far cry from the bright lights and big noise of the city, huh?"

Lily laughed, already sensing she was in for a lively conversation. "It's different," she admitted, glancing around at the peaceful surroundings. "A lot quieter."

"Oh, quiet's good, dear," Wilma said, her blue eyes still twinkling. "Lets you hear yourself think... or have a proper conversation without all that ruckus. You helpin' that rascal deliver groceries today?"

Andrew chuckled, hefting the brown paper bags full of groceries as he climbed the creaky stairs. "Yes, Miss Wilma. She's helping me out a little today. I'm thinking we might have to do something about this porch step of yours while we're here."

Wilma waved him off. "Aw, that thing's been threatening to give out on me for a while now. It's all bark, no bite."

"I'm not too sure about that," Andrew replied, setting the bags down inside the front door. "I'll check your shed to see if you have any extra lumber lying around, get some tools from the truck, and see if we can't give it a little CPR before it bites you back."

Without waiting for a response, Andrew nodded to Lily and gave a playful wink. "Hold down the fort with Wilma, would ya? I'll be right back."

With that, he jogged off toward what Lily assumed was a shed behind the house. Wilma's eyes followed his retreat before she turned back to Lily, an amused look on her face.

"You make sure he knows what he's doing. I don't see so good anymore," Wilma quipped, her cane tapping against the porch. "Sometimes these young men think they can fix anything just because they've got a toolbox and some muscles."

"Well," Lily laughed and said, "he seems pretty handy. I think he can handle a little step."

Wilma chuckled again, this time softer, her gaze turning back to Lily as she gave her another once-over, though this time with more curiosity than judgment. "So, you and Pastor Andrew... you two an item yet, or are ya just playin' it safe?"

Lily felt a gentle warmth creep up her neck. "We're not rushing anything," Lily admitted, smiling. "Just... getting to know each other."

"Mm-hmm," Wilma hummed knowingly, settling onto the wicker chair that creaked under her weight. "That's how it starts. You take your time, let things soak in, and before you know it, you get wrapped up in something you weren't expecting. It's the slow burns that stick—the ones that don't rush in, but simmer."

Lily smiled at that. "I like the pace we're going," she said.

Wilma nodded. "Smart girl. Ain't no use galloping when walking will get you there just the same." She leaned in a little. "But don't be fooled into thinkin' it has to stay slow forever. Sometimes life gives you a nudge, and you just have to run with it or risk missin' something good."

Lily met Wilma's gaze, and something softened inside of her. She could tell that Wilma had lived through her share of heartaches and joys, the kind of woman who had seen the world change many times and had made peace with it.

"Is that your way of telling me to run headfirst without thinking things through?" Lily teased.

Wilma grinned, a hint of mischief lighting her expression. "Oh, honey, no one can tell you how to feel or when to leap. But don't let nothin' keep you from what's in front of you. That boy's as solid as they come—even if he doesn't always know all the answers just yet. He's one of the good ones. And good ones don't wait around forever."

Lily gave a small laugh. "Yeah, he does seem like he's one of the good ones."

"Honey, you sure got that right." Wilma tapped her cane on the porch, drawing Lily's attention back to her. "But don't you forget—you're one of the good ones, too." Wilma's voice softened as she added, "It's easy to forget our worth when life tries to knock us down.

You've been hurt—I know you have, it's written all over you—but that doesn't mean you don't deserve every bit of happiness that comes your way."

"Thank you, Wilma."

With a dismissive gesture, the elderly woman brushed off the expression of gratitude as if it were mere dust. "Nonsense," she scoffed. "I'm simply speakin' common sense. It's a rare thing these days, with too few people willin' to speak the truth."

Wilma's piercing gaze, full of curiosity, focused on the woman. "Are you one of those slick, fast-talking city folk?" she inquired.

Lily chuckled. "I guess. You sort of have to be—everyone's always rushing in the city."

"Mmm, and you ain't in such a hurry here anymore, are ya?" Wilma gave her a look that said she already knew the answer.

"No," Lily shook her head, a smile playing on the corners of her mouth. "Not so much."

"Well, good." Wilma said, leaning back in her chair. "There's something deeply satisfying about takin' things slow. Gives you time to think straight."

Andrew reappeared. "Step looks worse up close," he announced with a grin. "Wilma, you've been tempting fate by walking up and down this thing."

Wilma laughed. "I'll get by just fine, I reckon. But you're offerin', and I won't say no to a little fix-up." She winked at Lily and said. "He's enjoying this handyman moment, whether or not he admits it."

Andrew rolled his eyes, already getting to work, prying up the broken step with the end of his hammer. "Yeah, well, better than letting it get worse."

Lily watched him. As the morning wore on and Andrew focused on repairing the step, Wilma and Lily continued their conversation, the older woman sharing stories from her youth. Lily soaked it all in.

After Wilma finished regaling Lily with the story of how her deceased husband had proposed to her under an apple tree in the middle of a thunderstorm, she leaned back in her chair, a satisfied smile on her lips. "Lily Reynolds, I hope you stick around here long enough to realize you're carrying a lot of joy inside you, just waiting to bloom. Don't let anything—or anyone—hold that back."

Lily smiled, the words meaning more than she could express. "Thank you, Wilma."

Andrew wiped his hands on a rag, finishing the repair on Wilma's sagging front step. "That should hold for now," he said with a satisfied nod.

"Looks good, Pastor, and I thank you."

Andrew smiled, his brown eyes warm with their usual ease. "My pleasure, Wilma. Should keep you safe for a while longer."

Wilma gave him an approving nod, but didn't let the moment linger. Her hazy eyes flitted over to the door with a knowing smirk before she raised a hand and pointed inside. "Now, what're you standing around for? Get those groceries in the kitchen so I don't have to stoop down and try to pick them up."

Andrew chuckled, setting the toolbox down on the porch. "Right, right. Won't take but a minute."

"Good boy," Wilma said, waving him off as he hurried inside.

Lily watched the exchange, an amused smile tugging at her lips. She could feel Wilma's eyes shift toward her once more, settling on her like the matriarch of the small town bestowing approval or suspicion upon its newest arrival. Lily shifted, feeling the weight of the older woman's scrutiny, but Wilma didn't seem fazed.

"So," Wilma began, her voice filled with a knowing tone of interest, "young lady. What've you got planned for the rest of your day?"

"We're heading to a farm nearby to pick up an order of mums," she explained. "They're for Grace's wedding this weekend."

"Ah, the wedding," Wilma replied, nodding as if she'd just confirmed some long-held thought. "You're picking up mums—watch out for the bees while you're at it. Flowers this time of year can still bring out a few stragglers. Those bees have a sting to 'em that hurts a bit."

"I'll keep that in mind," Lily said with a soft laugh, charmed by Wilma's straightforwardness.

"Groceries are all put away, safe and sound," Andrew informed Wilma with a wink as he came back out onto the porch. "Milk's in the fridge and the bread's on your counter. I put your candy in the jar by the couch in the living room, and I filled the cat's food bowl while I was at it."

Wilma gave a gruff nod, satisfied. "Good man." Then, her gaze shifted back to Lily as Andrew stood beside her, crossing his arms casually. "You kids get going then. Wedding mums don't deliver themselves, and I'm sure you've got your hands full enough without an old lady talking your ear off."

Lily shook her head. "It's been a pleasure, Wilma. Truly."

Wilma's face softened, her firm demeanor giving way for just a second. "You take care of that boy now," she said, eyes flicking between Lily and Andrew with a smirk. "Might be worth your trouble to stick around these parts."

Lily caught Andrew's eyes as they walked toward the truck, and he grinned, rubbing the back of his neck while pretending not to notice Wilma's not-so-subtle comment. "We'll see you next week," Andrew called to Wilma, waving as he opened the truck door for Lily once again.

"Watch out for them bees, kids!" she called.

With a puff of dust, they headed off toward their destination.

"Are you okay?" Andrew asked, glancing over at Lily.

Lily met his gaze. "Yeah. Now she was a character. I wonder what she meant with the bee analogy?"

Chapter 24

Lily hopped down from Andrew's truck bed, handing him another potted mum, its golden-orange petals glowing in the afternoon light. "Careful with this one," she said with mock seriousness, wiping her hands on her jeans. "It's the centerpiece. The crown jewel of the display."

Andrew gave an exaggerated nod as he took the flower, holding it up like a delicate artifact. "Oh, of course. Wouldn't want to bruise the crown."

Amused, Lily rolled her eyes and turned back to reach for another mum. "You know, for a pastor, you're pretty good at taking orders."

"Hey, now... I've been training under Pastor Eli for years," Andrew said with a quick grin that sent a flash of humor across his face, the kind Lily was finding more and more addictive. "I know how to follow orders when I need to," he added, his teasing tone holding just the right amount of charm, "and you're the expert here, after all, Miss Wedding Mastermind. I'm just the humble helper at your service."

Lily let out a low laugh as she hopped down from the truck once more, surveying the already growing line of pots they'd placed on the recreation hall porch. "Wedding Mastermind? That's a new one." Crossing her arms, she looked at him with a mock-judgmental stare. "What other made-up titles have you got for me?"

"Well, let's see. There's 'Flower Queen,' 'Wedding Wonder,' or…" He pretended to stroke an imaginary beard. "'Perfection Pioneer' since you seem to enjoy making sure everything is, you know, just… so."

"I'm sensing a little shade," she said, narrowing her eyes, though the affectionate teasing in her voice was undeniable. "Maybe I do enjoy making things look perfect. Unlike you, who seems okay with the idea of just tossing these things haphazardly around like some kind of 'flower hurricane.'"

Andrew gasped, clutching his chest dramatically as he sat down another mum on the porch. "How dare you accuse a man of such gardening sacrilege? Let's not drag my good name through the mud." His grin widened as his eyes twinkled. "I'd call my design aesthetic… relaxed. But sure, call it a flower hurricane if you like."

Once all the flowers were unloaded, Lily stood back, hands on her hips, surveying their work with a critical—and yet pleased—eye.

"Well," she said, wiping a hand across her forehead and turning to Andrew, "not bad."

Andrew, equally satisfied, stuffed his hands in his jeans pockets, grinning down at her. "Not bad? Come on, give me a little more credit than that!"

"Fine," she conceded with a smile. "You didn't completely mess it up."

He tipped an imaginary hat. "I'll take that."

She chuckled, the sound light against the backdrop of the soft rustling leaves. "So, Mr. Whitman," she asked after a beat, "what's your grand plan for the rest of the afternoon?"

Andrew's calm smile faltered just slightly—not enough for anyone else to notice, but Lily had spent enough time around him to pick up on the shift. He looked down for a second before he gently reached for her hand, his touch warm in the cool afternoon breeze. "Actually, I was hoping we could talk for a bit. There's something I want to share with you. Something that's been on my mind."

He didn't wait for an answer, just lightly tugged her toward the entrance of the recreation hall, leading her behind the kitchen area. Her curiosity piqued, she followed him without question, letting the warmth of his hand anchor the slight unease now swirling in her stomach. Whatever he wanted to talk about, it sounded... significant.

Andrew let go of her hand and walked to the fridge, pulling out two cold bottles of water. He handed one to her, their fingers brushing for one fleeting second before he gestured toward one of the round tables in the corner of the hall's dining area.

Lily sat down, taking a slow sip to steady herself. Andrew followed, but instead of his usual smile, his face was slightly more serious, contemplative—still kind, but carrying a weight she wasn't used to seeing. He twisted the cap off his water, took a sip, and leaned forward, resting his forearms on the table. "There's something I've been thinking about a lot," he began, his voice careful. "And I haven't really spoken with you about this."

Lily nodded, her heart thudding gently in her chest. She gave him an encouraging smile. "Okay. I'm listening."

Andrew's eyes flicked to the side, out the window, for a moment, as though finding the right words required searching the horizon. Then he took a breath, meeting her gaze again. "Pastor Eli called me earlier. It was while we were at Wilma's place—I was in the shed grabbing wood to fix the step when my phone rang."

Lily's brows knitted slightly. There was something in his tone—a tension he was trying to mask.

"He asked me to swing by the church office after we finished up here to talk."

"About what?" she asked, already sensing that this wasn't a standard meeting.

"I don't know for sure," Andrew admitted, setting his water bottle aside, "but I've got a feeling... he's retiring. Sooner than I expected."

Lily sat back, processing the words. Pastor Eli had been the senior pastor at Laurel Ridge Community Church for several years, she gathered from their earlier discussions. If Eli was retiring, it would be quite the transition for the congregation.

"And if he retires..." she began, her thoughts slowly unraveling the possibility.

Andrew nodded, picking up her line of thought. "I'd be stepping up. Full-time. Senior pastor."

The weight of what that meant settled, making the space between them feel both close and heavy. Lily saw the flicker of uncertainty in Andrew's eyes, the way he's always so sure of himself—so grounded—now seemed to give way to something else. "How are you feeling about that?" she asked quietly.

Andrew let out a breath he hadn't realized he was holding. "Honestly? My feelings are mixed. I've been working toward this since I felt called to ministry, and a part of me is ready—excited even—but another part of me..." He trailed off, rubbing the back of his neck. "Another part of me is terrified."

Lily tilted her head, locking eyes with him. "Terrified of..."

He let out a soft chuckle, shaking his head slightly, as though admitting this was some inside joke at his expense. "Terrified of letting everyone down. Of not being enough. I've been the assistant pastor for a while now—being the one people turn to for advice, handling youth programs, helping here and there—that's manageable. But leading an entire congregation? That's a lot. I mean... it's not just about the sermons on Sundays. It's the counseling, the leadership, the decisions, and the responsibility that comes with it all."

He paused, his voice quieter now. "What if I'm not cut out for it?"

The vulnerability in his voice caught Lily by surprise. For all the times she'd seen Andrew as this strong, steady presence, it hadn't occurred to her he wasn't impervious to doubt. But here he was, opening up, showing her the cracks in his armor.

She reached out, her fingers gently brushing his forearm. "Andrew," she said softly, "from everything I've seen, and from everything Grace has told me, you're already a leader. You've been guiding this community for some time now. And you? You're great at it."

Andrew's gaze was fixed, listening intently.

"The way you are with people," she continued, "how thoughtful you are, how you made me—this complete outsider—feel welcome and at home. That's more than just some checklist of responsibilities. You... you care about people. And that's what matters most."

Andrew's lips curved into a subtle, appreciative smile, though the tension in his eyes hadn't quite gone away. "Thank you, Lily. I... I guess I needed to hear that."

Lily tilted her head, her hand still lightly resting on his arm. "So why does it feel like there's more?"

Andrew sighed, letting his free hand rub at his temple, as though working through a knot in his mind. "It's not just about the responsibility. It's about what this position might require. The church here...

when you're the senior pastor, it's your life. I don't think Eli's taken a real vacation in years... and I'm sure some of that could be age... but, well, it's just a fact that his life revolves around the church. And that's not even the hardest part. The hardest part is... well, what if this ministry becomes my whole life?"

Lily blinked, surprised at the admission. "Isn't your ministry already a central part of who you are?"

"It is," he admitted, eyes softening. "But what if stepping into this role leaves no room for anything else? I mean, what if I spend so much time pastoring that there just isn't space for... a personal life? For someone like you?"

The unexpected vulnerability there took her breath for a moment. Andrew was leaning on her in a way she hadn't expected. There was weight in his words: this wasn't just about his position at the church. It was about them.

He cleared his throat and continued, eyes searching her face. "I'm afraid that if I take this on, if I pour myself into the role the way it needs to be done, there won't be anything left of me for anything outside of it. And I would rather not make promises if I'm not sure I can keep them."

Lily's throat tightened. She hadn't really considered the complexities of being in a relationship with someone in pastoral ministry—not just the demands on his time, but the emotional and spiritual workload that came with it. She could see how someone could feel torn between the two.

But this—what they had, the bond they'd been carefully building—this was something she wasn't ready to let go of.

"Andrew," she began, "I know you're in a really tough position. But I don't think God is asking you to choose between your calling and a life outside of that. I mean, isn't it possible that love—personal love—is also part of His plan for you? It seems to me that leading a church is still about leading with people, building relationships that only enrich your ministry."

Andrew swallowed hard, listening intently as she spoke.

She leaned in a little closer, her voice steady now. "Whatever He's calling you to in the church, that should only make you more capable of sharing your heart with someone. And I'd like to think... this thing between us? It's part of that bigger picture. A part that doesn't need to be sacrificed for the sake of ministry."

There was a soft pause as she gathered her thoughts, feeling her heart open even as the vulnerability of it clenched in her chest.

"I'm willing to be part of that," she said, her voice softer but unwavering. "If you want me to be."

Andrew's eyes softened, his hand reaching across the table to take hers in a warm, steady grip. "You really mean that?" His voice was quiet now, filled with the weight of the moment.

"I do."

The tension between them melted into something more profound, the shift from mild flirtation and quiet affection unfolding into something much deeper. This wasn't about just liking each other—it was about believing in each other.

Andrew offered her a warm but teasing smile as he leaned back slightly. "And here I thought I'd just have a quick chat with you and be on my way, but who knew I'd end up with free therapy?"

Lily half-laughed, the tension easing as warmth flowed back into the moment. "I mean, I didn't even charge for this session. You're lucky."

"Oh, I know." His brown eyes sparkled with gratitude.

Andrew rose from his seat and took Lily's hand, his grip gentle but secure as he helped her to her feet. "Come on," he said, his voice warm with sincerity, "How about I take you back to the cabin so you can grab your car? Then I'll head back here for my meeting."

"That sounds like a plan to me," Lily replied with a bright smile. "How about I swing by Martha's and pick us up a late lunch? Then, I'll meet you back here at the reception hall after your meeting with Pastor Eli?"

"That sounds like a perfect plan to me, Lily," Andrew replied with a smile.

<h1 style="text-align:center">Chapter 25</h1>

Inside the church office, the smell of old leather-bound books and stacks of sermons and reference materials greeted Andrew as he stepped through the weathered oak door.

The space had changed little in over three decades. A hand-carved desk sat in the middle, cluttered but not disorganized. Every item had a place, from the basket of unopened mail to the well-worn Bible that looked as though it had been opened a thousand times. Along the far wall, shelves were laden with books ranging from theology to gardening, and a few picture frames displayed black-and-white photos of the pastor and his wife, Clair, at various church events, their faces always full of joy and contentment.

Pastor Eli, with his graying hair combed neatly to one side, sat behind his mahogany desk. His kind, weathered face was lit by the glow of a small desk lamp. His wife, Clair, sat in a sturdy armchair, her hands folded in her lap, her warm eyes crinkling in greeting as Andrew entered the room. There was a deep comfort in their presence—a staple for anyone in Laurel Ridge who sought advice, solace, or just a calm conversation after Sunday service. This office has seen its share of laughter, tears, and quiet prayer over the years.

Andrew swallowed, feeling the weight of the moment the second he crossed the threshold. He wasn't just here for a casual afternoon chat. He had known it the moment Pastor Eli had asked him to stop by.

Eli's smile was the same as it always was—warm, knowing, and genuine. He motioned Andrew toward the chair across the desk, his words slow but filled with intent. "Come on in, son. Have a seat."

Andrew obliged and settled into the worn leather chair. The soft squeak of the chair's cushions groaned as he adjusted his position and forced a chuckle. "Smells like someone's been burning a candle again," Andrew joked, trying to ease his jittering nerves.

Clair stifled a laugh, shaking her head. "You'd be surprised how sentimental the smell of pumpkin spice makes people in the congregation around this time of year. We had Ladies Brunch earlier, and we all love a good fall scented candle as we study scripture," she said, her fingers playing with her silk scarf.

Eli's eyes twinkled in the soft light. "Not sure how much longer I can take the smell of it myself, but people seem to love it. Gotta keep the masses happy, right?" His gentle laugh was engulfed in the deep familiarity between them all.

Andrew chuckled, though he felt the tension in his shoulders. He took a deep breath, his gaze sweeping the room to meet Pastor Eli's kind but penetrating eyes. There was something coming—Andrew could feel it. Eli and Clair's peaceful smiles didn't quite hide the undercurrent of purpose pulsing between them. The old pastor had something on his mind.

"So, how's Grace's wedding shaping up?" Eli asked, leaning back in his chair, his hands resting on his stomach as he gazed at Andrew with his usual curiosity.

Andrew sat back, letting out a breath that he hadn't realized he was holding. "It's going well. Lily's doing an amazing job organizing everything." He hesitated, then added, "I don't think Grace has stopped smiling for over five minutes."

Clair's smile deepened at that. "Oh, Grace deserves every ounce of happiness. Ben, too."

Eli's eyes softened as they always did at any mention of Grace, an almost fatherly affection filling his weathered features. For a moment, the room was silent, save for the soft tick of the antique clock on the wall behind him.

But Andrew wasn't fooled by the small talk—it felt like a preamble to something more significant, something weightier. Pastor Eli had never been one for unnecessary embellishment for the business of the church or matters of the heart. There was always something deliberate in the way he approached tough conversations, and Andrew could feel it gathering now like a quiet storm on the horizon.

"How are you doing, son?" Eli asked after a pause, his voice dropping the playful tone it had held earlier.

Andrew's throat tightened. He didn't respond right away. He wasn't sure how to answer the question. How was he doing? Life had been moving at a speed he hadn't prepared for—Betty Sue's fundraiser last week, Wilma's front porch repairs this morning, and, of course, Grace's never-ending wedding checklist, not to mention his feelings for Lily.

But those things weren't pressing on his mind now—they weren't what he'd come here for.

"You know..." Eli started, leaning forward slightly, his elbows resting on the heavy wooden desk. "I've been thinking a lot lately about passing the torch."

There it was. Andrew blinked, the words hitting like a loud ripple of thunder.

Pastor Eli's smile softened and then stretched into something melancholy, though not sad. "Clair and I... well, I think it's time for us to step down officially."

Andrew felt the breath leave his lungs in a slow and drawn-out exhalation. Not that he hadn't seen this moment coming—Eli had been preparing him for years, allowing Andrew more and more space and responsibility within the ministry. But now that the words were being spoken aloud, actualizing it in real time, it hit Andrew like a weight.

"Step down... as in, retire?" Andrew said. The room felt smaller, almost shrinking in around him as the gravity of the words settled.

Eli nodded once, his face serene, albeit with the tiniest ghost of hesitation in his eyes. "Clair and I have been talking, praying... and we both agree its time. The old bones don't move quite as swiftly as they used to," he added with a gentle laugh, patting his arm as though speaking to his creaky joints.

Clair chuckled, though her gaze held a quiet intensity. "We've given our lives to this church, Andrew. This community, this flock..." She paused, her voice dipping. "But we're ready to visit our grandkids without worrying about getting back in time for Sunday service. We're ready for what comes next."

Andrew could tell that both Eli and Clair were at peace with their decision.

"It's happening... now?" Andrew asked, his voice tight.

Eli nodded once again. "I've talked it over with the deacons, and they're ready to support you in taking the lead. In fact,"—he paused, leaning forward—"we'd like you to officially take over this coming Sunday."

Andrew sat in silence for a few seconds, struggling to gather his racing thoughts. "I don't know what to say..."

"There is nothing to say, Andrew, you are ready," Eli said, his voice calm and steady. "I know it's sudden, but I also know you've been ready for this for a long time, even if you don't feel it yet."

Andrew swallowed hard, his mind bouncing between all the pieces that had yet to fall into place—the logistical concerns of running the church, the enormous shoes he felt he'd need to fill, and the underlying tension of how this new responsibility might affect his personal life—specifically with Lily.

Eli seemed to sense some of that internal turmoil because he leaned back and smiled—this one full of nostalgia and wisdom. "Let me tell you something about ministry, Andrew." He paused, his brown eyes twinkling beneath his gray, white brows. "There's never a moment where you'll feel you've got everything figured out. Something comes up, and you feel like everything is being held together with a bird's string and a little prayer. But somehow..." He let out a low chuckle, his eyes glancing toward the ceiling as if finding some hidden comfort up there. "God always pulls you through."

Andrew shook his head, half-laughing, his heart thrumming with a strange combination of nervousness and peace. "I just don't want to let anyone down."

"And you I know you won't," Eli replied, that fatherly tone kicking in again.

Clair reached over and covered Eli's hand with her own, giving it a gentle squeeze. "You're more ready than you know, Andrew."

Andrew's mind was spinning with thoughts of upcoming sermons, counseling appointments, weddings—his breath catching in his throat.

Weddings.

Lily.

As though reading his mind, Eli crossed his arms over his chest and raised an eyebrow. "You look like you've got more weighing on your heart than just this transition."

Of course, Eli would pick up on it. The older pastor had a way of always knowing when something else was bothering someone. Andrew certainly couldn't hide it.

He rubbed the back of his neck and let out a long breath. "It's... Lily."

Eli and Clair exchanged a quick glance, and Eli leaned forward, that kind but heavy gaze zeroing in on Andrew. "Go on."

Andrew hesitated, his gaze dropping to his hands resting on his lap. "I've... been spending a lot of time with her and my feelings for her are growing. That much is clear to me." He swallowed, another long breath escaping. "But with this new responsibility..." He paused, trying to find the right words. "I don't know how to balance being the leader of this church and trying to build a relationship with her."

Clair offered him a warm, understanding smile. "It's not easy, Andrew. Balancing love and ministry isn't something you figure out all at once, and there is definitely no instruction manual."

Eli nodded. "The weight of responsibility can feel overwhelming, son. But you don't have to carry all of it alone."

Andrew's heart thudded as he took in their words. Eli leaned forward, his voice steady and clear.

"You're worried Lily might not fit into the life you've chosen—or vice versa."

Andrew nodded, the fear settling in his chest once again. "I've had... things end badly because of this calling before."

Eli eyed him, nodding along. "You mean Sarah."

Andrew felt a jolt at hearing her name spoken aloud, followed by a deep sense of vulnerability. It had been years since Sarah had walked out of his life. Years since the engagement had been called off, and he was left alone. But the scars from that period lingered within him like a deep bruise that hadn't fully healed.

"I know Lily isn't Sarah," Andrew clarified. "But part of me can't help worrying that this path I'm on won't leave enough room for a relationship. Or that... she'll want a different kind of life."

Eli and Clair exchanged another glance before Eli spoke, his voice caring and full of fatherly concern. "Andrew, love and ministry don't have to exist separately. When they're founded on mutual respect and communication, they can coexist beautifully—even enhance one another." He smiled. "Clair has been my partner in every sense of the word. Having someone you love and trust walking beside you in ministry—it's not a weakness. It's a strength."

Clair nodded as she spoke. "I stood by Eli through every church transition, every tough season, every sleepless night. But he stood by me, too. We didn't have all the answers, and sometimes we didn't know how to balance everything perfectly." Her eyes softened as she met Andrew's gaze. "But what we did know... was that God had called us together. And because of that, He gave us strength in each other, not separate from the ministry—but through it."

The words settled within Andrew's heart, soaking in like rain over dry earth. He looked away for a moment, processing the truth of their advice. Could he really build a relationship with Lily? Could these two things exist not just in tandem but intertwined, supporting, and building up one another?

"If God is calling you to pursue this relationship with Lily, then He will make room for it within your ministry. It's not about one taking from the other—it's about both of them contributing to your purpose," Eli said.

Andrew nodded, his mind racing. The pieces were starting to make sense. He had been so focused on the fear of what might happen—that Sarah's story would repeat itself—that he hadn't allowed himself to trust in God's provision. To trust that maybe, just maybe, Lily wasn't here to take something away from him but to be a part of something bigger.

Andrew let out a long, slow breath, his shoulders loosening. "I've been afraid of things going wrong again in a relationship, and I know I shouldn't wonder and worry about those things, but I do."

"And that's normal, son," Eli said. "Fear is a very human response, but it doesn't have to dictate your choices. Faith—faith is trusting God even when the answers aren't clear. Even when there's risk."

Andrew turned his gaze back to Eli and Clair, his voice stronger now. "You're right," he admitted.

Eli's smile was wide and full of warmth. "God's plans for our lives rarely follow the script we expect, Andrew. But that's how we learn to rely on Him, isn't it?"

Clair nodded in agreement. "You've always trusted God with your ministry. Can you trust Him with your heart, too?"

After a beat of silence, he nodded. "I think it's about time I do just that."

The warmth in both Eli's and Clair's eyes was unmistakable.

"Andrew, there's something else Clair and I would like to share with you," Pastor Eli began, his voice gentle but heavy with the weight of untold emotions. He paused for a moment, his hands folded thoughtfully on the desk, as though searching for the right words. "We haven't brought up Sarah's name much over the years, not because we wanted to avoid her, but because we know how deeply she hurt you. Clair and I... we've been careful to tread lightly, out of respect for you."

Eli glanced over at Andrew, his eyes filled with both concern and understanding. Compassion laced his tone as he continued, "But it's time we talked about her."

Andrew sensed there was more. "I appreciate that, but you don't have to worry. She's your granddaughter, after all. I respect we need to talk about her occasionally."

He glanced between Clair and Eli. Something deeper was coming—he could feel it in the silence. Clair's eyes misted over, and she lowered her head, the weight of unspoken words heavy. Andrew's concern deepened, his gaze shifting back to Eli, waiting for what would come next.

"Yes... yes, she's our granddaughter, and we love her—always will. But Andrew, Sarah's been on a troublesome path these last few years. Since she left here... well, let's just say the devil's been busy steering her in the wrong direction." Pastor Eli paused, his gaze dropping to the papers scattered on his desk, as though the weight of the conversation pulled his eyes downward. After a moment, he continued, his voice quieter but firm.

"Andrew, Sarah's been in a rehab facility in Ohio for some time now. She's being discharged this afternoon. Her parents are on their way to bring her home—back here to Laurel Ridge." Pastor Eli's words hung in the air, thick with unspoken worries.

Andrew felt momentarily breathless, his thoughts scattering as he struggled to find the right words. For a few moments, he fumbled, uncertain how to respond. "Sarah's... coming back?" Andrew finally managed.

Eli nodded slowly, concern etched into the deep lines of his face. "Yes. She's been through a lot, Andrew. More than we realize, I'm sure.

Her parents have kept much of it quiet—trying to help her without drawing attention. But... it got to the point where they couldn't hide it anymore."

Clair shifted in her chair, her face softening with a mixture of sadness and hope. "We don't know all the details, Andrew, and we don't need to," she said gently. "What we do know is that she's asking for forgiveness. Not just from God, but from her family and from you. She's been carrying a lot of guilt."

Andrew felt as if the floor had tilted beneath him. For years, he'd carried the wound Sarah left behind, not knowing if she ever thought about him or regretted her decision. He had prayed for her well-being, but deep down, he'd tried to lock that chapter away for good. And now, suddenly, she was coming back—into the same town, into his life, or at least trying to intersect with it.

"Forgiveness..." Andrew said.

Eli exchanged a look with Clair before taking a deep breath. "She wants to make amends. That's what her folks said to me. But I don't know exactly what that means. All I know is that when she gets here, there's a chance... she might seek you out."

Andrew's head was spinning—old memories mingling with fresh confusion. This was the woman who had once shattered his heart, the same person who said she couldn't live this life with him, who couldn't be tethered to the church, to the ministry, to his future. Now, after all these years, she was coming back, looking for some kind of redemption or closure.

But then there was Lily. Steady, beautiful Lily, who was slowly breaking down all the walls Andrew had built from Sarah's betrayal. The idea of reopening old wounds with Sarah, especially when things between him and Lily were beginning to blossom—it felt complicated. Torn.

"I don't know what to say..." Andrew ran a hand through his hair, his thoughts spiraling.

Eli leaned forward, his voice gentle, fatherly. "Andrew, we're telling you this not to pressure you or confuse you, but to prepare your heart. Sarah's return... it doesn't have to undo everything you've built in her absence—whether in your ministry or your personal life. God's given you strength to grow beyond that pain."

Clair's warm hand reached out, resting on Andrew's arm. "What you've gone through with Sarah... it's part of your story. But it's not the whole story. It sounds like you and Lily are building something special—and you don't have to let Sarah's return derail that."

Andrew swallowed hard, feeling overwhelmed but grateful for their words. He had always admired how Eli and Clair seemed to see beyond the chaos and confusion of life, always finding the thread of faith that connected everything. But this... this was heavy.

"If she reaches out..." Andrew's voice wavered for a moment.

Eli smiled softly, nodding in understanding. "You don't need all the answers right away. But when the time comes, you'll be able to handle it because you've grown into who God has called you to be. You know your path now better than ever before."

"But don't fear putting boundaries in place," Clair added firmly. "If Sarah comes seeking closure for herself, her healing... that's her journey. You've got to protect yours."

Andrew sat quietly, absorbing their advice. He knew they were right. Sarah's return didn't mean undoing all the progress he had made—especially with Lily. He would need to be wise and careful, trusting God's guidance in this situation as well.

"I guess... I'll have to take it one step at a time." Andrew's voice came out steadier than he felt.

Pastor Eli nodded. "That's all any of us can do. One step at a time. And don't forget, Andrew, you're not in this alone. You have people who care about you, and most importantly, you have God walking right beside you."

Andrew exhaled slowly, feeling a slight release of the tension that had built up in his chest. "Thank you, Pastor Eli. Clair. I'll... I'll pray on it."

Eli smiled, his eyes full of wisdom and reassurance. "That's all you need to do for now. Just pray and trust that God's leading you exactly where you need to be."

Clair offered one final glance of encouragement as she rose from her seat, gently patting Andrew's shoulder. "You're going to be okay, Andrew. Better than you might realize."

Andrew stood, exchanging a few final words with them before saying his goodbyes.

As he exited the office, his thoughts lingered on Lily. She deserved to know the truth about Sarah's return. And she needed to understand that no matter what, she wasn't a second choice. Not now. Not ever.

He would have that conversation soon, he decided. The rest—the part with Sarah—he would leave in God's capable hands.

Chapter 26

Andrew's chest felt tight, constricted with emotions he hadn't invited. He had prayed for Sarah's well-being for years—hoping that she had found peace, that she had moved on the way he had tried to. Yet, hearing about her struggles with addiction, her time in rehab... that her parents were bringing her back to Laurel Ridge... it was like the wind had been knocked out of him.

He wasn't angry. Not at all. In truth, all he felt was sorrow for her. But what had cut deeper, more than the news about Sarah, was the heavy weight of uncertainty that now pressed on him regarding Lily. How was he supposed to tell her this? Would she understand? Would she—could she—be able to accept that this haunting shadow from his past might touch their future?

Andrew's heart twisted uncomfortably in his chest. And there was more—so much more. The responsibility of the church was now fully on his shoulders. Pastor Eli's words replayed in his mind. *I've talked to the deacons. They agree—it's time.*

Time for him to step up. The senior pastor. The one who would follow in Eli's steps and guide this congregation the way he had done for three decades. Andrew had always known this moment would come, that the torch would one day be passed to him, and now the time was here.

He drew in a deep breath and walked down the hallway. The door to the central part of the church creaked softly as he pushed it open, the light from the stained-glass windows spilling pale shades of burgundy, blues, and greens across the worn wooden pews. The cool stillness of the church enveloped him, its silent peace a stark contrast to the storm of emotions brewing inside him.

He stopped at the threshold, his eyes settling on the wooden cross that hung above the altar, illuminated only by the sunlight breaking through the windows. There it was—the symbol of sacrifice and grace, the cornerstone of his faith. Andrew came here often, to think, to pray, to unburden himself before God. Today, however, felt different. He didn't just feel the weight of his role as a pastor; he felt the crushing responsibility of everything—Sarah's reappearance, Lily, the church, his calling. It was all resting on his shoulders.

Help me, Lord.

The thought passed through his mind instinctively, without formality. It was simple and desperate. His feet carried him slowly down the main aisle, the echo of his footsteps bouncing off the wood walls. Each step felt heavy, difficult, as though the weight of everything he had been carrying was pressing down upon him even more with every stride toward the altar.

At the foot of the altar, he dropped to his knees, bowing his head over his folded hands.

He knelt there for a long moment, letting the stillness settle over him. His mind was a whirlwind of thoughts, but as he attempted to sift through them, he felt the one constant thread keeping his heart tethered to hope: God is with me. Even here, in the midst of uncertainty and overwhelming responsibility, God had brought him this far.

"Father," he whispered hoarsely, barely above a breath. "I don't know what I'm supposed to do. How do I bear all of this?"

The faint rustle of distant wind outside filled the silence in the church, but Andrew paid it no mind. His voice, steadying now, came again, more fervent. "I ask for Your guidance, Lord. I am prepared for this—the church, the ministry. But Sarah... her return... I didn't expect this. I don't even know how to tell Lily."

He shifted his weight slightly, his knees aching against the cold wood floor.

"God, please," he continued, his voice catching slightly. "I don't know what plans You have for Sarah—or for me. But... but I know You're good. I know You're sovereign over this, and I know You've carried me this far... I trust You'll carry me further."

He took a breath, his voice quieting as his thoughts turned toward Sarah. The memories rushed in—days spent dreaming of their future, her warmth by his side at church events, and the gut-wrenching pain when she told him she couldn't live this life. "Lord," he prayed, "I lift her up to You. Whatever path You have set before her, I pray she follows it. Please heal her broken heart. Forgive her for the things she has done and the decisions she's made. Walk with her now in the way she desperately needs. And help me... help me show her grace if she seeks it from me."

The tightness in his chest eased slightly as the prayer flowed out.

"And Lord, I pray for Eli and Clair," Andrew went on, his voice more controlled now. "I can't imagine this has been easy for them since Sarah left... and hearing that she's struggling so much. Please, God, grant them the wisdom to guide her now. Give them peace and understanding. They've been such... such good examples to me. They've loved me through this ministry, been like family. Keep them strong, Lord, in their faith and love for You."

Andrew's forehead dipped lower, pressing into his clasped hands. The overwhelming wave of emotion stirred deep within him.

"And for me, God," he whispered, barely audible now, "if I am to lead this church, then I will need You more than ever. I am ready. I know I am. Give me the strength to walk through this journey—in faith, not fear."

The vulnerable confession lingered in the still air, the weight of the prayer resting like a heavy, palpable release.

"And Lily..."

"Guide her, Lord. Let her heart be open to understanding, not to fear. I don't know how to tell her this, Father. I don't want her to think this changes anything between us because I..."

He stopped, his voice catching in his throat. Because he knew what he meant to say, what had been lingering beneath the surface. His feelings for Lily had deepened in ways that startled even him—but was this too much to put on her? So early in their connection? Would she walk away because of it?

"But I trust You, Lord. I trust You with her, too. Help me to be honest with her, to be clear... and help her receive it with mercy. If Sarah's return affects her, Lord, let there be grace between them."

Andrew's hands clenched tighter for a moment at the thought of it—Sarah and Lily in the same space, possibly sitting in this church at the same time.

The sound of quiet footsteps down the church's center aisle broke the delicate silence. Andrew didn't look up immediately but finished his last whispered words, "In Jesus' name, Amen."

Through the thin haze of uncertainty that remained, Andrew looked up and turned on one knee and saw that he wasn't alone. Eli and Clair stood a few steps behind him, their eyes soft as they took in the scene. Andrew felt the rush of residual emotion from his prayer, emanating from his chest like an open wound. He wasn't embarrassed, seeing them there—there was no shame in showing weakness, especially not here, not in the house of God, where they all came for help.

Eli moved first, taking the last few steps, and knelt slowly beside Andrew at the altar, despite the slight groan of his old bones. Clair followed, taking to the other side, completing what felt like a sacred circle of quiet fellowship.

No one spoke, not at first.

Eli placed a hand on Andrew's shoulder, his voice low and filled with calm authority. "Father," Eli began. "We come before You today, humbly seeking Your mercy and guidance."

Clair followed, her own voice soft but filled with years of seasoned faith. "We ask for Your forgiveness," she continued, "for our granddaughter... for Sarah. Grant her the strength to overcome her struggles and find joy in You again. Let her lean on You, Father, as we have all leaned on You in our times of need."

Andrew closed his eyes as the waves of their prayers washed over him—a communal surrender to God that brought a rich, almost tangible warmth into the room. There was power in each of their voices—all of them calling out to the same God, asking for different things: forgiveness, wisdom, and strength.

Eli's hand tightened slightly on Andrew's shoulder. "And God..." he continued, his voice growing more emotional, a slight tremble running through it. "Grant Andrew the wisdom and courage he'll need to lead this flock. I've watched him flourish, Lord. Watched him grow in

Your grace and service. He carries the weight of this new responsibility, but I know You've called him for a time such as this."

There was a brief pause, and then Clair's voice picked up once more, her words soft and fervent. "Let him lead with kindness, Lord, with wisdom and patience. And," she hesitated before pressing on, "Please, God... Bless his heart. Let the people in his life, especially Lily, see the man You've grown in him. Give her the strength to understand Sarah's presence—should it come?"

"Amen," they said in unison, their voices filled with reverence.

For a moment, no one spoke, the echo of the prayer still hanging thick in the air. Eli was the first to rise, albeit with some difficulty. Andrew followed, offering his hand to Clair to help her up as well. As they stood, stretching stiff joints and clearing their throats, something soft and unspoken hung between them. They had shared this moment, and it was more than prayer; it was a passing of strength.

"You good, son?" Eli asked.

Andrew looked away for a moment, the faintest smile playing on his lips. "No," he admitted, though there was a warmth in his voice. "But I will be."

Eli chuckled at that, clapping him on the back with a firm, paternal touch. "That's the spirit."

Clair came forward, her eyes gleaming with that familiar motherly concern, the kind she so often had for everyone in the congregation. She stepped closer, wrapping him in a soft, firm hug. "You'll be fine, Andrew," she said quietly. "Stronger people have waded through worse and come out on the other side."

Andrew chuckled. "Eli says that, too."

"That's because it's true."

As they parted, Andrew felt a sense of finality, but it wasn't heavy—it was light, filled with the hope that, somehow, everything would work out. Maybe Sarah's return wasn't about reopening wounds—maybe it was about closure. Maybe God was preparing him for something even greater.

As Eli and Clair walked toward the doors at the back of the church, Eli looked back at him one more time, that twinkle in his eye speaking volumes. "Remember, Andrew," he said, "you're not walking this road alone."

Andrew smiled. "I know."

Chapter 27

Lily balanced a large brown paper bag from Martha's Diner in her arms, the delicious aroma of buttery biscuits and fried chicken wafting up around her and curling into the air. The bite of the crisp autumn wind had left her cheeks a gentle pink, and a wide smile graced her lips as she pulled the door closed behind her.

"Sorry, it took me so long," she called out, her tone tinged with amusement. The echo of her voice seemed to dissolve into silence as she moved further into the recreation hall. "I ended up playing with Daisy for a bit—let her run some energy off in Grace's backyard before going over to Martha's."

As she walked further into the reception hall, she absentmindedly rambled on about Daisy's antics, the dog's playful energy providing her with some extra amusement for the day. There was a lightness in her steps, in her voice. She hadn't felt this comfortable—this happy—in a long time.

But as she neared the center of the room, where Andrew sat at one of the round, white-clothed tables, her words faltered, the gleam in her eyes dimming slightly. Something was off.

"Andrew?" she asked, more quietly, her smile fading as she came to a stop, still several feet away.

He didn't answer. Didn't even look up. His dark, wavy hair fell slightly over his brow as he gazed down at the open Bible in front of him, hands resting on either side of the weathered pages. His posture, usually so open and inviting, now looked strangely tight, as though he were folded in on himself, weighed down by something unseen.

Something was wrong.

Lily took a hesitant step forward, her earlier cheer quickly fading, replaced by a quiet unease. "I—I brought lunch," she tried again, her tone soft but slightly tentative, testing the waters. But still, nothing. Andrew's eyes remained fixed on the Bible. The room, once comfortably silent, shifted into something that felt oppressive.

When she reached the table, she set the brown bag down with a soft thud, her heart beginning to thump uncomfortably in her chest.

What's going on?

Lily's gaze flicked nervously between the Bible on the table and Andrew's face. The furrow in his brow, the quiet strain in his shoulders. The joyful determination she'd walked in with only moments ago now slowly unwound inside her.

"Hey," she whispered, the humor gone from her voice, replaced with cautious concern. "Andrew?"

Andrew looked up, his brown eyes meeting hers. And there, in the intensity of his gaze, reality hit her. His hand shifted slightly from the edge of the Bible, reaching toward her in a slow, tentative gesture. When his fingers met hers, it wasn't the reassuring touch she was getting to know. It was hesitant, almost apologetic.

"Can you... sit for a minute?" Andrew's voice was low and quiet now, the warmth in his tone seeping through the rough edges of whatever burden he was carrying.

Lily's heart sank into her stomach, but she nodded quietly, her legs moving before she even fully processed the request. She lowered herself into the seat next to him, her brow knitting together in a quiet frown, waiting for him to catch up to what was brewing inside him.

She knew Andrew wasn't someone to avoid tough conversations, but this... this felt different. His silence was unnerving in a way that made her stomach twist.

"I just came from Pastor Eli's office," he began finally, his voice rough around the edges, as if each word had to climb its way out.

Lily tilted her head, anxiety quickening in her chest. "Okay? Did... did something happen? You said it was just a meeting." She tried to keep her tone even, unsure of how else to respond.

Andrew took a slow, deliberate breath, his eyes flicking briefly toward her before returning to the Bible under his hands. "Sarah," he said, almost too quietly.

Without thinking, she muttered the name aloud, the taste of it foreign on her tongue. "Sarah?" Lily frowned, the question catching in her throat.

Andrew's grip on her hand tightened, giving her just enough balance to stay grounded. "Yeah. She's coming back to Laurel Ridge," he said. "Eli told me earlier today."

Lily blinked, processing the information—not just the name itself, but all the things that name carried. Sarah—the ex-fiancée. The woman who had left Andrew broken and questioning everything, the woman whose history was entwined with his in ways Lily could hardly imagine. And now she was coming back?

Her thoughts jumbled messily. She didn't know whether to feel angry, confused, or simply... sad. None of it made sense yet.

"She's... coming back?" Lily repeated slowly, her voice tightening just a little. "Why?"

Andrew's gaze remained in front of him, but Lily could feel his grip tighten once more.

"She's been through a... lot," Andrew began, his voice quieting further, but the words carefully chosen. "Addiction. It's kept her away from her family for some time. She's been in a rehab facility, and now... now she needs to come home. Her parents are bringing her back today."

The next breath Lily took felt sharp, catching awkwardly in her lungs. "Addiction?" Her thoughts immediately shifted, rearranging themselves like pieces of a puzzle coming into view, but they were blurry. She didn't know which emotion her heart wanted to cling to—anger at the intrusion this might cause in their budding relationship, or sympathy for someone clearly broken.

Her voice remained soft, her instincts focusing on Andrew rather than the woman she didn't know. "Oh, Andrew... I—" She faltered, unsure of what to say.

Andrew turned his head, his eyes clouded with so many emotions she could barely decipher them—from guilt to sadness, to what looked like fear. "I wanted you to know right away," he said, his voice rough, almost as if he was pushing the words out with difficulty. "I don't want this to be something I keep from you. And I... I don't want you to think that Sarah being back somehow changes things. Because it doesn't."

There was urgency in his words—something desperate that tugged at Lily's heart. Did he worry that somehow Sarah's return would undo everything they'd been beginning to build?

Lily tightened her grip on his hand, forcing herself to take a slow breath before responding. "Andrew," she began, her voice steady but her heart still thudding away in her chest. "Thank you for telling me... for being open and honest about this." She hesitated for just a second before continuing. "But I'm going to need a moment to process this. I... I just wasn't expecting it."

He nodded, his own body deflating just the smallest bit, as if bracing for her to take a step back—or worse, to walk away altogether. His eyes searched hers, full of both hope and uncertainty.

Lily took another beat, then scooted her chair closer to his, sitting up a little straighter and forcing herself to meet his gaze fully. "I know... I can tell this has hit you hard. I don't know Sarah or much about what she's been through, but I can't imagine how tough it must be for someone to lose their way like that."

Andrew blinked.

She pushed on, her tone thoughtful now, as if peeling away at something larger in her mind. "I mean, really... it's tragic. To go from someone who probably had dreams and goals to falling so far into something as destructive as addiction." Her eyebrows furrowed, sympathy seeping into her voice. "Drug addiction? It must be... it must be awful."

Andrew's hand flexed just slightly under hers, his lips parting as though he were about to speak, but no words came right away. When they did, his voice was quiet again. "I can only imagine that it is," he confessed, his gaze growing distant. "And the hardest part is knowing... I have to face her. Not just the past, but who she became—everything she went through since leaving. I won't lie, Lily... It's shaken me... I don't know how else to explain it. I'm just stunned."

Lily's heart squeezed, not just for Andrew's past, but for the pain this still caused him. Not because of lingering feelings for Sarah, but because of the gravity of a relationship broken and scarred by choices, neither of them had fully understood back then.

Carefully, as though testing the waters within herself, Lily shifted her hand to rest fully over his, offering what quiet strength she could. "I can't imagine what you're feeling right now. I'd probably be a complete mess if I were in your shoes."

Andrew attempted a weak smile, though the strain was still clear in his expression. "Aren't you? Even a little bit of a mess?" His tone was quiet, but there was the faintest trace of humor there.

And there it was—the opening, the room for her to allow herself to be honest, just as he had been.

Lily let out a soft, breathy laugh, shaking her head slightly. "Yeah, okay," she confessed. "I am a little bit of a mess. I mean, let's be real. I wouldn't be... human, probably, if a situation like this didn't bring out a little bit of jealousy and... protectiveness." She paused, looking down at their joined hands. "But that's just it, Andrew. I tend to be overly protective when I'm in a relationship... maybe insecure. And honestly? The idea of your ex-fiancée coming back into town? That does stir up some feelings for me."

Her admission was raw, real. It wasn't easy to say, but she didn't want to keep any secrets between them.

"But," Lily continued, her voice stronger now, "I will try." She squeezed his hand again. "I'm here, Andrew. And I understand that Sarah being back isn't something you have control over. This has nothing to do with who we are together... or who we can become." Her throat tightened when she added, "I know God makes paths in ways we don't always understand, and... and sometimes, people need a chance for redemption. Sometimes, they need forgiveness. And maybe Sarah needs that from you."

"Lily..." he whispered, his voice breaking slightly. "Thank you. I didn't know how you'd take this... and I was afraid it might make you feel—" He broke off, shaking his head gently. "I needed to tell you."

"I'm glad you did," she responded, nodding in return. "We both have pasts that are hard to shake. But that doesn't mean the future is out of reach."

"So," she added with a small, gentle smile, "where do we go from here?"

Andrew let out a soft chuckle, visibly lighter than before. "I guess... one step at a time."

Lily laughed softly, nodding in agreement. "Yeah... one step at a time."

"Lily, I need to tell you something else," Andrew began, his voice wavering slightly, "Sarah... she's Pastor Eli and Clair's granddaughter."

Lily's breath caught in her throat, her eyes widening slightly. She blinked once, twice, trying to process this new information. She opened her mouth to speak, but nothing came out at first.

"Sarah... she's their granddaughter?" She finally said the words, as if saying them aloud would help cement the truth. The revelation sent a ripple of surprise through her.

Andrew nodded, his gaze never leaving hers, his expression layered with apology and uncertainty. "Yeah," he said, his voice low. "I didn't mention it before now... not on purpose. I just never really thought about it."

Lily sighed, setting her hands on her lap and fitting them together so tightly that her knuckles went white. Her mind raced, trying to untangle the connections forming. It wasn't just that Sarah was coming back into Andrew's life unexpectedly—it was that she was also tied so intimately into Laurel Ridge's spiritual foundation. To Pastor Eli and

Clair. To Andrew's mentorship. To a family that had helped to shape and nurture him.

"And now she's..." Lily exhaled a long, slow breath as she placed her hands back on the table as if to brace herself. "She's going to be part of your life here... because she's part of the church and community family."

Andrew's thumb gently rubbed against her hand, his movements slow and modest, as though he could sense the turmoil she was wading through. "Lily, I need you to know... whatever happens with Sarah and her family, it doesn't change what's here. Between us." He hesitated, swallowing hard. "I'm telling you all of this now because I don't want there to be any more surprises. I want... us to have transparency."

Lily's heart pinched. It was new territory for them both, this level of vulnerability. Her natural defenses wanted to rise and shield her from the shock of the news.

"I appreciate that, Andrew," she said, her voice soft but steady. "I won't lie, though. This was... unexpected. I'm still wrapping my head around it."

Taking a steadying breath, Lily leaned forward a little, her eyes searching his. "But I'm still here. I'm not running away because of this. You... you're worth more than that to me."

Andrew's lips trembled, gratitude flooding his dark eyes. He squeezed her fingers lightly, then released her hand, lifting one arm to cup her face gently instead. When his fingers brushed her cheek, the warmth of the touch settled deep into her skin, grounding her.

"I don't deserve you, you know," he murmured, his voice barely above a whisper.

Lily offered a small, fleeting smile, the tension finally easing from her shoulders. "We'll see about that," she teased softly, tilting her head slightly toward his hand, finding comfort in the connection.

Lily turned fully toward him, her eyes bright yet thoughtful as she took in his strong, steady presence. "So... since our lunch is getting cold, how about we pivot back to something a little less heavy for a little while? We both need some time to process everything."

Andrew blinked, then let out a soft chuckle, his body relaxing with the shift in mood. "Okay? And what might that be?"

She smirked mischievously, leaning back in her chair again. "Well, Martha seems to think that fried green tomatoes were in order for our meal today. She included a double order with our meal. She sent along a message as well."

Andrew feigned a groan, but a playful glint lit up his eyes. "And what exactly would that message be?"

Lily narrowed her eyes playfully as she reached into the brown paper bag, pulling out the container of fried green tomatoes, setting it down on the table between them. "It seems our dear Martha has deemed these the crowning jewel of our meal. She said, and I quote..." Lily cleared her throat dramatically, "Tell Andrew to remember the old wives' tale about these fried green tomatoes and he better not let city girl miss out, or he'll have to answer to me.'"

Andrew let out a deep, rich laugh. "She would say that."

Lily raised her eyebrow. "Care to explain?"

"Fried green tomatoes, when shared by two, will keep their hearts forever true," Andrew said with a grin.

"Shall we put that old wives' tale to the test?" Lily asked with a sly smile.

Chapter 28

Andrew, Lily, Rachel, and Martha were busily stringing twinkle lights around the recreation hall, their cheerful chatter filling the space as they worked to create the perfect ambiance for Grace's wedding shower. Nearby, other congregation and community members helped Leslie with the floral centerpieces or hustled in the kitchen, preparing a few extra side dishes to complement the catered food.

"Careful with this one, Andrew." Rachel called from atop her ladder, holding her side of the string of lights as she nudged it into place. "Don't want it sagging in the middle."

Andrew, already stretching his height to its limit, raised an eyebrow. "Rachel, you realize I don't have eight-foot arms, right?" He stretched and affixed it to a beam as best he could. "There, shall we say it's symmetrical enough to pass inspection?"

Martha, standing beneath his ladder, chuckled. "You'd better hope so. Otherwise, Lily's going to have a thing or two to say about it."

From a few feet away, Lily stood on her own ladder, attaching the last section of lights near the front of the room. "You're all doing a great job," she said, glancing over her shoulder with a grin. "And yes, don't think I haven't been watching."

Martha let out a hearty laugh. "I knew it!"

Andrew shook his head, amused. "Guess I'll be held accountable for improper lighting configurations forever, thanks to your high standards, Lily."

Rachel smirked. "Better get used to it."

Lily climbed down from the ladder she was on, her eyes sweeping the room until they landed on the end of the last string of fairy lights. She walked over, picked up the strand, and couldn't help but grin.

"All right!" she announced with a flourish, plugging the lights in. "Let there be light!"

But the moment the plug met the outlet, things unraveled.

Popping sounds echoed through the room, followed by a heavy silence. And then—darkness. The entire room, once filled with light, was plunged into shadows.

Lily's stomach twisted.

Rachel blinked. "Wait... did we just... blow a fuse?"

"Oh, shoot..." Lily murmured.

"It's okay. It's probably just a breaker issue. I'll go check." Andrew said.

Lily stood frozen as Andrew left the hall to inspect the electricity. This wasn't happening—not on the day of Grace's wedding shower.

Rachel continued fiddling with some of the cords. "Maybe we should've gone with candles instead. You know, less chance of a power blowout."

Lily let out a nervous laugh, though her stomach wobbled with panic. "I don't understand what could have gone wrong. Every strand was working earlier. I tested them all."

Martha walked over. "Sweetie, you triple-checked everything like always. Sometimes, things just go haywire. No need to blame yourself." She said just as the overhead lights came back on, but not the twinkle lights.

Andrew returned, his brow furrowed but still calm. He walked over to check the nearest strand of twinkle lights. "The breaker's back on, but... I think most of these lights are fried."

Lily felt her heart sink to her toes. She wanted to scream or cry—something—anything to release the rising frustration. How could this happen now, after so much work?

Seeing the devastation on her face, Andrew stepped closer, lowering his voice. "Hey. Don't panic yet. We've still got time to figure this out."

"But—how?" Lily asked. "These are the only lights I brought with me. I don't have any backup supplies. Everything else is back in my office in Manhattan, and the nearest mega store that might sell lights is an hour and a half away."

Andrew placed his hands on her shoulders, his eyes full of quiet calmness. "We'll improvise."

"We could just use more candles." Rachel said.

Martha chimed in, already on her phone. "If you give me thirty minutes, I can have every tea light, lantern, and candle I own right here in this hall."

Rachel gave her a bemused grin. "Girl, nothing ever goes one hundred percent as planned. And hey, maybe this'll turn out even better than some fancy light show. You want ambiance, right? There's nothing more romantic than candlelight."

With a flurry of activity, everyone sprang into action. Martha called in reinforcements from her diner, asking an employee to gather all the lanterns and candles they could find. Rachel hurried to the church basement to search through the storage area for any candles, lighting, or lanterns. Meanwhile, Andrew and Lily began taking down the burned-out lights.

It wasn't exactly what she'd envisioned, Lily thought as she glanced over her shoulder to see Leslie arranging what candles they did have on hand into the centerpieces she'd so carefully crafted. She sighed, a hint of worry in her voice. "I just hope Grace isn't too disappointed when she arrives and sees the twinkle lights she had her heart set on... missing."

Andrew glanced over with a reassuring smile. "You know what I think?"

"What?" she asked, glancing up.

"I think she won't even give it a second thought. Look at how the room's transformed already. And besides," he added, nodding toward the candles, "Rachel's right—the candlelight is going to look beautiful."

Chapter 29

The bridal shower buzzed with the hum of conversation, punctuated by the occasional burst of laughter. The space had been transformed into what could only be described as a cozy, autumnal wonderland. From the twinkling lights that were still usable to the centerpieces filled with flickering candles, there was no mistaking that this celebration reflected the warmth and care that everyone in the community had for Grace. So many people had come earlier in the day to help decorate for this wedding shower. It amazed Lily to think about it.

Everything was running smoothly. The caterers had arrived on time, the pumpkin-spiced cupcakes from Taste of Heaven Bakery were displayed artfully on the dessert table, and the gift display looked like it belonged in a bridal magazine. She had to admit, even with the twinkle light debacle, everything had turned out beautifully.

The scent of cinnamon and hot apple cider lingered in the air, mingling with the fragrance from the fresh flowers in the centerpieces Leslie had arranged. From Lily's vantage point, she could see the gathered crowd—friends, family, and community members all enjoying themselves.

"Everything alright, boss?" Rachel's teasing voice pulled Lily from her thoughts as she leaned against the side of the dessert table, stretching her arm and snagging a cupcake. "You look like you're itching to do something."

Lily couldn't help but laugh. "Old habits die hard, I guess. But no, so far, everything seems to be running perfectly. I'm just enjoying watching everyone have a good time."

Rachel winked as she peeled back the cupcake wrapper. "It is pretty amazing to see the number of people who came. Goes to show you how much love there is for Grace in our town."

Lily glanced around once more, seeing church members making sure the other guests were comfortable and the youth group helping as well—everyone working in sync like cogs in a well-oiled machine, but with a kind of easy-going laid-back energy.

Rachel took a bite of her cupcake. "Mmm. These are fantastic! Shirley outdid herself this time."

Lily leaned against the table by Rachel and smiled. "I'll take your word for it."

Rachel's eyes widened in mock astonishment. "Wait, you haven't tried them? How have you been running around this place and not snuck at least one cupcake? It's practically sinful."

Lily rolled her eyes but grinned. "I taste tested them a few days ago at the bakery. I'm not in the mood for sweets right now. In fact, I usually don't even eat during a shower or wedding that I'm overseeing. I just kind of forget about it."

"You certainly have control," Rachel replied, waving her hand. "If there's food involved—I'm all in."

***

"You look like you've got something on your mind," Ben said as he stepped up alongside Andrew.

Andrew half-smiled. "Can't hide anything from you, can I?"

Ben chuckled, clapping him on the back. "Well, not with that look on your face. Let me guess..." Ben's eyes flickered across the room toward where Lily was chatting with Grace. "Lily?"

"No, Sarah," Andrew said.

"Wait, what did I miss?" Ben asked, his eyebrows raised in curiosity.

Andrew took a deep breath.

"Sarah is back."

Ben blinked, taken aback. "Sarah? As in, the Sarah?"

Andrew nodded. "Yep. She's been in a rehab facility for some time, and her parents... well, they picked her up and brought her home yesterday."

Ben let out a low whistle, leaning back as if digesting the news. "Wow, man... And I'm guessing this was all unexpected news to you?"

"It was definitely unexpected. I feel a deep sadness for the way her life has unfolded. I spoke with Lily about all of this yesterday. She seemed to be handling it well at the time, but today, I can't help but feel it might be weighing on her more than she's letting on. Honestly, it's the kind of thing that would be difficult for anyone to process," Andrew said.

"Wow, I thought she seemed a little off today. I just assumed it was stress from trying to make sure this wedding shower turned out okay," Ben said.

"No, I'm pretty sure that I added to Lily's stress levels when I told her the news. But she seemed to take it okay. Oh, and on a lighter note,

Pastor Eli's officially retiring. I'll be leading the services starting this Sunday," Andrew said with a smile.

"Congratulations," Ben said, grinning. "I'm genuinely happy for you."

Andrew returned the smile, but shifted his gaze back to Lily, who was now laughing at something Grace had said. His heart tightened. There was a lot left unspoken between him and Lily, things he wasn't sure even he fully understood yet. He'd seen the concern in her eyes yesterday, the way she had processed Sarah's return with grace—but he couldn't shake the lingering doubt that it was weighing on her more heavily than she let on.

Ben's voice pulled him back. "Listen, if there's one thing I've learned from all my years watching you chase after God's plan, it's that He doesn't leave us hanging. You're in a tough spot right now, trying to balance everything, but trust me, things will fall into place."

Andrew exhaled, nodding. "I know you're right. It's just... I don't want my past to interfere with my future, especially with Lily. She means more to me than I can even explain, and I don't want to do anything that might push her away."

Ben's eyes softened, his tone turning more serious. "That woman over there? She's tough. And I don't think she's going to break that easily. Just let her in. Be honest with her, like you've been doing. You'd be surprised how much God works in the uncertainties."

Andrew looked toward Lily again, watching as she bent down to fix one of the floral arrangements on a table.

"I know... You're right," Andrew said, straightening his shoulders.

Ben grinned again, giving Andrew one more reassuring slap on the back. "There ya go. Now, get over there and enjoy this wedding shower with Lily."

***

As the last of the guests trickled out of the recreation hall, Lily stood alone at one of the tables, picking up a forgotten plate, when she felt a warm presence beside her.

"I believe your work here is done," Andrew's said, a teasing lilt in his tone.

Lily groaned dramatically as she placed the plate on a tray she was balancing. "Almost. Just a few more things to clean up, and then I'm done for the day."

Andrew chuckled, taking the tray from her hands and setting it aside. "How about you let me handle the rest? It's the least I can do, considering all you've done for Grace and Ben."

Lily raised an eyebrow, crossing her arms playfully. "And what's your ulterior motive for this generosity, Pastor Whitman?"

Andrew smirked, leaning just an inch closer. "Maybe I have none. Maybe I just want you to relax for once."

Lily felt her heart do that familiar flip-flop. "Let's finish picking up the last few things together, then head back to the cabin. Grace and Ben are already on their way. We can all unwind and relax together before the big day tomorrow."

"Sounds like a plan," Andrew replied with a smile.

Lily refocused on gathering the remaining cups and plates scattered around the table, her movements brisk but thoughtful as she tidied up.

"Lily."

She paused, glancing over her shoulder. "Yeah?"

Andrew's brown eyes held hers, his expression soft with something deeper—more deliberate—than before. "Thank you."

"For what?" Lily asked, squinting at him, unsure what he was getting at.

"For... everything," he said. His eyes never left hers. "For yesterday. For today. For..." He paused, rubbing the back of his neck nervously. "For letting me in."

Lily turned and walked toward Andrew, a gentle yet determined smile on her lips. Her hand found its way to his forearm, a light, reassuring touch. When she spoke, her voice was soft but steady, full of quiet conviction.

"Andrew, you never have to thank me for any of that."

Lily reached out with both hands, gently cupping the sides of Andrew's face, her fingers brushing against the hint of stubble on his jaw. His breath hitched as their gazes locked—words unsaid swirling in the space between them, thick with emotion. The world seemed to still for a moment, shrinking down to just the two of them.

Slowly, deliberately, Lily leaned in closer, her eyes fluttering shut as her lips met his in a tender, unhurried kiss. It was soft at first, and hesitant—like testing the waters of something both fragile and profound.

Andrew responded just as gently, his hands finding their way to her waist, holding her with the same tenderness she'd come to know in him. The kiss deepened subtly, not with urgency, but with the quiet intensity of two hearts finally speaking the same language.

When they pulled away, their foreheads touched, and for a moment, they simply breathed together—hearts syncing in the quiet aftermath of something that already felt like more than just a kiss. With her eyes still closed, Lily whispered, "I... I wasn't sure I'd ever feel this way again."

"Neither did I. But maybe... maybe this was always part of the plan."

Lily smiled, a small, quiet smile, not weighed down by the fears that had once kept her heart guarded. She knew now that trusting in love—like trusting in faith—was risky. But standing here, in his arms, she no longer wanted to protect herself from the very thing she'd been craving all along.

Love, however fragile it might be, was worth the risk.

Chapter 30

The stillness of the church wrapped itself around Lily like a comforting quilt, the silence both familiar and foreign. It wasn't the silence of loneliness or tension, but the kind that felt welcoming, full of untapped possibilities—like the pause before a melody. All morning, community members had come and gone, everyone helping to create a perfect wedding day for Grace. She could hear the flurry of movement from various rooms behind the sanctuary. Grace and her maid of honor, Rachel, getting their makeup and hair done. She could hear the gentle teasing between Ben and Andrew as they tried to wrestle into their tuxes and keep each other calm in another room.

Lily walked down the center aisle of the church, her fingers trailing along the smooth oak edges of the pews, her gaze bouncing between the cross hanging in the sanctuary and the wooden arch decorated for the wedding in front of it. The stained-glass windows threw a patchwork of jewel-toned light across the floors.

She sighed, a mix of contentment and something a little bit deeper settling into her chest. She had made it here, all the way to this moment—not just in location, but within herself. Months ago, she would have shaken her head in disbelief at the Lily who now stood in this church contemplating love and faith. Her heart had been so locked up in bitterness and doubt, her mind festering with distrust—not just in men, but in God. It had taken every last ounce of courage to show up in Laurel Ridge, and now, more than ever, she was glad she did.

Her eyes traced the front of the room, where Grace and Ben would soon exchange their vows. The wooden arch was decorated with a few white roses, miniature sunflowers in various autumn colors, and a mass of wildflowers draped in green vines. Colorful fall mums were scattered around. It was perfection. Normally, she would be darting around the church and recreation hall, checking, and rechecking every detail. She'd have her clipboard, her cellphone, her emergency kit full of hairpins and double-sided tape. But today?

Everything was already perfect.

The hustle, the stress, the endless worry she used to drown herself in—it was all muted now. What was the point in scrambling for control every second of the day? Lily couldn't pinpoint when exactly it had changed for her, maybe somewhere between Grace's calming reassurances or Rachel's off-handed jokes about planning a wedding being a bit like herding glamorous cats, but at some point, she'd begun to let the reigns go a little. And it felt good. Scary. But good.

She smiled to herself. This work, helping others celebrate love, had carried her through part of her life. But there was so much about love she hadn't embraced... not yet. Not fully.

As she moved closer to the altar, a deep warmth stirred in her chest. Something unspoken, but palpable.

Faith.

She noticed the wooden cross again, hanging perfectly centered at the back of the sanctuary, a quiet testament to its place at the heart of the church. So too, she thought, should God always remain at the center—steady, aligned, unshakable. As she closed her eyes, she drew in a deep breath, letting the stillness of the sacred space wash over her, grounding her in its quiet certainty.

For so many months, she had struggled with faith—buried it under the weight of broken promises. But now...

Now it felt like something living inside her again.

And Andrew.

Her heart fluttered at the thought of him. He'd supported her, listened to her, challenged her to think beyond what was broken. He'd done all of that just by being his gentle, grounded self. Andrew hadn't pushed. He hadn't pried. And, like sunlight breaking through a fog, she had let her guard down. Let him in.

Lily paused at the pew closest to the altar. Her palms were cool against the wood. She just stood, watching the way the light danced on the cross.

With a slow exhale, she slipped into the pew; the wood creaking ever-so-slightly beneath her. Her hands folded in her lap, and her gaze traveled once more to the front of the sanctuary.

Closing her eyes, Lily let out a soft, shaky breath, her hands clasped tightly together in her lap. For a moment, she simply sat there, gathering herself.

Hesitant at first, her voice broke the silence in a whisper. "God," she began, "I don't really know where to start."

"I've been... angry," she admitted, her tone laced with vulnerability. "Angry at the world, at love, and, if I'm honest, at You. I questioned whether You even had a plan for me anymore."

The words came a little easier now, as if releasing them was loosening the knot in her chest.

"But now... now I realize I've been so focused on control—on trying to keep myself from getting hurt—that I forgot. I forgot that You're in control, not me."

"Thank You," she whispered, her voice more certain now. "For bringing me here to Laurel Ridge. For Grace... for her not giving up on me, even when I was giving up on myself. Thank You for the way she's always been there—always believed that I could heal, that I could trust in love and in You again."

A soft smile tugged at her lips as her thoughts wandered to the people she had come to care about in this tight-knit community—Martha, Rachel, Ben, Andrew, and so many others. They had welcomed her, flaws and all. They had seen the guarded woman she was and loved her, anyway.

"Thank You for these people," she continued, her smile growing a little wider. "For the wonderful people of Laurel Ridge. They didn't have to, but they took me in, showed me kindness, and made me feel like... like I belonged. I'm grateful for every one of them."

"And Andrew..." she whispered, her voice soft as her heart swelled with emotions deeper than she'd realized. "Thank You for him. For his patience... his kindness... for the way he believed in me, even when I couldn't believe in myself."

"God, I don't know what's ahead of me," she admitted, her voice trembling just slightly. "I don't know what Your plan looks like—how it will unfold. But I'm asking for Your guidance. Help me to trust that You are paving the way—help me to trust You with my heart and to trust You with Andrew."

The admission felt raw, real. A tear slipped down her cheek, but this time, she didn't rush to brush it away.

"I'm scared," she whispered, her vulnerability echoing in the quiet. "I'm scared of getting hurt again. Of opening myself up and... possibly losing it all. But I'm ready, God. I'm ready to trust You again. And I'm ready to fall in love again, with You guiding me… With Andrew beside me. I'm ready to trust that You've got me."

Her voice quivered, the fear and hope blending together in a mix of emotions.

"Thank You for bringing me this far. For not giving up on me. For showing me that love—that Your love—is bigger than my fears. I don't know what tomorrow holds, but I'm trusting You to guide me through it. I'm trusting You to lead me in my relationship with Andrew, and my relationship with You."

"Thank You," she whispered once more, "for all You've done."

In the sanctuary's quiet, the words lingered. And something shifted in Lily's heart—the sense that maybe, just maybe, she was right where she was supposed to be.

"Amen," a familiar voice said, soft but sure.

Lily's eyes flew open, her heart jolting in her chest at the sound.

Spinning around, her blue eyes locked onto Andrew, who stood at the back of the church. His posture was casual—arms folded across his chest, one shoulder leaning against the door frame—but his expression… the warmth, the tenderness in his gaze made her stomach flip.

"Andrew?" she said, her voice shaky. "How long have you—"

He smiled. "Long enough."

Her cheeks flushed.

Scrambling to recover her composure, she stood readjusting the hem of her dress, her nerves on high alert.

"I didn't mean to—I mean, you weren't supposed to—" she stammered, wishing her cheeks weren't turning several shades darker.

"I wasn't supposed to hear my name?" He stepped closer, his playful tone cutting through her embarrassment, but there was sincerity in his eyes.

"No, not like that!" She let out a frustrated breath. "It was just—you weren't supposed to hear any of it, Andrew."

Deep down, she knew whatever Andrew had heard, he wouldn't judge her. If anything, he looked... proud—happy even.

He stepped forward. That quiet warmth she loved settled into his eyes. If there was one thing that steadied her, it was his ability to be so calm, so patient.

"I'm sorry," he said. "But I'm not sorry." His smile widened. "I'm really glad I heard what I did."

Lily swallowed hard. "It wasn't exactly meant to be a public performance."

"I know." His gaze softened. "But thank you for sharing it with Him. And... trusting Him enough to say what you did."

Her breath caught in her throat at the intensity of his words. The air between them shifted—heavier but warmer, filled with something thick and beautiful.

Lily's eyes stung as a quiet laugh escaped her. She didn't know what to say—what do you say to the man who had somehow seen through every layer of you, even when you hadn't wanted him to?

Her voice found her. "Well... I was completely honest," she murmured, meeting his eyes now.

His smile deepened. "Yes, you were." He stepped a little closer, closing the gap almost completely now. "And that's what I love about you."

Lily inhaled sharply, reeling as his words landed between them, heavy with meaning. "That's what you what?"

Andrew chuckled. "Lily... you don't get it, do you?"

"Get what?" she asked, her voice softer than before.

"How incredible you are." His gaze held hers like an unspoken promise—steady, unshakable. "I never wanted to push you, Lily. If you weren't ready—you weren't ready. And I wasn't about to risk it by rushing into something you couldn't trust with all your heart. But now…"

Her heart thudded, her pulse quickening as she watched him.

"But now," Andrew said, his voice dropping an octave, "I think you're ready."

The weight of his words made her knees feel wobbly.

"I'm trying," she whispered, her voice barely a breath.

"I know," Andrew replied, his hand brushing against hers for just a moment—a jolt of warmth. "And that's all I could ask for."

"I'm still… scared."

"I think that's what faith is." He smiled. "The not knowing."

She opened her eyes again, meeting the steadiness of his gaze.

"And I have faith in you, Lily. In us."

Chapter 31

Lily stood in the churchyard. She scanned the area, noting the final touches for the wedding. The tall, arched stained-glass windows of the church were aglow with sunlight, casting colorful, dancing patterns onto the whitewashed exterior. Mums—burnt orange and deep red—bordered the walkway, and the soft flicker of candles caught her eye through the church doors. Everything had come together.

And remarkably, so had she.

At any other wedding in the past, this would be the moment where her hands trembled from the weight of perfectionism. But not today. Perhaps it was the sight of the church—so much a part of this community, so much a part of Andrew—or maybe it was Grace and Ben, their joy infecting every detail no matter how small.

But as she stood there, she knew the truth.

It was more than just the wedding. It was everything. She was the one who had changed.

Since being in Laurel Ridge, she'd uncovered a part of herself she thought had been lost—her trust, not only in others, but in God. The pieces of her life she'd so carefully controlled and clung to for months...years even... she was learning to loosen her grip. To let go. And today, that peace radiated from within her.

"Lily!" Grace's voice rang out, pulling Lily back from her reverie.

She turned to see her cousin hurrying across the churchyard, her white dress sweeping slightly against the dewy earth. There was a brightness to Grace's face—a glow that came with happiness, with certainty in what lay ahead.

Lily hadn't stopped marveling at it all morning.

"Oh no," Lily said with playful horror, her hand to her chest, "are you supposed to be seeing me right now? Don't you know it's bad luck for the bride to see the wedding planner before the ceremony?"

Grace laughed, her cheeks flushed from both excitement and the chill in the air. "Do we have time for me to peek inside the church?"

"Of course." Lily smiled and gestured toward the steps.

Grace moved past her in a swirl of white lace, satin and radiant energy, only pausing once inside the church.

Mums in deep autumn hues were tucked at the end of each pew, echoing the colors of the season. Lanterns with candles in each sat next to the mums down the aisle. Long ivory and burgundy ribbons trailed gracefully down the aisle, woven with sprigs of greenery chosen to complement the understated decor. At the front of the sanctuary stood the wooden arch, meticulously decorated and positioned so that, from the pews, the cross on the wall appeared perfectly centered within the arch's frame.

"Oh, Lily..." Grace's voice broke, as she stood at the back while tugging her shawl snug around her shoulders. "It's even more beautiful than I imagined. Everything feels..."

"Perfect?" Lily finished for her, stepping up beside her cousin with a knowing smile.

"Yes." Grace nodded, her eyes a little misty. "Exactly that."

Lily wrapped her arm around Grace and pressed a gentle kiss to her temple. "You deserve nothing less."

Before the moment could grow too sentimental, Andrew appeared from one of the side doors. His hair was slightly tousled, and his face was flushed from the cool air, but the grin that broke out when he saw them was like a warm ember in the chill morning.

"Well, if it isn't the two most beautiful women in town," Andrew said, his deep voice playful, but the warmth in his eyes unmistakable.

Grace gave him a mock frown. "Andrew Whitman, you're supposed to be with Ben."

Andrew laughed. "I was with Ben, but he said he needed a moment to himself, so I took that as my cue to leave him to it." He winked at Lily before adding, "Don't worry, I made sure he wasn't thinking about skipping town."

Lily shook her head while she laughed.

Grace groaned a little, but her eyes twinkled with affection. "That man... there will never be a dull moment with him."

"That's how it should be." Andrew added, his gaze shifting to Lily.

Andrew cleared his throat with a bit more gravity now. "You two should probably get moving. Ben's going to be standing at the altar soon."

"Oh, right!" Grace flustered for a moment before pulling Lily into a hug. "Thank you. For all of this. For making it perfect. Now... it's time to go get married!"

***

The church brimmed with anticipation. The murmur of guests filled every corner. Music echoed softly through the air as Pastor Eli stepped forward, flanked by Andrew and Ben, who looked nearly too excited to stand still.

Lily had to stifle a laugh at her cousin's fiancé—his usual calm, outdoorsy nature, temporarily replaced with the barely controlled energy of a giddy groom. Ben's fingers drummed against his leg, his cheeks flushed with excitement, and the smile that spread across his face when Grace appeared at the back of the church lit the entire room.

The music swelled as Grace walked down the aisle with her dad by her side. Her eyes, luminous with affection, were locked onto Ben's. And the light coming through the stained-glass windows seemed to dance—ripples of color moving across her dress, painting her like some fleeting, ethereal vision. The congregation could only watch, still and enraptured by the moment.

As Grace reached the altar, Ben's hands reached out immediately, squeezing hers with a fervor that made her smile in adoration.

Lily felt a prick of emotion in her eyes. She wasn't one for overt sentimentality—she rarely had the luxury for it in this line of work—but watching Grace and Ben standing together, exchanging those loving, nervous, joy-filled glances... it hit her in that tender place. Weddings were about more than plans and perfection. They were about this. The love.

Pastor Eli cleared his throat, drawing everyone's attention once more.

"We gather here today," Pastor Eli began, his voice rich and authoritative, yet soft as age and wisdom gave it a certain gravity, "to join together two souls, Ben and Grace, in the covenant of marriage. This is a sacred union, one that reflects the same love that Christ has shown

His church. It's a love that endures, serves, sacrifices, and stays steadfast through all seasons. And today... we celebrate what God has made."

Lily glanced over at Andrew, his deep brown eyes focused on the ceremony with a look of reverence. His gaze flicked toward her, catching her watching him, and a subtle smile curved his lips.

The ceremony moved forward with quiet elegance, from Pastor Eli's heartfelt words to the shared laughter of Ben as he fumbled his vows, pledging that he'd never leave Grace behind on any trail hike—not even the steep ones.

Laughter rippled through the church, and Grace's eyes sparkled with affection.

"I love you, Ben Turner," Grace said, her voice brimming with emotion. "And I'll walk every trail with you, no matter how steep, as long as we're walking it together."

Pastor Eli announced them "husband and wife," Lily felt the entire congregation release a collective sigh of delight. The couple swept down the aisle, bubbling laughter rising from Grace as Ben scooped her into his arms, twirling her once before setting her back on her feet under the shower of autumn leaves the children gleefully tossed over them.

Lily stood there, watching with a smile. Beside her, Martha Kincaid reached down and squeezed Lily's hand, offering a knowing, grandmotherly smile.

Lily chuckled, shaking her head. "What?"

"Oh, darlin'," Martha said, her voice filled with that salt-of-the-earth charm as she wiped tears away from her eyes. "That was a beautiful wedding, Lily... you did good. And... I think your time's coming round sooner than you think."

Lily couldn't help but laugh. "Please, Martha. One thing at a time."

Martha gave Lily a wry grin, her mischievous blue eyes sharp as ever. "If you say so, honey. But something tells me you won't be calling yourself Miss Lily Reynolds much longer."

Lily's heart skipped at the implication, her mind thinking back to the way Andrew had looked at her earlier—like there was something waiting for them beneath all this joy. She smiled, giving Martha's hand a squeeze before looking back toward the happy couple. "Maybe, Martha. Maybe."

***

The reception was every bit as joyful as the wedding had been, if not more. The recreation hall was pure elegance, yet simple and charming. Between the autumnal centerpieces of colorful mums and rustic burlap table runners, and the laughter that filled, everything felt cozy, intimate, and just right.

The warm scent of pumpkin-spice cupcakes and mulled cider filled the air, mixing with the rich, freshly baked bread that several ladies from the church had prepared in the kitchen. The wedding cake was indeed a masterpiece.

Laughter broke out periodically, accompanied by the clang of plates and light conversation. It was all a glorious, joyful hum of life—from the children giggling to the elders quietly reminiscing.

"Need me to pinch you?" Rachel asked, leaning toward Lily with a saucy grin on her lips as she snagged another cupcake from the dessert table and winked. "Because this turned out to be a real-life fairy tale dream wedding."

Lily laughed. "Guess that means my job here is done."

Rachel studied her for a moment, eyes twinkling, then glanced across the room. "Not quite."

Lily followed Rachel's gaze to where Andrew was standing at the head table next to Ben, finishing his toast to the happy couple. Andrew was grinning mid-chuckle, holding his glass of cider high as Ben attempted to recover from a humorous mention about one of his early dates with Grace. Mid-laugh, Andrew's eyes moved toward Lily, catching her gaze with one of those unintentional yet intentional looks that sent a warm flutter through her chest.

Rachel quirked a brow. "Mm-hmm. Yep. Your job is definitely not done."

"Would you stop?" Lily grinned, nudging Rachel in response.

"I'm just saying." Rachel said as she licked some icing off her finger with raised brows.

***

Dinner flowed seamlessly into the cake cutting, where Shirley's towering, buttery vanilla masterpiece crowned with sugared berries stole the spotlight. But, as was bound to happen, Ben's playful side got the best of him, and he ended up with a bit more icing on his face than on his plate, sending the guests into fits of laughter.

"Oh, Ben..." Grace chided through giggles, dabbing frosting from his nose with an oversized napkin, trying her best to look serious.

"C'mon, let me live a little, honey!" Ben protested, leaning away from her napkin. "I'm still learnin' this... married-life etiquette."

The laughter swelled again, filling the room with warmth and joy.

Soon, the tables were pushed back to make room for dancing, and the sound of music filled the hall.

Ben and Grace swayed under the lights in their first dance as husband and wife, moving as though the rest of the world didn't exist.

The song filled every corner of the room, the lyrics speaking of trust, and love, and believing in a greater plan.

When it was time to invite the others to the dance floor, Andrew wasted no time making his way over to Lily. His brown eyes were warm, kind, and without a trace of hesitation.

"May I have this dance?" he asked with sincerity, offering his hand. "Please?"

She smiled as she placed her hand in his.

As he led her onto the floor and pulled her into the soft rhythm of the music, the world seemed to soften around them. His hand rested on her back, and the other was wrapped around her hand, like he was cradling something fragile and precious.

***

The evening ended with Grace's bouquet soaring through the air, landing with a not so surprising plop in none other than Lily's hands.

Cheers erupted, and Lily blushed, shaking her head as shouts of encouragement rippled through the hall.

Andrew stood nearby, arms crossed as he leaned casually against a table, clearly pleased. "Well, would you look at that?" he said with a grin, his tone a mix of pride and amusement.

"Yeah, would you look at this," Lily said, holding up the bouquet with a smirk?

Andrew raised an eyebrow. "I believe God planned this perfectly, wouldn't you?"

Leave A Review

If you enjoyed this book, please consider leaving an honest review on
Amazon or Goodreads.
Visit Our Website:
www.tarabaisden.com
Visit Our Amazon Author Page HERE

Find Us On Social Media:
Facebook
Instagram
TikTok
Pinterest
GoodReads